My Heart Stood Still

LORI COPELAND

HARVEST HOUSE PUBLISHERS

EUGENE, OREGON

Cover by Garborg Design Works, Savage, Minnesota

Cover photo © Chris Garborg, Bigstock / Richard McMillin

MY HEART STOOD STILL

Copyright © 2015 Lori Copeland, Inc.
Published by Harvest House Publishers
Eugene, Oregon 97402
www.harvesthousepublishers.com

Library of Congress Cataloging-in-Publication Data
    Copeland, Lori.
    My heart stood still / Lori Copeland.
       pages ; cm
    ISBN 978-0-7369-6167-7 (pbk.)
    ISBN 978-0-7369-6168-4 (eBook)
    I. Title.
    PS3553.O6336M9 2015
    813'.54—dc23

2014021860

Printed in the United States of America

      15 16 17 18 19 20 21 22 23 / BP-JH / 10 9 8 7 6 5 4 3 2 1

Abigail, Anne-Marie, and Amelia McDougal are smart and pretty enough to turn any man's head, but marriage isn't for them. They'll stick together through thick or thin. The trouble is, the thin times are coming faster than the thick times.

The nuns who run the mission in Mercy Flats, Texas, do the best they can with the three orphaned girls, but they are constantly glad to know the Lord forgives, since those three need a huge dose of tolerance daily.

In book one, Sisters of Mercy Flats, *we witnessed how Abigail had Barrett Drake scratching his head with bewilderment. So sit back and hold tight as Anne-Marie attempts to tame Creed Walker, a man who has no intentions of being tamed...*

One

A large chestnut stallion galloped headlong across the dusty plains, carrying two riders pressing low against its sides. Man and beast had ridden hard for over an hour and the animal's side was heavily lathered, its flanks heaving from exertion.

Anne-Marie McDougal locked her hands around her rescuer's waist and held on tightly, praying she would survive this newest catastrophe. Her sisters, Abigail and Amelia, had been rescued from a jail wagon and carried off in different directions, and Anne-Marie was in the hands of a stranger. A very large, intimidating man, who had plucked her off her feet and now raced along the road at a frightening clip. Glancing over her shoulder, she saw no sign of the band of youthful braves who had been chasing them. Perhaps they had tired of the pursuit and broken away.

The Comanches, the sudden flight from the jail wagon, and now galloping across the countryside with a savage was like an awful dream, but Anne-Marie knew it wasn't a nightmare. It was really happening.

She tightened her grip around the Indian's waist and wondered about this uncivilized being who had swooped down from the heavens to save her from a fate worse than death.

Her heart raced with alarm. Who were these men who had seized her and her sisters, Amelia and Abigail, to safety, and then sprinted in opposite directions?

A new, more disturbing thought came to her mind. What if the three Samaritans had not come upon them? Anne-Marie shuddered to think where she would be now. Scalped…or dead.

She held tight as the Indian cut the chestnut off the trail and pushed the animal up a steep ravine. If only she had thought the last scam through more carefully. She had warned Amelia and Abigail it would be risky to make a fool of A.J. Donavan. He was an intelligent man, and she had sensed that he couldn't be tricked as easily as the others.

Panic welled up inside her. She had never been apart from Abigail and Amelia. She and her sisters had always faced life together, afraid of nothing, anxious of no one. If anything happened to them she couldn't bring herself to go on.

But she couldn't allow herself to entertain such thoughts. Optimism was her strength; she couldn't lose it now. She had escaped unharmed, hadn't she? She wasn't bleeding or wounded. And the two men who had rescued Abigail and Amelia were white men, not a savage like her defender.

The Indian's stoic silence was beginning to grate on her. Obviously he neither understood nor spoke a word of English, but she would have to find a way to communicate soon. She had to make him understand that he must help her find the nearest stage or rail station so she could return to Mercy Flats, Texas, immediately.

There, by the grace of God, she and her sisters would be reunited—provided her sisters' rescuers had been as cunning in eluding the Comanches as her protector. But was he her rescuer? She had no assurance that he wasn't as intent on evil as the band of young warriors chasing the wagon.

No. She must believe that he had good intentions and that Abigail and Amelia were safe. At this very moment they might be as confused and frightened as she was, but they would be back together soon—very soon. And they would continue providing funds for the orphanage in Mercy Flats as they always had.

Leaning closer against the man's powerful back, she shouted above the racing wind. "It's getting colder. Can we stop soon—is there a town nearby?"

When he showed no signs of responding, she sighed, realizing that communication was impossible. He didn't understand a word she said, but it didn't matter. She would forgo small talk if only he was skilled enough to get her to safety with her scalp intact.

She was limply clinging to his waist by the time he finally angled the horse down a gulley and through a deep thicket. She tensed. This was the moment she had been dreading; this was the hour he would prove his intent. He was either her defender or her adversary. Her heart tripped in her chest and she sucked in a deep breath.

Half turning, the man grunted, pointing toward the ground.

When she was slow to comprehend, he grasped her by the arm and eased her off the back of the horse. She had been astride the animal for so long that her legs threatened to give out. When she stumbled, a strong hand reached out to steady her.

Motioning her to a nearby log, the man slid off the horse and set to work. In a surprisingly short time he had a fire going, its warmth gratifying in the deepening twilight. The day had begun warm and balmy, but during the afternoon clouds had formed overhead and now the biting wind carried a hint of snow.

Anne-Marie tried to ignore the grumbling in her stomach. She hadn't eaten since sometime early this morning, and she had no idea where her next meal would come from. The Indian appeared to have little provision for travel—a canteen tied to his saddle and a bedroll. His tribe could be nearby, yet if that were true, considering the worsening weather, why hadn't he elected to seek shelter with them? But if he planned to do her harm, he was certainly being a gentleman about it.

"I'm hungry," she said, patting her stomach to convey her misery. "I'm hungry and *cold*," she added, using the same insistent gesture, hoping he would comprehend her need.

Giving her a brief, vacant stare, the man moved closer to the fire.

In the light he looked wild and uncivilized. He was large, and his buckskin shirt and trousers smelled as if he hadn't washed in months. Thick black shaggy hair blew in the wind. Nut-brown skin stretched tightly over high, hollow cheekbones. In the deepening shadows, he appeared even more ominous.

Her eyes traveled the length of his ragged form. He was from an impoverished tribe. Even the leather moccasins he wore were old and threadbare.

Pity momentarily flooded her, and her compassion deepened when she saw that he was shivering from the cold.

Drawing a deep breath, she glanced about the campsite, wondering if either one of them would make it through the night. She didn't see how. They had nothing, virtually nothing, to protect them from the elements.

"Do you have a blanket?" She mimed rubbing her shoulders.

His gaze fixed on the shower of sparks shooting up from the dry timber.

"Perhaps we should huddle together. We have to do something or we'll both die!"

The man remained stoically silent.

She thought for a moment and then tried again. Pointing at the fire, she lifted her brows in question. Food? Surely he could understand that. They had ridden for hours. He had to be as hungry as she was. Didn't his kind run down rabbits on foot or catch fish with their bare hands? She glanced around the campsite and her heart sank when she spied a stream that was little more than a trickle of water. There would be nothing in there to ease their hunger.

She rose and began to pace around the campfire, her frustration mounting. She had to try to think of a way out of this. If she had to be stuck with a man, why couldn't it be one who understood simple English? The other girls would surely have a laugh when this was over and Anne-Marie told them about her captor. At least Amelia and Abigail had been rescued by men who undoubtedly spoke or understood a common language.

Positioning herself on a rock, she focused on the sounds coming from the bushes. She wasn't squeamish. It took more than rustling sounds in the thicket to spook her, but she had never been out alone much at night.

And she had never depended on a man for anything.

She didn't like the fact for the time being that she was dependent on one now—and especially this particular man.

She bit her lower lip. If it weren't so late, she'd scare up her own supper. Her eyes returned to the dense thicket, but it was extremely dark.

Not a hint of moon shone through the bare tree branches. In another few minutes she would barely be able to see her hand in front of her face, and she didn't have a gun.

Shivering, she burrowed deeper into the woolen nun's habit she'd been wearing as a disguise during the caper that had landed them in the jail wagon. The shrieking wind reminded her of how little protection the disguise was in a full-blown blizzard. Her gaze returned to the Indian. At least her habit was warmer than what he was wearing.

He stirred, adding wood to the fire, seemingly oblivious of her presence.

Miniature snowflakes began to form in the air as the two forlorn figures huddled close to the fire.

Long minutes of silence passed when Anne-Marie decided to take matters into her own hands. She was so hungry she couldn't sleep, even if she wanted to, which was impossible in such deplorable conditions. She had no idea what she would find beyond the rustling bushes, but she—

She stiffened as the corner of her eye caught sight of something slithering across the ground. A lizard seeking the warmth of the fire.

She lowered her eyes to the toe of her boot, and her throat squeezed so tightly with fear that she couldn't make a sound.

A pair of reptilian eyes stared up at her.

There were few things in life Anne-Marie dreaded, but a lizard was one of them. As a child, she had slipped into an abandoned well and spent the next hour in a bed of various species of lizards before Father Luis and Sister Agnes had been able, with the help of a long rope, to pull her out. For years afterward Anne-Marie couldn't close her eyes without reliving the horror of that old well and the slithering reptiles that had mercilessly crawled over her body while she lay paralyzed with terror.

Cold yellow-green eyes stared back at her while she attempted to find her voice. She squeaked, and then squeaked again, trying to gain the Indian's attention.

The man calmly piled more wood on the fire.

By willing her vocal cords to move, she succeeded in making a small, barely perceptible noise pass her lips as her eyes riveted on the intruder reclining on the top of her left boot.

Glancing up, the man finally caught Anne-Marie's anguished stare. He rose slowly to his feet, his eyes warning her not to move. The hairs on the back of her neck rose when she saw the glint of a blade appear in his hand.

With catlike stealth, he advanced on the lizard. The knife blade reflected the fire's dancing flames, looking more sinister than any gun. The man's black eyes glittered as he concentrated on his prey. Anne-Marie's gaze beseeched him to move faster, but he showed no signs of understanding. Instead he crept closer, each step methodically calculated.

While still a few feet away, he took aim and let the knife find its mark.

Anne-Marie's eyes rolled back in her head, and with a soft whimper she slumped to the ground in a lifeless heap.

～

Snow had started to fall heavily when the Indian knelt beside the sister to check her pulse. He laid his fingers on the base of her throat, his eyes softening when he detected a strong heartbeat. For so small a sparrow, the sister had much spirit. His gaze traced her delicate features. It had been some time since he had seen such a lovely woman.

Bending forward, he gently picked her up and moved her closer to the fire.

His gaze lingered on her beauty when he slowly straightened. Snow was gathering on her dark lashes, and in the flickering firelight her face radiated a childlike innocence.

Kneeling again, he tucked the skirt of her habit around her tightly, making sure the wind could not penetrate her small frame.

When he stood, his eyes moved regretfully to the bushes where he had thrown the lizard carcass. Too bad she was so afraid of the creature; it would have made an adequate meal.

His eyes once again returned to the sister. She was such a beautiful woman to have chosen to live out her life in a convent. He briefly speculated as to why. Dedication like hers was not often found in one so young.

A moment later, carrying his knife, he disappeared into the heavy thicket.

✑

Anne-Marie opened her eyes to see large, cottony white balls floating down in the moonlight, settling like feather down on her cheeks. For the longest moment she couldn't remember where she was.

Staring up, she saw a layer of white coating the tops of the trees, their branches decked out in glistening winter finery. Icicles dripped from the boughs of cedar trees, turning branches into dazzling Christmas tree ornaments.

She lay drinking in the magnificent sight. The night was so silent she could almost hear smoke drifting from the fire.

When her memory rushed back she bolted upright. Where was the Indian? The campfire blazed brightly, but he was nowhere in sight. Panic seized her and she called out, her voice hollow in the icy stillness. She sat for a moment, trying to collect her thoughts. Had he left her? What if he had taken the horse and ridden off, leaving her to fend for herself? A groan escaped her when she remembered the lizard and the speed with which the Indian's knife had killed it.

A sound drew her attention, and she glanced up, catching back a shout when she saw the man returning. He was carrying something in his right hand.

"There you are!" she called out. "I was afraid you'd left me here—alone."

Her eyes focused on the meat he was carrying, and her stomach rumbled with hunger. "Thank goodness you found something." She wasn't sure what he held, but by now it didn't matter. She'd settle for anything to appease her empty stomach.

Moving to the fire, the man deftly skewered the meat and hung it over the hot flame.

"What is it?" she asked, not expecting a response, but just to hear a voice breaking the unnerving silence. "Well, no matter, it looks delicious," she added a moment later.

They sat in silence, surrounded by falling snow and the occasional sound of fat dripping into the fire.

When the meat was nearly black, the Indian removed it from the spit and laid it aside to cool.

After a while he tore the fare into chunks and handed her a portion. She couldn't hide the trembling in her hands when she took it from him.

His eyes darted to hers briefly, and she smiled back in gratitude. "Thank you. It smells wonderful."

Picking up the crusted meat, she told herself to be grateful for the kindness he had shown her. Maybe they couldn't communicate, but at least he had treated her with respect, and she should consider herself fortunate.

He paused as if waiting for something.

When she returned his gaze vacantly, his eyes fell away, and he began eating.

Later he tossed the last bone aside and settled near the fire and closed his eyes.

Anne-Marie rolled herself up in a blanket he provided from his saddlebags and lay down near the fire. Was there a woman somewhere tonight concerned about his welfare? Tall, sleek muscle ridges showed through the rugged buckskin. He was handsome to be sure—or he could be most striking with the proper care. A good scrubbing, a pair of scissors, and a shave would make a big difference. She looked away when her cheeks heated. What thoughts! Abigail would think she'd lost her mind.

She studied the worsening weather. "Maybe we should sleep close together." The offer came out louder than she'd intended. She didn't mean anything improper by the suggestion. If he planned to hurt her he would have done so by now. If they combined their body heat, they might survive the night.

In the distance coyotes—or something worse—howled. She wasn't going to dwell on that fact for fear that panic would set in again.

"With the weather worsening, the good Lord would not hold us accountable for trying to survive the elements," she continued, more to herself than to him, because he didn't appear to be listening. The suggestion was brazen and dangerous but he couldn't take offense. He didn't understand a word she was saying. They would be frozen carcasses by morning, and if she dared creep closer to him for warmth she might very well end up in the bushes with the lizard carcass.

The wind howled through the bare tree branches when she rolled to her side and stared at the fire. She was safe. She huddled deeper into her habit. He thought her to be a holy woman. She was only using common sense; she didn't want either of them to freeze to death. At the moment he was her only hope of reaching a town alive, and the thought of anything warm, no matter how unkempt and smelly, appealed to her survival instincts.

"Well…you can let me know if you should change your mind," she said over her shoulder. Then she sat up to see if he had heard.

Rolling to his side, the man presented his back to her.

Sighing, she closed her eyes, the weight of the world heavy on her shoulders.

She didn't know about his plans, but her goals were clear. She must stay alive. The McDougal sisters were the primary support for the mission, and without them, the mission would have to close.

ᶜ∿

Dawn lit the sky, and the Indian doused the fire long before daybreak. The snow had tapered off to occasional blowing flakes, but bitterly cold air encompassed the campsite. Only the golden sunrise filtering through the trees promised a pleasant day for traveling. The orange ball of sun, now beginning to top the trees, brought a smile to Anne-Marie's face and a renewed optimism when she accepted the Indian's hand and he pulled her up behind him on the chestnut.

Reining the horse, he set off, riding south.

It was late morning when their stallion topped a rise. What a strange sight they must be—a nun and an Indian together on a horse.

Peering anxiously around the man's shoulder, Anne-Marie couldn't hold back the shout that bubbled to her throat when she spotted the small community spread out below them. "Holy smokes!" They'd made it! They'd beaten the elements, and she was going to live!

The Indian glanced over his shoulder at her, and for the first time since they'd met, she thought she detected shock on his perpetually stoic features.

Catching herself, she added a perfunctory "Thank the Lord," and hurriedly crossed herself.

Nudging the horse forward, the Indian rode into town.

Two

High Bluff, Texas, was an ordinary border town. The steady clang of the blacksmith's hammer rang out from the livery, the mercantile sat next to the cafe, and the hotel was facing east so it wouldn't bake in the late afternoon sun.

The saloon, the Gilded Dove, was just beginning to come to life as the Indian and nun rode through the center of town.

An occasional head turned when the couple passed, but for the most part folks were accustomed to strangers. The train ran straight through town every Tuesday and Friday morning, regular as clockwork, so the comings and goings of outsiders never caused much of a stir.

Although a nun riding horseback with an Indian wasn't an ordinary sight.

Reining the horse in front of a hitching post, the Indian swung down and then lifted a hand to help the sister.

Adjusting her rumpled skirts, Anne-Marie glanced up and down the street, relieved to see they weren't attracting the curiosity she'd feared they might. "I want to secure a room at the hotel right away," she murmured.

Looping the reins around the hitching post, the Indian pointed to the train depot.

Anne-Marie located the hotel near the large water tower and nodded. "Oh, yes—thank you so much for all your trouble."

Her words dribbled off when she realized she was talking to his retreating back. He disappeared into the mercantile, closing the door behind him.

Straightening her habit, she turned with quick, determined steps and headed for lodging. She would rent a room, order a hot bath and a hot meal, and then lie down in a soft bed and sleep for hours. Who knew how long she'd have to wait for the next train? She wasn't ready to presume that God was on her side today. Dare she ask for His help when so much of her life was lived in deceit?

She shrugged off the troublesome questions. Whatever the reason, she'd survived another day. Although she was rumpled and penniless, she was still wearing her disguise, and any God-fearing man or woman would be eager to provide a woman of the cloth with food and comfortable quarters while she waited.

⌒

Minutes later the front door opened and Anne-Marie stepped out, drawing a deep breath as she straightened her veil. There wasn't a single room available.

So much for God-fearing charitable souls. "May they all get a blood blister today," she muttered as she crossed the street.

Turning to her right, she headed for the mercantile where the Indian had earlier disappeared.

When the bell over the door tinkled, the proprietor turned from stacking boxes on his shelves. He climbed slowly off the ladder, wiped his hands on his apron, and walked toward her, smiling. "Afternoon, Sister."

"Good afternoon." Anne-Marie glanced around the room, trying to locate the Indian. He was standing near the back, studying a knife display in a glass case. When he glanced up and recognition registered on his face, he quickly stepped away from the counter and disappeared behind a tall stack of dry goods.

The kindly-looking clerk skimmed the nun's rumpled habit, still smiling pleasantly. "Something I can help you with today?"

She leaned over the counter, trying to see around the stacks of woolens and linens. Was it her imagination or was her benefactor actually trying to avoid her? "Nothing in particular. I'm just browsing, thank you."

"If you see anything you want, I'll be happy to get it for you."

"Thank you, I'll let you know."

Moseying toward the bolts of colorful ribbons and lace, she kept an eye on the Indian, who—no, it wasn't her imagination—was making himself conspicuously absent. Apparently he understood enough to think his part in the rescue was over, but since he had rescued her and she now found herself without a cent to her name and not a single room available, he might take pity on her.

Turning pleading eyes on him, she was annoyed to see he was returning her silent reprimand with a surprisingly astute one of his own, one that clearly suggested that he considered his part finished.

Done.

Through.

Stepping to the counter, the Indian pointed to an expensive-looking rifle.

Climbing off the ladder again, the clerk said, "You want to see the Sharps carbine?"

The man gave a brief nod.

"You got enough wampum to purchase it?"

He nodded curtly.

"All righty." The clerk took the rifle off the shelf and handed it to him.

After a cursory inspection the Indian nodded, indicating his approval.

"Guess you'll be needin' shells? A box do you?"

The man nodded.

Anne-Marie watched the exchange with growing interest. The Indian seemed to have no trouble understanding the clerk. No trouble at all, yet he'd pretended he hadn't understood a word she'd said for the past twenty-four hours.

Laying the cartridges on the counter, the clerk totaled up the purchase. "Looks like you owe me forty dollars."

Anne-Marie's lips parted indignantly when she saw her rescuer produce a small leather pouch attached to his breeches and calmly remove several gold coins. Judging from the lumps in the pouch, there was more where they came from, maybe a lot more. Why, the man had enough money to burn a wet mule! She felt her cheeks turn red. What was he doing with that kind of funds? He didn't have a penny an hour ago—her eyes narrowed—or did he?

The proprietor tossed a few coins of change onto the counter while glancing at Anne-Marie. "Finding everything you need, Sister?"

"Thank you, I'll just be looking today. Does the stage come through here?"

Picking up his purchases, the Indian turned and walked out the door. Anne-Marie's teeth worried her lower lip as she watched him leave.

"The stage? Sure does, once a month, just like clockwork."

"What about the train?"

"Twice a week regular as clockwork."

The man seemed to have a fixation on clocks. "On what days?"

"Tuesdays and Fridays."

Her frown deepened when she watched the Indian cross the street. "Today is Saturday, isn't it?"

"That it is, Sister. Saturday."

Two whole days in town without a penny. She smiled, bowing her head subserviently. "Thank you, you have been most kind."

Plucking an apple from a barrel, the proprietor polished it on the sleeve of his shirt before handing it to her. "An apple a day will keep the doctor away," he offered with a twinkling eye.

Nodding, Anne-Marie jammed the fruit into her mouth and stepped out of the store.

Now what? She stood looking up and down the unfamiliar street, munching on the apple. Her eyes located the Indian, who was walking in the direction of the sheriff's office, and a sense of injustice struck her. Where did he think he was going with his pouch full of coins and a new, expensive rifle? Her eyes followed him as he strolled past a saloon. He'd rescued a woman in distress and now he planned to leave her still in danger?

Since he had taken it upon himself to be her protector, the very least he could do was see that she was properly protected. What was she to do about the price of a train ticket and, for that matter, where was she supposed to stay until the train got here? Men. No matter what color skin, they were all alike.

Taking another bite of the tart fruit, she made a face, stepped off the planked sidewalk, and crossed the street, falling into step behind the Indian. If he had understood that clerk, then he could understand her—and he was going to be made to comprehend in no uncertain terms that he wasn't going to desert her now.

"I would like a word with you, Mr. Indian!"

When his footsteps didn't falter, she articulated more loudly. "I know you have money, and obviously I don't, so don't you think that since you appointed yourself my rescuer, it's only fair that you see to my well-being until the train arrives on Tuesday?"

He walked on.

Anne-Marie's temper flared. "I know you can understand what I'm saying—you understood the clerk at the mercantile perfectly."

He crossed the street and picked up his pace.

Following him, she grabbed the apple out of her mouth and hurled the uneaten portion at his back, thumping him soundly between his very impressive shoulders.

"Answer me! Do you hear me? I said, say something!"

The door to the sheriff's office opened and a deputy cautiously stuck his head out, eyes trying to locate the ruckus.

At the sight of the lawman, the muscles in Anne-Marie's stomach tightened. For a moment she had forgotten her disguise. Nuns didn't fling apples at Indians' backs and demand a response.

"Afternoon, Sister," the deputy called when she walked past.

Nodding severely to the deputy, she marched on, passing the jail-house door, still dogging the Indian's steps.

She told herself to calm down when the deputy continued to stare after her. Neither she nor her sisters had ever been in High Bluff, so no one could possibly recognize her as one of the three women who had been operating con games in the area.

"Oh, Sister?"

Anne-Marie froze, not particularly liking the tone of a second man's voice that had suddenly joined the conversation.

"Oh, Sisterrrr?" repeated the mocking voice.

The Indian's footsteps picked up and he walked faster.

Anne-Marie was close on his heel when the voice sang out again, "Sister!"

Turning around slowly, Anne-Marie swallowed when she saw a large man with a silver star on his chest striding toward her. A man in a brown suit followed on his heel, breathing like a charging bull.

"Sister, I wonder if I might have a word with you?" the sheriff inquired pleasantly when he approached.

Shoot! Shoot! *Shoot!* A.J. Donavan, the man she and her sisters had scammed just a few short weeks earlier, was accompanying the sheriff, his swarthy features molten with anger.

Whirling, Anne-Marie started to make a run for it when she suddenly felt the cold barrel of a .32 caliber Colt resting lightly between her shoulder blades. "Now, now, what's your hurry, little lady?"

She jerked upright. "Sir, how dare you—"

"Is this the woman, A.J.?"

"That's her, all right. I'd know those green eyes anywhere!"

"Now, Sheriff," Anne-Marie began, and then immediately piped down when she saw that the deputy had cornered the Indian and was pushing him back, at rifle point, in her direction. Donavan had a grudge. She and her sisters had sold him cattle that didn't belong to them—but how had he found her so quickly?

She straightened her veil. "Now, see here, how dare you treat a woman of the cloth—"

A.J. sneered "Save your breath, woman. We've got you dead to rights. No con artist sells me a herd of stolen beef and lives to brag about it!"

The sheriff ushered the Indian and the nun down the sidewalk over Anne-Marie's loud and spirited objections.

Entering the jail, the sheriff steered Anne-Marie into a cell.

The deputy snatched a key ring from a hook on the wall. "What are you, mister? Crow?"

The Indian lifted his head, black eyes spirited, and nodded.

"How did you fall in with the likes of this woman?" He shoved the man in the cage and turned the key.

"I demand you release me this instant! You can't grab innocent people—" Anne-Marie glared accusingly at A.J. Donavan. "Innocent nuns," she amended. She turned pleading eyes to the sheriff. "You can't just grab me off the street and treat me like common riffraff because some wild man is making ludicrous accusations about—cows."

"There's two more of 'em around somewhere," A.J. warned the sheriff.

"We'll find them, A.J. They couldn't have gone far."

Glaring at the Crow, Anne-Marie warned him silently that if he could speak, he'd better be doing it.

The Indian refused to meet her eyes.

The sheriff smiled reassuringly. "Now, don't you be worrying your pretty little head, ma'am. You and the Injun will have yourselves a fair trial. I guarantee you that."

"I demand proper legal representation! Get me an attorney!" Anne-Marie shouted as she clasped the bars with both hands.

"Why certainly, ma'am." He turned to A.J., smiling. "I believe the lady would like a word with you, A.J."

Anne-Marie frowned. "He's my lawyer?"

The sheriff nodded. "Yes, ma'am, but don't you worry none. Not only is A.J. the town's finest attorney, but he's the onliest."

Anne-Marie's heart sank. "Onliest what?"

"Onliest attorney." The sheriff's smile widened. "He'll be speaking on you and your friend's behalf."

Three

Anne-Marie sank down on the cot opposite the Indian, frustrated. It had been weeks since they'd sold Donavan that herd of stolen cattle, and she'd have sworn she'd seen the last of him.

Springing back to her feet, she started talking under her breath as she paced the small cell. "Just don't—how—the man—Amelia—then Abigail said—rotten luck. Pure rotten luck."

The front door opened and the sheriff came in with A.J. trailing behind. Hooking his hat on a peg, Ferris Goodman walked over to the woodstove and poured two cups of steaming black coffee.

"Sheriff," Anne-Marie called, "can I have a word with you?"

"No ma'am."

Handing A.J. a cup of coffee, the sheriff sat down behind his desk. "Now, A.J., tell me again what happened."

A.J. pointed an accusing finger at Anne-Marie. "That she-devil and two others dressed just like her sold me a herd of stolen beef."

"You're certain it was this woman."

"As sure as hair grows on a pig's back!"

"And the Crow?"

"I don't know nothing about the savage, but the way I figure it, he was with her when they rode into town, so they must be in cahoots."

"Well, your word's good enough for me." The sheriff got up and walked to the cell where Anne-Marie stood, gripping the bars. "Don't suppose you plan on telling me where your sisters are?"

"That's what I wanted to speak to you about. I don't know where they are."

"Then by the authority vested in me by the great state of Texas, I hereby sentence you and your friend here to hang at sunrise."

Anne-Marie's jaw dropped. "Now, just a minute! What happened to my fair trial?"

The sheriff met her eyes with an unwavering gaze. "You just had it."

"Just had it?" They'd had it, all right, but good.

Returning to his chair, Ferris took a swig of coffee, peering over the rim of the cup at A.J., and raised his voice to talk above Anne-Marie's vehement protests. "You know, A.J., I'd still like to know how you let yourself get swindled by a woman. Don't rightly seem like you."

Red crept up Donavan's neck. "I hate to admit it, but the woman snookered me slicker than glass. She told me the cattle had been a gift and they had to sell them because the mission couldn't afford to feed them. Some orphanage they ran needed money, not cattle, she said. Well, Ferris, who's going to question a nun, much less three of 'em?"

"Well now, I might have questioned getting a top head of cattle for hundreds of dollars below market value," Ferris argued.

"No, you would have fell for it just like me," A.J. grumbled. "It sounded on the up-and-up, so I marched myself right over to the bank and got the money real quick like before the sisters could change their minds."

"Guess you wish you'd marched a little slower?" Ferris appeared to be having a hard time hiding a grin behind the rim of his cup.

"I was there to buy cattle, and the price was right," A.J. said sullenly.

Ferris broke out laughing. "And you never once suspected them women were pullin' a fast one on you?"

"Do I look like an idiot, Ferris? Of course I didn't know I was bein' played for a fool! Why, that one over there even wrote me out a bill of sale, right there in the saloon, big as all get out." He snorted. "I should've known something was wrong when they hightailed it out of town as soon as they had the money in hand. No one's seen hide nor hair of 'em since—not until I saw that one ridin' into town with the Indian, the both of them as brazen as a two-bit floozy."

The Crow suddenly got to his feet and walked to the front of the cell.

His black eyes pinpointed Anne-Marie. "Gentlemen, twenty-four hours ago I didn't know this woman existed."

Anne-Marie's jaw went slack and she stared back at him. "What?" Had he said what she thought he'd said? Why, the *nerve*—

"I said"—the man's eyes locked with hers and he repeated in perfect English— "I am not with this woman. I do not know her; I do not want to know her."

She knew it! He had been deliberately making her think that he couldn't understand English, and now he not only understood it, but he was speaking it as flawlessly as a professor.

Chairs scraped against the floor. Ferris and A.J. got to their feet.

"You were sure enough with her in the mercantile a while ago," A.J. reminded him.

"True, but it appears that Mr. Donavan and I have met with the same misfortune, that of being taken in by a wolf in sheep's clothing…or"—the Indian's eyes returned to Anne-Marie—"as is the more applicable case, a thief in nun's clothing."

"Care to say how she took you?" the sheriff inquired, clearly surprised by the sudden turn of events.

The muscle in the Crow's jaw tightened visibly. "I rescued her from a jail wagon."

"Rescued her from a jail wagon, huh?" Goodman and Donavan exchanged amused looks.

"The wagon was being pursued by Comanches. When I saw what I assumed to be three nuns in danger, I rode to their aid."

"And the other two nuns?" Ferris smirked. "Where might they be?"

"I don't know. Two other men rode to assist the women at the same time I did."

"My, my, was that a stroke of luck on them women's part or what, A.J.? Three men, all ridin' in to help them nuns at the exact same time?"

"More than a stroke of luck, Ferris. I'd say it was a miracle." A.J. crowed.

The Crow gripped the bar tightly. "I'm telling you exactly what happened."

"Well, Injun, you speak real educated-like, but the fact is you rode in the company of a cattle thief, and right now, since I've got no way of knowing if you're telling me the truth about all this jail-wagon and band-of-Comanches stuff, I'm bound by the law to let my decision stand."

"You are making a mistake," the Indian warned.

"Could be, but if I was you, I'd just sit back and keep quiet." Ferris glanced at A.J. and winked. "You and the little lady got yourselves a big day ahead of you tomorrow. Sal?" He spoke to the deputy lounging in the corner. "Keep an eye on things whilst me and Donavan visit the café."

The man nodded and stretched.

"Well, if that doesn't beat all." Anne-Marie whirled to confront the Crow when the door closed behind the two men. "How dare you make me think that you didn't understand a word I was saying?"

"How dare you pose as a nun?"

"What difference does it make who I am?"

"The difference is that I wouldn't have given you or your friends a second thought if I hadn't believed three nuns were about to be scalped."

"But I was about to be scalped!"

"But you're not a nun."

Ripping aside her veil, Anne-Marie freed her long hair to tumble loosely over her shoulders. Her usual way of worming out of tight situations wasn't working, so it looked like she would be forced to resort to drastic measures. No man, no matter how infuriating, could resist a helpless, simpering female.

Covering her face with her hands and dropping her chin, she began to sob. After a few moments of theatrics, she spread her fingers, peering out to witness the Indian's reaction. He was ignoring her. Completely ignoring her.

Discarding the tactic, she switched to her wounded look, a method absolutely no man could survive, no matter how unsympathetic. "Some protector you are," she accused with trembling lower lip.

Walking back to the cot, he sat down. "Why should I protect you?"

"Because you appointed yourself my protector when you rescued me from the jail wagon yesterday."

"Today I unappoint myself your protector."

"You can't do that."

"I believe I just did."

"Fine." She sat down on the cot, crossing her arms and giving him a cold stare, another surefire tactic to bring a man to his knees, no matter how mean and hateful he was. And this man was the meanest one she'd ever had the misfortune to meet.

"Fine," he said, and met her cold stare with icy contempt.

They sat in stony silence, staring at each other.

Finally Anne-Marie heaved an aggravated sigh and loosened her confining collar. Reaching into the large pocket sewn into the front of her shirt, she pulled out a piece of ribbon and tied her hair back out of her face.

She caught his glancing look. "Who are you and why did you pretend not to understand English?"

His gaze slid over her impersonally. "Have you no shame? Why would you choose this disguise?" he asked.

"Don't you question my integrity. I have my reasons."

His eyes darkened to a dangerous hue. "Only godly women wear the habit. It is a sign of their devotion to the Lord's work; it is not worn as a ruse to steal from unsuspecting men."

"I have no idea what that A.J. person was talking about," she said.

"I haven't duped anyone out of anything and I didn't sell any cattle. It's all a mistake, I tell you, a big mistake." She wasn't proud of her actions but sometimes a person had to do what she could to survive—and it wasn't as though she hadn't cringed a few times when she wondered how the Lord would judge her means of support. Abigail said that since the money went to a worthy cause it wasn't really stealing—they were just helping people make donations.

The man shook his head. "Do I look gullible enough to believe that?"

"Well, it could be that you're no more Indian than I am a nun. You certainly had me fooled into thinking you didn't speak a word of English."

He settled back on the cot, leaning against the wall. "At least I'm not impersonating a priest."

He did for the world look exactly like a full-blooded Indian, but he sure wasn't acting like one.

"You're not a normal Indian," she scoffed. "And if you are, you're not uncivilized and uneducated like you want everyone to believe."

He laughed—a cold, mirthless sound in the small cell.

"What do you find so amusing?" They were sitting in a cell, hopeless for the moment. She didn't have money for bail and he wouldn't help her. She might sit here for weeks. The sheriff couldn't be serious about hanging them, of course. He was just trying to scare her.

The Crow shifted. "If what I've gotten myself into couldn't be judged ignorant, I don't know what would. I'm sitting here in jail with a con artist, waiting to be hanged at sunrise."

"They'll never hang us," she said. "By morning they'll realize their mistake…" Her voice died away as the sound of hammering reached them. Stepping to the windows, she peered out, her heart filling her throat when she saw the large platform being erected in front of the jail. "Will you look at that," she whispered. "What do you suppose they're building?"

"A gallows."

Her cheeks burned. "You're not serious."

"Do I look like I'm attempting to amuse you?"

She turned to glance over her shoulder at his solemn features. He didn't look like he was teasing; he looked dead sober.

Shuffling back to the cot, she sat down, sighing. She had always been smart, too smart for her own good, so if the two of them put their heads together, they could think of a way out of this. "Who are you, honestly?"

He shook his head. "It is not important that you know."

"Tell me your name." If she was going to die with him, she'd at least like to know his name.

"Creed Walker."

"That isn't an Indian name."

"I didn't say it was."

"What is your Indian name?"

His eyes fixed straight ahead. She'd met stubborn men, but this one took the prize.

"Did you hear me?"

"Has anyone ever mentioned that you talk too much?"

"No. Never."

"Consider yourself informed."

"You look like an Indian, but you don't sound like one," she said. He was just a man. A rather striking and dangerous one, it would seem, but still a man.

Stretching his full length on the bunk, he closed his eyes. "Let's assume I've not been living among my people for many years."

"Why did you pretend not to understand me when I talked to you?"

"Because it suited my purposes."

"Well, Mr. Walker, does it suit your purpose to get us out of here?"

His brows drew together autocratically and he sat up. "What can I do? In case you haven't noticed, those are steel bars I'm looking at."

"We have to do something. We can't sit here and let them hang us."

He looked at her, shaking his head with disbelief. "Hasn't it sunk in yet? We're not getting out of here. The jail is too tight, the sheriff is too crooked. We are going to hang."

"Pooh. Something will happen—it always does." After all, yesterday when her circumstances looked bleak, God had rescued her. He still looked out for her, didn't He? If only Abigail were here—she'd figure a way out of this.

They glanced up as the front door opened again. An unkempt man entered this time, followed by a black man. He was wearing the fanciest duds Anne-Marie had ever seen. He must be a gambler. From the top of his black derby to the equally black patent-leather shoes, he reeked of success. The dark broadcloth suit fit his physique like a second skin. There was a slight bulge beneath the red satin vest, and Anne-Marie surmised that the man was heavily armed. A brown cravat that matched the color of his eyes accentuated his flawless white shirt.

The man grinned as he spotted Anne-Marie and the Indian huddled together on the dirty bunk.

"Yes sir, that's her all right. She's the woman who stole Grandma Edna's brooch and then took off like a scalded cat. She's the one."

Striding over to the cell, the stranger pointed his bejeweled finger at Anne-Marie. "Thought you'd get away with it, did you, Sister? Well, I can promise you this, I'm not going to let you, you hear me? Now hand it over."

Wide-eyed, Anne-Marie backed deeper into the cell. She'd never seen this man before in her life, much less swindled him out of a brooch. "I…don't have Edna's…brooch—"

"She's lying. Sir, I insist you open that cell door and search this thieving wench. She stole my grandmammy's brooch, and she's not going to get away with it. I have my papers; I'm a free man and I refuse to be treated this way."

The man narrowed his eyes. "I am Cortes, and I will decide how you are to be treated. Now, *Señor*—what did you say your name was?"

"John Quincy Adams, sir."

Cortes studied the dandified man. "John Quincy Adams?"

"That is correct. My mother named me after the president. Now, here I was, showing the nice sister my dear ol' grandmammy's brooch—she's dead now, God rest her sainted soul—the very brooch her dear sainted mammy had given her, when the sister, she says, 'Oh, it's so lovely, may I share its unusual beauty with Sister Louise, who is this minute buying flour and molasses in the mercantile?' Well, like the fool I can be, I handed it to her and I says, 'You and Sister take your time looking at the fine piece of jewelry while I go over and sit down under a tree and wait.' And I wait and I wait for her to get back, but she never gets back. She up and disappears. Gone, vamoosed!"

"I don't know what this man is talking about. I haven't stolen any brooch!" Anne-Marie's fists balled into tight knots and the blood vessels in her temple throbbed. What was he babbling about? She hadn't taken a brooch!

Apparently John Quincy Adams had said all he intended to say on the subject. "Open the cell door, Cortes, and we'll see who's telling the truth."

"I do not know. Sheriff Goodman is across the street—"

"Won't take a minute to clear up the matter. All I want is my brooch back and I'll be on my way."

"Well." Cortes glanced out the window. "I will search her, but you'll have to stand back and let me do it."

Adams nodded. "Fine with me. All I want is my brooch back."

"I don't have his brooch!" Anne-Marie protested when the deputy slipped the key in the lock and opened the cell door.

She gasped when she heard a sound thump. Cortes slumped to the floor, unconscious.

"Now, you have youself a nice little snooze, Mr. Cortes," the man said calmly.

"What took you so long, Quincy?" Creed snapped when Adams handed him a pearl-handled pistol.

"What took me so long? I've been trailing you from the minute you got involved with this woman—which, I might point out, was pretty reckless —and then when I saw you were in this fine mess, I had to go rustle up some clothes and come up with a plan to break you out."

"We don't have time to discuss the merits of my decision," Creed interrupted. Striding to the window, he said, "Ferris and Goodman are busy hammering nails into the scaffolding. Get us out of here."

Anne-Marie listened to the men's exchange, her bewilderment growing. "Do you two know each other?"

The men ignored her.

"We'll have to make a break for it," Quincy said in a low tone, and it suddenly occurred to Anne-Marie that his speech was as educated as the Indian's.

Why, those low-down, conniving—these men topped her when it came to deceit.

"If we're quick, the sheriff won't notice a thing," Quincy predicted. "With all that banging and sawing, we should be able to get out of here without causing a stir. Let's go."

Creed stepped out of the cell and the two men headed for the door.

Anne-Marie watched, dumbfounded. They were going to leave her.

"Wait a minute! Aren't you going to take me with you?"

When they didn't answer, she scrambled to her feet. "Oh, no you don't. I'm not going to hang!"

Racing out of the cell, she pressed against Creed's back when he opened the front door a crack and peered out.

"There's a buckboard sitting in front of the bank."

Quincy rolled his eyes. "Too risky. Let's separate and make a run for horses."

Creed studied the nearly deserted street. "Not a chance. We take the buckboard."

The three shoved through the door at once and raced toward the wagon. Anne-Marie shot a glance toward the men at the gallows. The sheriff looked up and straightened. "Run faster!" she shouted, panic raising her voice an octave. *"Run!"*

∾

Dropping his hammer, Ferris shouted, "Hey! Where do you three think you're going?"

Anne-Marie held her skirts high and raced toward the wagon, fighting to keep her footing in the rutted street. She didn't fool herself into thinking Creed would rescue her a second time if she fell.

Scrambling aboard the buckboard, Creed reached out and grabbed Anne-Marie's hand. With a mighty push, she heaved herself up beside him as Quincy scrambled for a position on the small board seat.

"Hold on!" Creed shouted as he swung the horses into the street. Anne-Marie felt a hard jab in the ribs when Quincy reached for a shotgun lying on the wagon floor.

"Hee-ya!" Creed shouted. The buckboard raced past the newly constructed platform, scattering lumber, nails, and men in its wake.

A burst of gunfire rained over the careening wagon as it rolled out of town.

Clinging to the wooden seat, Anne-Marie clamped her eyes tightly shut. The buckboard bumped and banged along the rutted road as Creed cracked a whip over the horses' heads, urging them on to even greater speed.

Quincy attempted to hang on to the shotgun as the wagon lurched crazily across the countryside.

Glancing over her shoulder, Anne-Marie felt her heart pounding. There were riders in the distance, hot on their trail.

"Faster, faster, they're gaining on us!"

Creed swung the whip harder, snapping it smartly over the ears of the team.

The old buckboard wheeled along. A tarp covering two wooden boxes in the wagon bed came loose and began flapping in the wind.

Before Quincy could secure the rope holding the tarp, the canvas ripped free.

Anne-Marie's eyes widened when she spotted the two strongboxes with *Wells Fargo* emblazoned on the sides.

Quincy glanced over his shoulder and yelled, "Holy moly!"

"What's wrong?" Creed shouted.

Quincy shook his head, his eyes frozen on the two strongboxes. The buckboard hit a deep rut and bounced awkwardly on its side. Quincy and Anne-Marie held on for dear life.

The wagon struck another rut and the gun flew out of Quincy's hand.

Anne-Marie made a grab for the firearm and the gun discharged, the explosion propelling the shotgun to the floor of the buckboard.

The Indian yelled, grabbing for his right thigh. The reins fell to the wagon floor. Anne-Marie scrambled to retrieve them as the stench of burning gunpowder filled her nostrils.

Climbing back on the seat, she gasped when she saw the crimson patch of blood soaking above the knee of Creed's breeches.

"Now what'd you do?" Quincy yelled when he grabbed the leads from Anne-Marie's hands.

Before she could deny that she'd done anything, the buckboard sprang up again, pitching Creed off the seat and out of the wagon.

When she whirled to look back her heart sank at the sight of the Crow's lifeless form sprawled in the middle of the road.

Brother, this was *not* her day.

Four

Quincy scrambled over Anne-Marie while the buckboard bumped and crashed its way through the heavy underbrush. Half standing, he hauled on the reins and pulled back.

Gripping the sides of the wagon, Anne-Marie held on as Quincy gained control of the team. Gradually he angled the buckboard around until he had the horses on the road again.

Creed was lying on his side groaning when Quincy brought the cart to a halt beside him. Jumping down from the seat, Anne-Marie ran to assist the injured man.

"Are you hurt?" How inane she sounded; of course he was hurt. Blood seeped from his wounds. His features contorted into a pained mask.

"Yes, I'm hurt! You've nearly blown my leg off!" He lay back, agony and fury fighting for dominance on his usually stoic features.

"Oh, my goodness." She reached toward the gaping wound and then quickly drew back her hand. "What should I do?"

He motioned for her to bend closer. "Take one of the horses and ride as hard and fast as you can in the opposite direction." Groaning, he struggled to sit up, wincing when he focused on the gory injury.

"Sir, it would be my pleasure," she snapped, glancing over her shoulder to see how close the posse was. "But you'll have to endure me awhile longer, because if we don't get out of here fast, none of us will live long enough to argue about it."

Creed collapsed back to the ground, moaning in agony.

"Riders are moving in fast," Quincy warned. He reached to pull Creed back to his feet. "Come on, brother, we've got to get you back into the buckboard."

"Go on without me." Creed's jaw tightened with another spasm of pain.

"I can't do that," both Quincy and Anne-Marie said in unison.

After all, the man had saved Anne-Marie from certain death not once but twice in the past twenty-four hours, and if the sheriff and his men caught up with him, he was certain to hang.

Creed gripped his blood-soaked thigh. Anne-Marie stared at the widening crimson pool, knowing he had to have help soon or he would bleed to death. Biting her lower lip, she tried to think. What would Abigail do? She would seize control of the situation.

"Mr. Adams, please help me move him into the wagon. I can stem the flow of blood with my hands if need be until we can properly cleanse and bandage the wound."

The Crow opened his eyes and glared at her. She glared back. She was only trying to help.

"I know you are in a great deal of pain, but we must get you aboard and leave."

"You and Quincy go on. I'll make it to the underbrush. No one will see me."

"Oh, no you don't. Don't even think of leaving me alone with this woman," Quincy warned him.

Rolling to his side, Creed tried to sit up. When Anne-Marie shifted to help him he sharply drew back, his black eyes glittering. "I can manage on my own."

Stepping up, Quincy gently grasped him beneath his arms and steadied him. "Lean on me until I can get you back to the buckboard." Riders approached at a fast gallop.

Quincy supported Creed's weight and walked him back to the wagon. Creed was barely lucid now, his features contorted by pain. He lost his fight for consciousness when they reached the wagon bed. Realizing that he would need some sort of covering, Anne-Marie quickly retraced the wagon tracks to search for the canvas that had blown off the strongboxes. She located the crumpled tarp several yards away, and then she raced back to the wagon and tucked the covering around Creed's limp body.

Aware they had to move quickly, she motioned for Quincy to drive the team when she jumped aboard the wagon.

With a shrill whistle, John Quincy Adams flicked the whip over the horses' heads, and they were off again, the posse hot on their trail.

❧

Loyal Streeter, High Bluff city councilman, paced his office above the millinery. "What do you mean you don't know what happened? It's your job to know what happened!"

Cortes's face darkened as he tried to explain to his boss what had just taken place. Even he didn't believe it. Cortes had never let a gold shipment get away. Never.

"I say to you, *Señor* Streeter, I do know what happened. One minute the buckboard is loaded and waiting, the next minute it is—how do you say?—vamoosed." He shrugged.

"Gone?" Loyal Streeter asked in disbelief. The outlaw hadn't been right since he was kicked in the head by a mule years earlier, but he'd always carried out the jobs Loyal gave him. Until today. "A hundred thousand dollars of gold, just gone?"

Cortes's features heated. "*Sí, señor*, vamoosed!"

"Who grabbed the gold?"

"The Indian, black, and nun! Before Cortes can say what is happening, they grab the gold and ride out of town."

Loyal ignored Cortes's ridiculous Spanish phrases. Cortes and his gang were loyal and did Loyal's dirty work with a patriot's zeal. Now Loyal swore heatedly. He should never have put this simpleton in charge of such an important shipment. "Where was Ollie when all this was taking place?" Not a one in Cortes's gang had the sense God gave a goose.

Cortes's eyes carefully avoided the boss's piercing gaze. "He run after the gold, *señor.*"

Sheriff Ferris Goodman, who was sitting at Loyal's desk, quietly reached for his hat and rifle.

"You put every man you got on this, Ferris," Loyal ordered when Goodman stood up and walked to the door. "Whoever took that gold couldn't have gotten far."

When the door closed behind the sheriff's back, Loyal stalked back to his desk. "Bunch of incompetent fools. A hundred thousand dollars' worth of gold, gone."

Cortes's eyes focused on the floor. "*Sí, señor.*"

The councilman's scowl turned blacker than coal when Cortes stood there. "Shouldn't you be out there looking for that wagon instead of standing here *sí señoring* me?"

Cortes's boots thundered across the floor now, his stubby legs pumping. "Do not worry, *Señor* Streeter. As you say, they no can get far. When Cortes find the *hombres,* Cortes string them up by their heels and return the gold to you, *pronto.*"

Streeter's features flexed with fury. "You have that gold back here by sundown. You understand me?"

"*Sí.* Sundown, *señor.*"

∾

"Do you have the slightest idea where we're going, ma'am?" Quincy had been pushing the team hard for over two hours, and they seemed to be getting nowhere.

"No, but I'm thinking." Anne-Marie turned to check on Creed again. The wound oozed bright red blood and no matter what she did she could only slow the flow, not stem it. At the moment she was at a loss as to what to do for him. If she could get him to Old Eulalie, she would know what to do. *Eulalie.* Why hadn't she thought of her sooner?

"Mr. Adams, do you know approximately what vicinity we're in?"

"No, ma'am, I come from Alabama. I just work here."

"I wonder if we're anywhere near Addison's Corner." Her gaze roamed the area as the buckboard flew down the road. She should know these parts; she and her sisters had roamed far away from the mission on some of their excursions.

"Saw an arrow for Addison's Corner pointing down a road about a mile back. Why? You know the authorities will have someone checking out any small settlement around here." Quincy gradually slackened the horses' pace to a ground-covering trot. There'd been no sign of riders for over an hour now. Adams had proved adept at eluding the posse, cutting corners and driving through rough ravines, but that didn't mean they could relax their vigilance.

Anne-Marie mused. "Have you ever heard of a woman called Eulalie?"

Quincy visibly paled. "You mean that strange old woman who lives with all those cats?"

"Oh," she scoffed, "Eulalie isn't strange; she's just…different."

Quincy kept his eyes fixed on the road. "Yes, ma'am, I've heard of her. Stories abound about that old woman. They say she's crazy as a loon."

"Do you think you could find Eulalie's cabin?"

"Why would you want to go looking for her house? Haven't we got enough trouble?" Quincy shook his head. "No, ma'am, don't you go expecting me to go within ten miles of that woman."

"Oh, shame on you. Eulalie wouldn't hurt a fly, and if you think anything of your friend at all, you'll help me find her house before he bleeds to death. She's the only chance we have of keeping him alive."

Quincy eyed her curiously. "How do you know that old woman? You're not one of her kin, are you?"

Anne-Marie sighed as she fondly recalled her friend's goodness. "No, she and I go back a long way."

The woman known as Old Eulalie was something of a mystery and a legend in this remote region of Texas. The valley where she lived was well known to the locals, but neither the Indians nor the whites bothered her. Eulalie was regarded as a person to fear rather than a source of help when it came to health issues.

But Anne-Marie knew that if anyone could save Creed Walker, Old Eulalie could.

She turned and continued, "Anytime we pass through the area we visit with her, but"—Anne-Marie's eyes continued their search— "nothing looks familiar to me."

"That's because we're coming in the back way to the old woman's cabin."

Anne-Marie laid her hand on Quincy's arm. "We have to go to her, Mr. Adams. We have no other choice."

Quincy groaned. "I don't know how I get myself in these messes." But Anne-Marie noticed he was turning the buckboard around and heading toward a break in the terrain she had not seen before.

It was a long time before they spotted the gnarled cedar that marked the entrance to the small valley where Old Eulalie lived. A light mix of rain and snow began to fall, and Anne-Marie frowned, glancing at the darkening sky. With everything that had happened, the threat of another snowstorm was all they needed.

Mr. Adams drove the team down the furrowed path. Anne-Marie glanced over her shoulder to find Creed already damp and cold.

The buckboard rattled to a stop, the door to the shanty opened, and the barrel of a shotgun appeared.

"Who's there?" a gravelly voice demanded.

"It's me, Anne-Marie, Eulalie! I need help!"

The barrel of the gun vanished and the door immediately swung open.

"One of the McDougal young'uns? Well, land sakes—haven't seen you in a coon's age." A scarecrow of an old woman shuffled onto the porch and made her way down the rickety steps. Anne-Marie counted three sweaters and a heavy coat the woman was wearing—plus overalls and work boots. Eulalie wasn't one for fashion.

Jumping down from the wagon, Anne-Marie ran to the back of the buckboard, jerking the tarp off the still-unconscious Creed.

"What brings you out this way, child?" Eulalie approached the wagon. "Sakes alive, girl! You're going to catch your death out here." Her eyes fixed on Quincy, who was nervously holding the reins of the exhausted team.

"Git on in by the fire, son, and I'll fix something to warm your innards."

Quincy glanced at Anne-Marie, shaking his head.

Anne-Marie shot him a look. "Mr. Adams, Eulalie has graciously invited us to share the warmth of her fire. Now get down off that wagon seat and help me get Mr. Walker into the house!"

Quincy set the brake and then climbed reluctantly down.

Though Eulalie moved with a shuffling gait, she appeared ageless. Her grin was topped by eyes twinkling with intelligence. She had black waist-length hair intertwined with silver streaks. She'd never said why she'd chosen to hide herself in a hovel built from lumber scraps and tin she'd found by the wayside, and Anne-Marie had never asked. Eulalie survived by trading her healing herbs with locals, but for the most part, people thought her a fright and left her alone.

Quincy pulled Creed out of the wagon, giving Eulalie a wide berth when he carried the unconscious man up the rickety steps.

Upon entering the cabin, Anne-Marie was reminded that Eulalie wasn't the tidiest of housekeepers. She would gather up anything and everything that she found or traded for, so the furnishings inside the cabin were as much a hodgepodge as the structure itself.

"Who is he?" Eulalie asked, inclining her head toward Creed.

"An acquaintance. I accidently shot him."

"Shot him?"

"Eulalie, he's lost a lot of blood. Can you save him?"

"Only the Lord can save him." The old woman looked deeply into Anne-Marie's eyes. Anne-Marie hated admitting it, but she wouldn't lie to Old Eulalie.

"All right, we were trying to outrun the law," she murmured.

Eulalie cackled. "Outrun the law, you say? Well, put him on the kitchen table and I'll take a look at him."

Anne-Marie trailed Quincy as he carried Creed to the sturdy wood table.

"Shoo! Get out of here! Shoo!" Eulalie waved her hands at the dozen or so cats that had converged to greet them. "Anne-Marie, light another lamp so I can have a look at that wound."

The cabin reeked of cooking odors and pungent animal droppings. Quincy deposited Creed on the block and then stood to the side. Anne-Marie tried not to stare at the wounded leg, but she couldn't tear her eyes away.

The leg was swollen, as if all the blood from Creed's body had pooled in one place. Eulalie's gnarled fingers probed the torn flesh and Creed moaned.

"It's bad...real bad."

"Can you help?" The man couldn't die. For some odd reason, Anne-Marie felt he was the only security she had at the moment.

"Can't promise anything, but I'll do what I can."

The smells combined with the sight of the woman poking fingers into the wound appeared to be too much for Quincy. Eulalie and Anne-Marie turned when they heard a soft thud. Quincy had passed out cold on the dirt floor.

"Well, I'll make him some good strong tea when he comes to," Eulalie said. Drawing Anne-Marie aside, she murmured, "Get me some hot water and some rags from the kitchen shelf."

The warmth from the fire seeped into her weary bones, but at that moment Anne-Marie was too concerned about Creed to enjoy it. A scratching in the corner of the room momentarily drew her attention to a small raccoon who had taken up residence; he peered back at her with alarmingly resourceful eyes. A mother cat and four kittens rested on a rug in a corner near the fireplace. As usual, Eulalie had a collection of critters that believed the cabin to be their own.

Pouring a pan full of hot water, Anne-Marie carried it and the clean rags to the table, stepping over Quincy in the process. He would come around, or she and Eulalie would drag him to the couch later.

Using Creed's knife, Eulalie slit the Indian's breeches from ankle to thigh and peeled the buckskin aside.

"That buckshot's got to come out." Eulalie motioned for Anne-Marie to move the light closer. "Hold the lantern higher."

Creed stirred "What's happening?"

Anne-Marie bent closer. "Don't be alarmed; we're at a friend's cabin."

"Where's Quincy?"

She pointed to the crumpled heap lying at the foot of the table. "He fainted."

"Never could stand the sight of blood," he murmured. His eyes closed, and then briefly opened to focus on Eulalie hovering above him. "What's going—who?"

Grasping his hand, Anne-Marie held it tightly. "You're going to be fine. Eulalie is going to help you."

His eyes clouded with doubt. "My leg…" Long, dark lashes drifted shut.

"He's out." Eulalie noted. "Good. Shoo. Get away from here," she scolded, nudging two of the felines out of the way with toe of her boot. Turning back to the wound, she talked as she worked. "Where are Amelia and Abigail?"

Sighing, Anne-Marie said wearily, "Eulalie, you wouldn't believe what's happened." While Eulalie dug buckshot out of Creed's leg, Anne-Marie filled her in on the events of the past few days.

"What do you think? You think Abigail and Amelia are safe?" Anne-Marie asked once the tale had unfolded.

"Can't say," Eulalie admitted, "but you girls have a way of coming out on the good end of trouble."

Anne-Marie swayed with exhaustion as she held the lamp closer to the bleeding wound. "I hope so, Eulalie. Abigail and Amelia are all I have."

Eulalie picked out three large pieces of shot, each one plinking loudly in the enamel pan lying beside the table. When her fingers probed the torn flesh Creed moaned, his teeth clenching as the point of the knife discovered yet another fragment. Each one that clinked into the pan made Anne-Marie feel guiltier as she watched his face turn pale as a ghost's even though he was thankfully unconscious.

"Will he be all right?" She leaned closer, praying that he would recover. She should be afraid of this strange man, but she wasn't. He was her defender, and the thought made her slightly giddy. She'd never had a man's protection, not that she'd ever needed one. Abigail said that no woman needed a male hanging around, but sometimes when she was ranting on about the subject Anne-Marie thought, deep down, that maybe some women might. Men were strong and often kind and they could cut a cord of wood or clean a stringer of fish in less time than it took all three of the McDougal sisters.

"For sure he's a might stronger than his friend there," Eulalie said.

"I pray he will recover."

Eulalie bandaged Creed's thigh and cast another look at Anne-Marie. "I'm guessing he ain't your young man."

"No, he was just kind enough to help me. And look what I've done to repay him."

"He's strong; all he needs is a few days to mend. And from the looks of you, a good rest wouldn't hurt you any either. Let's get him into bed, and then you try to get some sleep. And while we're at it, let's get you out of that nun clothing. It ain't fittin for you to pretend to be something you ain't."

"Yes, ma'am."

When Anne-Marie tried to move Creed he stirred, weakly pushing her away. Awake now, he turned defensive. "I can get to the bed on my own."

The cats gathered, meowing as though they wanted a better look at their guest.

"Leave him alone, girls. He needs his rest."

Between Eulalie and Anne-Marie, the two women pulled Creed off the table and eased his body the few steps to the small cot in the corner of the cabin. But no sooner had they gotten him settled than they heard a moan coming from the man on the floor.

Quincy sat up, grasping his head with both hands. "What happened?"

"You fainted," Anne-Marie said.

"Fainted?" Quincy scrambled to his feet. "No, ma'am, I didn't faint. I must've tripped over one of those cats, or something."

"Yes, that must be what happened." Anne-Marie and Eulalie exchanged amused looks.

Quincy spotted Creed lying on the cot. "Is he going to make it?"

"Eulalie thinks he'll be good as new in a few days."

"That's good news." He reached up gingerly to probe a knot the size of a goose egg forming on the side of his head.

"It wouldn't hurt any of us to get some sleep," Eulalie said.

Quincy edged toward the front door. "Well, I'll just be going out to the lean-to. If you need anything, I'll be close by."

Eulalie met his eyes, understanding passing between them. "It's not necessary for you to sleep out there. Plenty of room in here where it's warm."

"Thank you, ma'am, but I'd be more comfortable sleeping in the lean-to."

"Suit yourself. Just wanted you to know you're welcome." Shuffling to the stove, Eulalie took the lid off a pot and drew in the smell of the steamy contents. "Better have a bite to eat before you go. Mornin's a ways off."

"Thank you, ma'am, but if it's all the same to you, I'll be going now." Giving Anne-Marie a cursory nod, he strode quickly out the door, latching it behind him.

The occupants of the shanty settled down for the night. Eulalie provided a skirt and worn feed-sack blouse, and Anne-Marie gratefully shed the disguise before she made herself a pallet beside the bed. Eulalie moved to the fire and lowered herself into her rocker with a mug of homemade tea.

Stretching out on the pallet, Anne-Marie closed her eyes and put her toes to the fire, absorbing the warmth. She was conscious of hunger pangs, but she was too tired to do anything about them.

Fatigue swiftly claimed her, and she drifted off to the faint smell of wood smoke in the air.

Five

The sound of a rooster's crow shattered the cabin's sleepy silence. The boisterous *Cock-a-doodle-do!* was accompanied by a weak ray of sunlight struggling to penetrate the dirty windowpane.

Rolling to her side, Anne-Marie came awake slowly. Creed was sleeping now, having tossed and turned the better part of the night.

Eulalie was standing at the stove dishing out portions of cornmeal mush for the cats. She stirred the bubbling mixture with a heavy wooden ladle.

"You must be hungrier than a polecat," she called when Anne-Marie stirred.

"I am. Whatever you're cooking smells wonderful."

"Nothin' fancy—just plain old mush, but it'll keep starvation off your doorstep."

Getting up, Anne-Marie tried to step over and around several cats and the raccoon as she crossed the room. The animals were scattered around, their heads buried in various bowls of scraps.

A tap sounded at the front door and Anne-Marie called out, "Come in, Quincy!"

Quincy appeared in the doorway, his coat dusted with light snow. "Morning, ladies."

"Mornin'," Anne-Marie and Eulalie called back.

"Snow about over?" Anne-Marie asked.

"Yes, ma'am, seems to be tapering off." His dark eyes moved to the cot in the corner. "How's he doing this morning?"

"He's quieter now." Eulalie motioned for Quincy to have a seat at the table, now clean and set with bowls and cups. "Hope you like mush."

"Yes, ma'am, I do." Quincy sat down, and shortly thereafter Anne-Marie set a steaming cup of chicory in front of him.

"I hope you were warm enough in the lean-to."

"I slept just fine, ma'am."

Eulalie and Anne-Marie sat down and the three bowed their heads as Eulalie prayed. "Bless us, O Lord, and these Thy gifts, which we are about to receive from Thy bounty, through Christ our Lord. Bless the poor and the sick and the hurting. Amen."

Anne-Marie picked up a knife and spread butter on her bread, hesitantly broaching the subject that worried her most. "What do you think we should do about those strongboxes, Quincy?" She wasn't sure if she should call him by his given name, but at the moment the small liberty felt proper.

Keeping his eyes on his plate, Quincy said quietly, "We have to keep them, ma'am."

"You don't have to be so formal; you can call me Anne-Marie."

"Thank you, ma'am."

"You really think we should keep the strongboxes?" Anne-Marie took a bite of bread, chewing thoughtfully. It was a high risk. Those strongboxes belonged to Wells Fargo. The last thing she wanted or sought was more trouble. That gold wasn't theirs and needed to be returned. "Wouldn't that make us thieves, though we took the boxes by accident?"

"I suppose it would, but I don't see we have much choice but to keep them. I wouldn't advise turning them over to anyone we didn't know for certain. That would create too much risk of them falling into the wrong hands."

"How so?"

Quincy looked up, his dark eyes respectful. "Doesn't it seem coincidental to you that those two strongboxes were in that wagon?"

"No. The boxes could be the railroad payroll being delivered to the bank."

"Could be, but I don't figure so."

Anne-Marie sat up straighter, her interest piqued. "Are you suggesting something unlawful is going on?"

He shrugged. "Someone might have been transferring those boxes to their wagon instead of delivering them. Lot of thievery going on in these parts. Guess most anything's possible."

Anne-Marie looked at him, skepticism forming in her mind. "Exactly why are you and Creed traveling together?"

The combination of an educated black man and Indian keeping company seemed suspect to her, unless there was an underlying motive, one the men had failed to mention.

Accepting another hunk of bread from Eulalie, Quincy busied himself buttering it.

"What were you and Creed doing when Creed rescued me?" she repeated.

"I think Creed should explain that, ma'am, not me."

She studied him, trying to decide why he was so evasive. "Friends, maybe?"

"Yes, ma'am." He glanced up, smiling. "We're that all right. Met years ago and formed a tight friendship."

"Where?"

"Where what?"

"Where did you meet and form a tight friendship?"

"Through our work."

"You work together?"

"I didn't say that we worked together—I said we met at our work."

"Which is?"

"Can't tell you." He glanced at Eulalie. "Ma'am, could I have some of those strawberry preserves?"

"You work together," Anne-Marie pursued, "but you can't say where?"

"Miss Eulalie, ma'am." He spooned thick preserves on his bread. "These are quite possibly the best looking preserves I've ever seen. You put these up yourself?"

Eulalie smiled. "I shore do, and I got more where those come from. Before you leave remind me to give you a jar..." The two went into great detail about jams and jellies.

Anne-Marie's gaze narrowed on him. He was clearly avoiding the subject of Creed and their friendship. But why? She butted in on the preserves conversation. "Is it possible that you know something about that particular gold that you're not telling me?"

Was that why he was choosing his answers so carefully?

"Ma'am, I guess when it comes right down to it, I don't know much of anything," he conceded. "I just eat my preserves and thank the good Lord for giving me another day."

"Well." Anne-Marie sighed, biting into her bread. It was apparent she wasn't going to get anything more out of him than his overwhelming desire for more jam. "I suppose Creed will know what to do about the strongboxes once he's awake."

Quincy kept his eyes on his plate. "Yes, ma'am, I expect he will."

She watched as he ate the meager fare with appreciation, convinced he was hiding something from her. Obviously he and Creed were in cahoots, but she wasn't going to get anything out of Quincy. Not this morning. Turning to Eulalie, she said quietly, "We'll have to stay a few days—long enough for Creed to get back on his feet."

"Stay as long as you like. Be happy to have the company."

Turning to Quincy, Anne-Marie tried to gauge his reaction to her suggestion. "Is that okay with you, Mr. Adams? You don't have to be anywhere at any particular time?"

Now she had him cornered. If he was up to something, he'd have to tell her or he wouldn't be able to finish whatever he was up to on time.

"Fine with me, ma'am."

Oh, he was smart, all right. If he and Creed were working together, she'd never hear it from John Quincy Adams.

The morning turned to one of waiting. Snow cleared and a cold wind rattled the old dwelling. Eulalie waited for bread and pies to come out of the oven, while Anne-Marie and Quincy waited on Creed's return to consciousness. Eulalie wondered aloud if she'd baked enough bread for everyone and had put enough cinnamon in her apple pie; Anne-Marie wondered if Creed was really going to be all right and why Quincy was deceiving her; and Quincy wondered what he and Creed were going to tell Anne-Marie to satisfy her curiosity when his friend finally woke up.

It seemed the whole world waited on Creed Walker.

e~

Creed drifted between awareness and unconsciousness. In lucid moments he recognized the smell of cinnamon and baked apples, but that wasn't what Anne-Marie and the old woman were forcing down his throat. When he tried to swallow the bitter concoction, he was reminded of the time he'd been sick with the white man's fever and the medicine man had forced something equally vile through his parched lips.

Occasionally he could hear Anne-Marie voice his concerns.

"He's so weak."

"He's as strong as an ox," a gravelly voice answered from somewhere above him. He felt a small, cool hand touch his face when the noxious brew was once again raised to his mouth.

"Will he live?"

Creed wanted to assure the voice that he would, but he couldn't force the words from his throat.

"He'll make it," Eulalie confirmed.

Occasionally he could hear pounding in the background and could only surmise that Quincy was trying to repay the old woman for her charitable hospitality.

Mercifully he dropped into unconsciousness, his last thoughts being that of a lovely young woman with emerald-colored eyes.

⁓

By late afternoon Anne-Marie had grown weary of the wait. She decided the patient needed a good washing, if not for him, then out of respect for those around him. Armed with soap and hot water, the angels of mercy scrubbed, lathered, scoured, and powdered until they had the Indian, in Quincy's stated opinion, smelling like a girl. He stood close by, trying to converse with a lifeless Creed. "I'd spare you this appalling exhibition of maternal clucking, but I am powerless to prevent it."

"Don't be so smug, Mr. Adams." Anne-Marie filled the hot water kettle and set it on the stove. "You're next."

Quincy headed for the door but Anne-Marie blocked his efforts to flee. "You're not going anywhere until you bathe. I'm sick of smelling you and your friend—and lay your clothes by the doorway. I want to scrub them too."

Not long after, the freshly bathed Quincy excused himself and escaped to the lean-to, wearing a pair of clean breeches and a shirt Eulalie had provided.

Later, Eulalie settled down in the rocking chair and Anne-Marie decided to read a book of poems by the popular poet Walt Whitman. She loved poetry; she'd even written one or two poems herself—though they weren't all that good.

"Where did you get a Walt Whitman book?" she asked, thumbing through the yellowed pages of *Leaves of Grass*. She would never think that Eulalie had a literary side.

"Can't rightly recall." Her host glanced at the book. "Don't look familiar to me. You're welcome to read it if you like."

A gust of wind rattled the old shanty as Anne-Marie lost herself in Whitman's words. The sound of a strangled snort distracted her, and she glanced up to see Eulalie's head starting to nod.

Shaking her head, Anne-Marie returned to "Song of Myself" as the clock on the mantel methodically ticked off the long evening.

᧬

Smoke. Creed opened his eyes when the smell filled his nostrils. Coughing, he struggled to sit up.

Angry, red-hot tendrils licked a trail from floor to ceiling, devouring the dry timber. Heat suffocated him and he groped for the edge of the bed.

Where was he?

Rolling to the floor, he gritted his teeth when a white-hot pain shot up his leg. Through a thick blanket of haze he saw the old woman's sleeping form slumped forward in her chair, the roaring flames, like a pack of wild animals coming closer.

He threw his arm up to shield his face from the scorching heat while his eyes searched the room. The flames were spreading, leaping across the dry timber, destroying everything that stood in their way.

"Quincy! Are you in here?" he called in a cracked voice. His lungs burned, and his eyes blurred when he rolled off the cot and tried to crawl across the room.

"Over here." Anne-Marie's barely perceptible voice came to him above the sound of the roaring inferno.

"Where are you?"

"Over here, near the kitchen table."

"Can you crawl to me?"

He heard her gasp when she slid off her pallet and began to crawl on hands and knees across the floor.

"Where are you?" Creed insisted.

"Where are you? I can't find you!"

Filled with panic, he searched the inferno. "Anne-Marie!"

He was so weak he could barely move. He had to get to her...

Quincy. Where was he?

"Over here—take my hand!" He blindly groped, hoping to feel her flesh.

Long moments passed before he felt a small hand latch firmly onto his. Relief filled him.

"Where's Quincy?" he yelled.

"Outside—lean-to!"

Struggling across the floor, he half dragged, half pulled Anne-Marie along behind him. Every muscle in his body felt like hot coals. Gritting his teeth, he silently cried out against the pain but he held tight to her hand.

The fire raged out of control. Flaming arrows of destruction stuck him when rafters rained down on their heads.

"Eulalie!" Anne-Marie cried out. She struggled to break away but he held tight. "Where's Eulalie?"

Clasping her hand, Creed felt his way across the plank floor. When he located the door, he realized he didn't have the strength to reach the latch.

Rolling to his side, he gritted his teeth and kicked the door with all of his might. The panel gave way with a splintering sound. Flames gained new life when fresh air sucked into the room.

Grabbing Anne-Marie around the waist, he rolled out onto the porch and down the log steps onto the snow-packed ground.

ᘒ

Drawing in deep breaths of fresh air, Anne-Marie staggered to her feet and scrambled away, nearly falling over half a dozen cats in the process when she sought refuge beneath a nearby oak.

Collapsing, she remembered Creed and crawled back to help him to safety. As they fought for breath, she saw Quincy burst from the lean-to, leading the frightened team of horses.

Moments later the roof of the cabin caved in, and the shanty was engulfed in a ball of fire.

"Eu-Eulalie!" Anne-Marie buried her face in her hands and sobbed, her shoulders heaving. Eulalie had seen her through many a lonely time in life. The world wouldn't be the same without the kindly woman who always made her feel like family.

Bracing his hands on a snow pack, Creed bent forward as a spasm of coughing choked him. When he could speak, he crawled to his feet.

Anne-Marie's hand blocked him. "Where are you going? Creed!" she shouted when she noticed that he was already making his way back to the house. Relief surged when she spotted Quincy leaning against the horse rail, catching his breath.

❧

"What happened?" Quincy shouted when Creed limped toward him. The wild-eyed animals shied away from the fire, and the man struggled to hold them. "How can you be on your feet? You were near death two hours ago."

"I woke up and the cabin was in flames." He fixed on Quincy. "Eulalie's still in there. I'm going in after her."

"Not alone, you're not." Quincy fell into step behind him and the two men disappeared into the flames.

❧

Anne-Marie sat on the ground staring, praying, hands clasped tightly to her chest when Quincy returned carrying a limp Eulalie. Creed leaned on his shoulder, coughing. Laying the woman at the base of a tree, Quincy gently leaned and blew breath back into her body. After several moments, Eulalie stirred, coughing.

"Oh thank You, God." The grateful sob slipped from Anne-Marie softly. "She's alive."

Creed carefully made his way to where she sat. Reaching out, she helped him to the ground. "You risked your life to save her," she whispered.

"Appeared that she meant a great deal to you."

"Eulalie was—is—the mother I never had." She caught back a sob. "One old woman couldn't possibly mean anything to you, but she meant everything to me. Thank you." She turned to look at him. "Do you or Quincy know how the fire started?"

He wiped a sooty hand across his face and she winced when she noted that blisters were forming on his palms. "It's hard to say—a stray spark on the rug. Maybe one of the animals dragged something too close to the flames."

Fighting back tears, Anne-Marie longed to reach over and put her arms around his neck and comfort him. She'd made such a mess of this whole ugly incident, and she knew he rued the day he had stopped to help her.

He turned to face her, his features and chest streaked with smoke, his hair slightly singed, his—

Her hands flew up to cover her mouth and drew Creed's attention from the flaming ruins. "What's wrong?"

Not trusting her voice, she averted her eyes and took two deep breaths. How was she going to tell him in a respectful way?

"Well?"

"I'm sorry…but it's you," she admitted, keeping her gaze fixed on a line of bare thorn bushes.

"Me? I fail to see how anyone could find anything funny about this situation. We're lucky to escape with our lives."

A hysterical giggle escaped her. Once started, the laughter took over and she couldn't stop. Bending forward, she buried her face in the smoky folds of her skirt.

"You!" she burst out, losing complete control when her eyes swept him from head to foot.

Understanding finally dawned on his stoic features. Creed Walker was a funny sight in the blood-soaked nightshirt—not to make light of the situation. He could have died going back in for Eulalie, but still…

She bit her lip until she tasted blood and finally stepped away until she could get her giggles under control, painfully conscious that she didn't look so good either.

❧

"You blame me for all the trouble, don't you?"

Creed's features remained stoic.

"You do, don't you?" she persisted.

"I don't blame you."

"And about me shooting you, it was purely accidental," Anne-Marie said.

"So you say."

"It's the truth. And I certainly didn't—"

"Enough!" Creed roared. "If you say another word, I am going to turn this wagon around and deliver you straight into the hands of the law. I'm sure they'll be glad to see you."

She drew back. "Sorry."

"Well," Quincy announced, "I'm going to leave you two lovebirds alone while I see to the horses."

When he walked off, Anne-Marie settled back to watch Creed lace the material. "I could do that."

"Have you sewn men's britches before?"

"No, there's never been a need, but I imagine I could."

"I'll do it myself."

She focused on the tiny stiches. He was very good. Obviously he had sewn his clothing often. She knew there was more to Creed Walker than met the eye. Somewhere in his background he had been highly educated.

Creed glanced up to study the remains of the smoldering cabin. "What's your friend going to do once we leave? The shack is gone."

"She said she'd have it built back up in no time. Eulalie's used to hard conditions. Now that her head is clear, you would never convince her to leave."

His gaze scanned the pile of worthless rubble. "It won't be hard to gather enough to build shelter until spring arrives."

Sighing, Anne-Marie stared at the burned-out hull of the shanty. "There's nothing left but ashes."

"We can bury that cat she loved, if you want."

"Marbles. Eulalie loved all her pets, but Marbles has been with her the longest. She would take great comfort if we buried the animal for her."

With the dawn, the heavy layer of clouds had parted and the sun broke through. A few timid rays held no warmth. A cold breeze whipped the limbs of an old cedar, a reminder that spring was not yet here.

"Quincy and I will get the cat. Someone's bound to have seen the smoke and will come to investigate. We need to move on."

"But you're still so weak—"

"Quincy will do most of the work."

While Creed located the cat, Quincy positioned the shovel and then shoved the blade into the ground, digging a hole beside the river. They completed the work quickly, and then Anne-Marie cleared her throat.

"Lord, we thank You for bringing us safely through the fire. Bless Eulalie, Father, as she rebuilds her home. Send her friends to help her and comfort her in her time of distress. Amen."

"Amen," Quincy repeated. "Your words were real heartfelt. That should do it, Sister." He covered the hole with dirt. "I'll get the wagon and team."

Later the three prepared to leave. Eulalie gave Anne-Marie a big hug. Her strength had returned and color was back in her cheeks. "I've been on my own longer than you've been alive. Don't you worry about me. You take care of yourself."

⚮

"Now what?" Anne-Marie asked when the wagon pulled away from the shanty.

"You're the one with the ideas. What do you suggest?" Creed winced when the wagon hit a deep pothole. "Quincy, can you manage to hit deeper ruts? I could use more agony."

"Sorry—these horses go out of their way to hit holes."

Heat flooded Anne-Marie's cheeks. She did not appreciate Creed's attitude toward her this morning. The wound had left him cranky and difficult. She hadn't put those potholes in the road. "Are you asking me what I would do?"

"Am I speaking French?"

Well now. She could be just as testy as he could. "I would suggest that we each take a horse and go our separate ways, but we only have two horses—and the gold." The wind whipped her hair into her face and she brushed it aside. "So I don't have any ideas."

"Do you want to separate? Because we can. One horse will pull the buckboard, so you're welcome to the other."

He was baiting her but she wasn't falling for his trick. She hadn't asked to be involved in that gold shipment, but she had just as much invested in this escapade as these two. If anyone other than Wells Fargo got that gold, she was going to get her share. She was smart enough to know that Creed and Quincy were her best hope for rejoining her sisters in Mercy Flats. Whether she liked Creed Walker or not, she had no reasonable choice but to stay with him for the time being.

She blew out a pent-up breath. "That's not what I want."

At the moment, what she wanted was to be home with Abigail and Amelia, drinking hot tea and eating warm muffins in the sisters' kitchen that always smelled of roasting meat and baking bread. In a few days, the nuns would start to worry about the missing McDougals. The kind women were accustomed to the girls' short, unexplained absences, but Mother Superior often noted that the McDougals were of age to do as they willed. Only the nuns' goodness still provided meals and a roof over the three sisters' heads. In return, the girls worked hard to repay the nuns' compassion.

For the moment, Anne-Marie had little choice but to accept her circumstances, a bitter pill to swallow. "What are we going to do?"

Creed shifted. "With the gold?"

"The gold—and getting me back to Mercy Flats."

Creed and Quincy made eye contact before Creed turned to confront her. "Why do you suppose two strongboxes from California, full of gold, were sitting in front of the bank with no guard?"

"Quincy asked me the same thing; I didn't know then, and I don't know now. Is there some significance to the coincidence?"

Creed mused out loud. "The way I figure it, a gold shipment means guards, several guards. This particular shipment of gold was sitting there vulnerable. Agreed, Quince?"

Quincy nodded. "That's how it looked to me."

"But the sheriff—" Anne-Marie interjected.

"—wasn't concerned about the gold," Creed said. "He was working on scaffolding."

"Well, maybe he didn't know about the gold and that's why he wasn't concerned about it."

Quincy and Creed exchanged looks again. "Maybe," Creed conceded, "but that's unlikely. A good sheriff knows everything that goes on in his town, and a man responsible for a shipment that size should be vigilant every moment unless he knows the gold is safe."

"Maybe he isn't a good sheriff."

"Right now it doesn't matter if he's good or bad." The wagon hit another pothole and Quincy gave the team a sharp warning whistle. Creed winced. "The sheriff thinks we stole it."

"And if they were going to hang us for stealing cattle, then they're bound to hang us for stealing gold, whether we meant to or not," she murmured.

Creed and Quincy's eyes met again.

She brightened. "Why don't we just go back and explain what happened?"

"And how do you propose we do that?"

Quincy shook his head. "We can't prance back into town and walk up to the sheriff and say, 'Sorry, Mr. Sheriff, we've done taken your gold by mistake.'"

"Don't tempt her, Quince."

Anne-Marie narrowed her gaze on Creed. "Very amusing. My sisters and I have managed to pull off some pretty brilliant cons—"

"I noticed how brilliant the three of you looked screaming your pretty little heads off in that jail wagon," he noted.

"There you go again, insinuating that if it wasn't for me, we wouldn't be in this—"

"I'm not insinuating, I'm telling you flat out, if it wasn't for you—"

"Look." Quincy dropped the reins and threw up both hands. "Right now it doesn't matter who had the gold. We've got it now."

"You mean we're going to keep it?" she asked incredulously. She picked up the reins and put them in Quincy's hand.

"Yes, we're going to keep it."

The cold finality of Creed's tone concluded the conversation.

Easing to the back of the wagon, he stretched out, giving a low moan.

Anne-Marie turned to help. "Here, let me do that."

"Woman, leave me alone."

"You are so…so churlish!"

"You *make* me churlish—whatever that means."

"I do not. That's a horrible thing to say to a woman."

Quincy whipped the reins. "Both of you are giving me a headache."

❧

Cortes and his three *compadres* topped the horizon. The disheveled horsemen focused on the smoldering ruins of what once had been Eulalie's cabin.

"Looks like there's been a fire," Butch observed.

Turning slowly in his saddle, Cortes glared at him. "What is your clue? The smoke still curls from the ruins."

"Well, guess that settles it. The Injun, the nun, and the black ain't down there," Ollie said. "Guess we won't be stirring up that scary old crone anytime soon."

Cortes's gaze strayed to the mound of fresh dirt located near the stream. "We no know the *indio* hasn't been here. We will see for ourselves."

Ollie, Rodrigo, and Butch passed a series of uneasy looks. Ollie bent and muttered out of the corner of his mouth to the other two men. "What do you think?"

Rodrigo thought for a moment and then said, "Even being touched in the head, he's still had the smarts to get us into and out of plenty of schemes, but lately he does seem odder than usual."

"Better do what he wants," Butch advised. "That's a lot of gold."

Ollie snorted. "'Pears to me that one of them there meteors must have hit 'em instead of a horse kicking him in the head."

Nodding, the three men slowly fell in behind Cortes and rode toward the old crone's shack.

When the outlaws reached the creek, Rodrigo reined his horse around a bucket sitting on the bank. "Must be the old lady's water bucket."

"Maybe." Cortes chewed the stub of the cigar absentmindedly. "Maybe, no." He stood up in the stirrups, spotting the set of wagon tracks leading away from the shanty. "Someone has been here." He kneed the horse forward.

The riders approached the smoldering ruins with caution. Climbing off their horses, the men stood for a moment, assessing the situation. The place was deader than a cemetery.

"Can't we just leave?" said Butch. "It's plain to see the shanty burned down. There's nothing living around here now."

Cortes set his jaw. "Our outlaws could have buried the gold here, planning to come back later and get it."

"But where? No sir, I 'spect they've got the gold with them right now. If it were me, well, I wouldn't let that gold outta my sight for one minute." Butch looked around. The other men were nodding silently.

"Idiots!" Cortes's dark eyes narrowed with contempt. The *indio*, the negro, and the *monja*. They would pay for making Cortes look the *estúpido*.

Oh, they would pay.

Six

I'm worried." Anne-Marie drew her brows together when she turned from checking on Creed again. He had slept since they'd left Eulalie's, and she had barely been able to rouse him throughout the day. "His fever's come up."

"I'm not surprised." The buckboard rattled along the rutted road as Quincy scanned the back roads.

"What are you looking for?"

"Southern patrols."

"Creed needs proper food and warmth."

"I know."

There was no shelter or food to be found. Huddling deeper inside a buffalo robe Eulalie had given them, she watched the passing scenery. Patches of dirty snow littered the hillsides, but a thin sun made the temperature bearable.

A back wheel hit a pothole, jostling Creed. Upon hearing his groan, she quickly turned around, shooting Quincy a censuring look.

"Be careful."

"I am, ma'am, I am."

Turning around, she wrapped the heavy buffalo robe around herself tighter in an effort to block the wind. "It wouldn't do us any harm to have a nice meal and a warm bed, either, you know."

"No, ma'am, it wouldn't." Quincy's eyes softened. "Are you warm enough?"

"Yes, thank you." She was only being polite. The robe helped, but a fierce wind stung her nose.

"Do you have any ideas?" They couldn't just wander the countryside like gypsies. They had no food, no clothing, no shelter, and it would be dark before long.

"I've been thinking…there's a mission up ahead. Creed and I overnighted there during a rainstorm a few months back. We could hole up there until Creed's leg is better."

"How far?" She frowned. "It'll be dark soon."

"Three, maybe four miles. I figure we'll take shelter in some rancher's barn tonight and then start out first thing in the morning. There's always an egg lying around for the taking. We'll be warm and fed, and then with a little luck, we'll reach the mission by late tomorrow afternoon."

Anne-Marie turned to look over her shoulder at Creed again. "I don't know, Quincy. The nuns are so busy with prayer and…he needs care, and soon."

"The mission is deserted now, ma'am—by the looks of it, has been for years. I don't know what else we could…" Quincy's voice faded when the buckboard rounded a bend, and they found two young, strong Indian warriors sitting astride war ponies in the middle of the road.

"Oh, give us grace, oh Lord," Quincy murmured.

Anne-Marie sat up straighter when Quincy set the brake on the wagon. The old buckboard clattered to a halt a few feet in front of the horses. "Who are they?" she whispered.

"Look to be Apache. They must be from the encampment."

The Indians, wearing war paint, regarded the three travelers, their dark eyes traveling slowly over the wagon and its occupants.

"Do you suppose they understand English?" Anne-Marie whispered.

"The way our luck's been running? No, ma'am, not a word."

The four sat in the middle of the road, sizing each other up.

Finally one of the Indians broke away, kneeing his horse to the back of the wagon. Anne-Marie closed her eyes when he slowed, peering into the wagon bed.

"Oh, Lord, Lord, Lord," Quincy agonized in a low whisper. "Miss, if you got any pull with the Man upstairs, now might be a good time to use it."

Anne-Marie winced. She didn't have any pull; chances were the Man upstairs was pretty put out with her right now. Would He even want to keep caring for her when her choices brought trouble everywhere she turned? The nuns who'd raised her would say yes. They'd claim no one was irredeemable. But after the events of recent weeks, Anne-Marie wondered if she'd tested His patience too far.

The Indian shouted in a tense, guttural tone to the second Indian.

Surprise flickered across the warrior's features. Cutting his horse around the wagon, he joined his companion. The two men gestured at Creed as they conversed in animated tones.

"What are they saying?" Anne-Marie longed to turn around and look, but she was too scared to move a muscle.

"I'm not sure we want to know."

One of the warriors trotted back to the front of the wagon and leaned over to grab the horse's bridle.

"Have mercy," Quincy groaned when the Indian started leading the team down the road.

℮

A young man led the buckboard into camp and a crowd gathered. Anne-Marie had never seen so many Indian men, women, and children—and all were peering at her curiously.

The lead warrior shouted orders, and two young braves scattered to various tents. The women crowded closer, some touching Anne-Marie's skirt, eyes bright with curiosity.

When the wagon rolled to a stop a tall, lean man wearing breech-cloth stepped from his tent to view the spectacle. Parting the crowd, he made his way to the back of the buckboard. Surprise and gladness registered on his handsome features when he apparently recognized the injured man, followed closely by worry when he focused on the blood-soaked bandage around Creed's right thigh.

"Who is that?" Anne-Marie asked.

Quincy bent closer. "Can't say for certain, but I'd guess it's the tribal chief."

Issuing a harsh command, the man motioned for help. The flap of a tepee parted to reveal a startlingly beautiful girl with doe-like eyes. The girl hurried to the wagon to peer down at the man's unconscious form. Worry flooded her features. Leaning over, she gently touched his face and whispered, "Storm Rider."

His eyes opened, and he smiled at her.

Anne-Marie noted the exchange, surprised to feel a trace of envy. When Creed gazed at the young woman Anne-Marie could see something akin to love reflected in his eyes before they slowly closed again.

"Berry Woman, go with Storm Rider to the medicine man," the chief said. Two braves stepped forward to lift Anne-Marie from the wagon. Without ceremony, she was taken to a colorful tepee in the center of the camp. She stood by helplessly when Quincy was led to a tent on the opposite side of the circle.

The two warriors loaded Creed onto a travois as Berry Woman hovered near his side. Slowly they made their way to the medicine man's tent.

It was over an hour before anyone returned to Anne-Marie's tepee. During that time she had sat huddled near the fire, feeling no particular sense of fear. Obviously Creed was acquainted with the Apache band, and if they were going to harm her, they would have already done so.

Her thoughts returned to Creed and the young Indian maiden. She'd hated the way her stomach had cramped up when he looked at the girl. Obviously he knew her well enough.

The flap on the tepee parted and Berry Woman entered, carrying a wooden bowl of stew. Although Anne-Marie was famished, she was more concerned about Creed.

"How is he?" she inquired.

The maiden's eyes met hers coolly. "You need not concern yourself with Storm Rider. I will see that he is cared for."

"You speak English?"

"When necessary." The edge in her tone told Anne-Marie that they were not destined to become friends.

Berry Woman turned to leave, and then apparently changed her mind. "How was Storm Rider injured?"

"I shot him. Accidentally."

The girl's eyes grew more opaque. "You shot the man who will be my husband?"

"Husband?" Was there no end to the surprises concerning Creed Walker?

"We have been promised to one another."

"Since when?" Anne-Marie didn't know why she had this sudden urge to cry, but it was all she could do to control the impulse.

"Since a long time ago. The arrangement is sealed." Her eyes skimmed her clothing. "You have no expectations concerning Storm Rider."

"No...of course not. Creed hasn't mentioned that he is...spoken for." Of course he hadn't mentioned anything about his life, so the news shouldn't startle her. "You...and Creed," she clarified, just to make certain she understood, and she dearly hoped that she had.

"Storm Rider and I. And since he is soon to be my husband, his welfare is my concern. You are welcome to our fires." Dipping her head, she backed toward the tent opening.

Anne-Marie felt compelled to add. "My only concern is Creed's well-being."

The young woman nodded.

"But I do need to talk to him, if you have no objections."

Berry Woman hesitated, apparently weighing her trust. "Perhaps. Tomorrow. When his wound has been treated and he is rested."

The two women openly measured each other.

"Thank you—you will tell me when he awakens?" Why Anne-Marie felt this protective urge she wasn't sure. She barely knew the man, and their brief time together had been less than ideal. Still, if it were not for her, Creed Walker would be dead by now. Maybe she ought to point that out to this woman. And then maybe not. She'd caused Creed enough trouble.

The young woman bent her head. "I will send for you when he is stronger."

"Thank you. You're most kind." Anne-Marie's thoughts swirled with the past hour and the abrupt change of plan. She was truly alone now, and in a place so foreign to her that she swallowed back rising terror. She couldn't fall apart. She still had long miles to cover to reach her sisters.

Berry Woman turned, parted the tent folds, and exited, leaving Anne-Marie to wonder where her fate now lay. Surely in God's hands, but also in Quincy's protection? He had been a gentleman in every sense, but would he be good enough to see her back to Mercy Flats? She lay back on a soft buffalo pelt, weary and discouraged. And yet sleep eluded her. She longed to cry but she wasn't a quitter. The McDougals never gave up. Creed was safely with people who would care for him now and she could rest. And yet she couldn't deny that deep within her heart she longed to look into those warm dark eyes and be comforted, but Creed Walker belonged to another woman.

Cortes's swarthy features flamed. Veins bulged in his neck. No one bested Cortes!

Pacing beside his horse, he went over his predicament. He must find that gold, and *pronto*. He was Cortes! Finding gold was his heroic mission. Not to mention Streeter would have his hide if he didn't. They'd been following the buckboard tracks for hours and they were getting nowhere. Either that *indio*, black, and nun didn't know where they were going, or they were taking the long way getting there.

"They no fly like a bird. You no look *muy bueno!*"

"We have so looked good. We've spread like bad news and covered every inch of that wagon track trail, but the folks is wily, boss, just plain wily," Ollie accused.

"Weren't our fault," Butch declared. "The truth is we've just plain lost 'em."

"How can we lose a negro, a *monja*, and an *indio*?"

The men hung their heads.

Cortes thought he had met up with some stupid people in his past adventures, but Ollie, Butch, and Rodrigo were just plain idiots. He glanced up to study the worsening weather. "They no go far. They are here somewhere, you'll see."

"Maybe they found somebody to help 'em," Ollie volunteered.

Cortes's eyes narrowed. "Do you know of anyone who'd help an *indio*?"

The men swapped stumped looks.

"Well, what do we do now?" Butch asked.

"What we do *ahora*?" Cortes slapped his forehead. "We search, fool!"

Squinting, Butch nodded. "What do you suppose Walker's doing with a nun? Last I heard he had joined up with the North."

"I cannot read the man's mind!" Climbing back in the saddle, Cortes spat his cigar on the ground. "There's a band of Apaches camped out not far from here. Maybe Walker's party is holin' up there."

Butch frowned. "I ain't real crazy about the idea of snooping around a bunch of Apaches. That could be risky business. Real risky. We could get ourselves scalped poking our noses in them Injuns' business."

"Are you a little girl? We no get scalped," Cortes snapped. "We ride that direction and wait to see who comes and goes. If Walker and the woman are there, they have to leave sometime, *sí*? No hole up forever." A silver tooth glistened like armor in the sunlight when the outlaw's lips parted in a smile. "And when they show their faces, we greet them with hot lead."

"What if they don't come out?" Butch insisted.

"Yeah, what if they ain't even in there to begin with? We could lose time just waitin' here like a bunch of sittin' ducks," Ollie said.

Cortes exploded. "My brain! You make it pound! If they are there, they come out sometime!"

"If Walker doesn't, the woman will." Rodrigo entered the fracas. "And when she does, we grab her."

Butch nodded. "What about the black?"

"We don't worry about the negro," Cortes snarled. "We can handle him."

Nodding, Ollie said, "Then we take the gold. You think Walker and the woman's still got it with 'em?"

Wedging a cigar between his teeth, Cortes struck a match on his thumbnail. "He's got it. He wouldn't let it out of his sight." He swore as sulfur flared, searing his thumbnail before he could drop the flame.

"And if they don't have the gold, we use the woman for bait to get the Injun to tell us where it is." Butch shook his head. "Once we get the gold back, we leave the three for the buzzards."

"Leave a nun for buzzard fodder?" Rodrigo shook his head. "I'd have to give that some thought."

Sucking his blistered thumb, Cortes growled. "*Silencio*! Find that gold!" Reining his horse hard, Cortes spurred the animal and galloped off in the direction of the Apache camp.

Butch, Ollie, and Rodrigo exchanged resigned looks, shrugged, and then rode after him.

ᴄᴏ

Berry Woman parted the tent flap and paused to focus on Anne-Marie. "Bold Eagle inquires about your comfort."

"Bold Eagle?"

"Our chief."

"I'm fine. Creed?" She met the young girl's eyes. "Is he…"

The young woman nodded. "He lives. Walks-in-Morning will bring your food."

"Wait!" She reached out when the woman turned to leave. "Has…he asked about me?" She knew the question would not sit well with the young maiden, but so much of her time had been invested in his care. She'd earned the right to know if he was concerned even a tiny bit about hers.

"He does not speak, but you need not be concerned about Storm Rider. Soon Bold Eagle will provide someone to take you away from camp."

Anne-Marie's pulse thrummed. Exactly what did that mean? And where was Quincy? She should be allowed to speak with him.

"Where is the man who came with us?"

"He is comfortable."

"I want to talk to him. He…he can take me away from here."

Gratification showed in Berry Woman's eyes. "Storm Rider is an honorable man. He will arrange your departure when he has healed."

Anne-Marie's thought swirled. She switched subjects. "You speak English well. Both you and Creed."

The young girl clearly grew weary of the conversation. "Creed taught me when he and Bold Eagle became blood brothers."

"Blood brothers?"

"When my brother Bold Eagle was attacked by a band of marauders, he sought refuge in the fort where Creed was living with Father Jacob. Together, Creed and Bold Eagle rode to meet my brother's enemies."

So, Bold Eagle was her brother. Imagination swept her and her mind conjured a thought. Could it be one brother was repaying another by providing a wife? A very lovely, winsome bride who must surely be the object of every young man's eyes?

"How long ago was this?"

"Many moons ago—five years."

So Creed had spent part of his life at a fort among white men, Anne-Marie mused. "How is it that Creed speaks such good English?" The question had plagued her from the moment he had spoken to the sheriff in the jail cell.

Sighing, Berry Woman sat down, crossing her legs. Her features remained stoic but the expression in her eyes softened. Perhaps she was lonely and needed to converse with someone outside the situation, or maybe she sensed that Anne-Marie wouldn't give up until some questions were answered. Either way, it seemed she was reluctant but willing to provide answers. "When Creed lived at Fort Walters, Father Jacob taught him English. He learned everything—reading, writing, history. There are many among the Apache as well who are willing to learn the white man's ways." Her eyes lowered as she continued, "Though Creed and I prefer the ways of our fathers. When we are one, we will live among our people."

Nodding, Anne-Marie decided that Creed's wife-to-be wasn't so bad. She was very pretty, and she spoke in soft, bird-like tones. If Creed must marry, this young woman would be an ideal choice. "If I can't see Creed, may I speak to Quincy?"

"You speak of the dark-skinned one?"

"Yes, I want to talk to him."

"I will tell my brother of your wish." Berry Woman reached for the pail of water sitting by the door. "Your pail is nearly empty. I will bring fresh water from the spring."

She left, dropping the flap back into place behind her. Apparently simple courtesy demanded that she provide a bed and food, even to those she didn't trust.

Anne-Marie turned back to the fire seconds before she heard a hushed but heated exchange break out between Berry Woman and another female.

A moment later Walks-in-Morning entered the tepee carrying a steaming bowl, which she sullenly extended to Anne-Marie. Turning on her heel, she left as quickly as she'd entered.

Sitting down on the pallet, Anne-Marie began to eat the unidentifiable fare. The mush was very spicy. It made her eyes water and her nose run, but she continued eating, aware that she had to keep her strength up. When the wooden bowl was empty, she fanned her mouth, muttering when she realized Berry Woman had not returned with her water.

Lying back on the pallet, she would have sworn someone had put hot peppers in her gruel.

ℰ

Bright sun filled the tent when she next opened her eyes. Exhausted by the lack of sleep, she had dropped off shortly after breakfast and slept the morning away.

Drawn to the trails of sunlight shining through the tent top, she focused on the sound of hunters returning to camp. She lay for a moment, idly scratching her arm. Her mouth still tingled from the wretched breakfast and the pit of her stomach was ablaze.

Rolling to her side, she scratched her neck and then her shoulder. Before she knew it, she was itching all over. Springing to her feet, she slapped at her clothing, finally realizing that something was terribly wrong.

She stripped off her blouse, her temper flaring when she saw red ants running in a zigzagging frenzy throughout the material.

Muttering, she jerked the pallet aside, confirming her worst suspicion. Berry Woman had made the pallet over an anthill, the inhabitants of which were now crawling over and through the bearskin and blanket as well as every stitch of her skirt.

"Very funny, Berry Woman," she muttered, shaking the ants out of the soiled material.

By the time Berry Woman returned, she'd had enough of her antics. "I want to see Creed," she demanded.

"Storm Rider is ill and cannot be disturbed."

"If I can't see Creed, then I demand you let me leave."

Actually, she'd never insisted on anything in her life but getting back to her sisters. The words felt foreign and hostile—exactly her thoughts at the moment.

Smiling, Berry Woman lowered her head submissively. "If this is your wish."

Anne-Marie paused, uncertain she'd heard right. She was giving her permission to leave? Her eyes narrowed. There had to be a catch. A really sneaky catch. "You will arrange for a horse and enough food and water to last me for two days."

"If that is your wish."

"That is my wish. And I want to take Quincy with me."

The girl dropped the tent flap into place.

"Well, this is just dandy," Anne-Marie fumed as she dressed. Now what had she let herself in for? Exactly where did she intend to go— and would Quincy agree? If he and Creed were best friends he might very well be comfortable in his new surroundings, and she was terrible at reading maps. Abigail was the navigator. Anne-Marie merely followed.

Pacing, she tried to formulate a plan. With a good horse and the proper provisions, she could make it on her own. But would Berry Woman provide a good horse—or merely a nag that would give out somewhere along the trail? She couldn't trust her safety to this woman. Yet if she could make it to a town that had a stage or a train... The sisters had been in this fix many a time and rallied. Reaching Mercy Flats couldn't be that hard, but she'd need money.

The coins.

There were two strongboxes full of gold sitting on the buckboard. So much gold that one or two coins would never be missed, and it was quite likely that Wells Fargo would pay a handsome reward when the strongboxes were returned. She would just take her share now—a meager portion—and be on her way.

ॐ

Quincy glanced up, his eyes widening when Anne-Marie burst into his tent. "Quick, where's the gold?" she blurted breathlessly.

He sprang to his feet. "What are you doing here?"

"I haven't got time to argue, Quincy. Berry Woman is arranging a horse for me. You can do what you want, but I'm leaving and I need money—and you, if you'll go with me."

"Why would Berry Woman be getting you a horse?"

"Because she dislikes me—and she's envious because she thinks that I have…eyes for Creed. You could clearly persuade her otherwise if there was time, but there isn't. I have to leave. Now."

Next time she found something strange crawling in her pallet it might be worse than ants.

He shook his head, snapping his suspenders into place. "Don't be a fool, girl. You're not familiar with this area, and what with the war going on, you could run into all kinds of trouble wandering around out there alone."

"I can't stay here and sleep on ants and eat pepper gruel."

"What?"

"Never mind." She turned back to face him. "Where's the gold? All I need is a couple of coins to see me back to Mercy Flats."

He stiffened. "You're not to touch that gold."

"You're acting like it's yours when all of us took it. I'll only take two pieces. You and Creed can split the rest. That's fair."

"Well, for one thing your assumption is dead wrong. That shipment is mine—in a way." Judging his grave tone, she realized that he'd said more than he meant to. His eyes snapped back to the fire.

"Yours?" She stalked toward him, her eyes tapered with a promise of menace. "What is going on, John Quincy Adams—if that's even your real name. And don't tell me you don't know, because you

obviously know more about that gold than you've led me to believe."
She crept closer. "Are you going to tell me, or am I going to have to
wheedle it out of you—which, I warn you, I can do? And you're going
to hate every agonizing minute of it, Mr. Adams." She stomped in
front of him. "Start talking. I'm a real good listener."

"Woman, you are mean—just plain mean."

"I assure you, I can get meaner."

"All right, all right!" Glancing about uneasily, he lowered his voice.
"You got to promise not to mention a word of this."

"A word of what?"

"Of what I'm about to tell you."

"All right, I promise not to tell anyone."

"Creed and I are working for the Union Army."

"Working for the Union Army? You mean you're federal spies?"

He straightened. "We are paid agents. We were on our way to
intercept that gold shipment when Creed decided to ride to your
rescue."

Anne-Marie took a step backward. "You and Creed knew about
the gold?"

Quincy rubbed his neck. "We knew the gold was going to be con-
fiscated by someone in High Bluff to further the Confederate cause.
What we didn't know was that it would be on that buckboard we stole."

She turned and paced the confines of the tepee. "And you
happened along when someone was in the process of stealing the
shipment."

"Creed and I were as surprised to see those two strongboxes on that
wagon as you were." He loosened his collar.

"So that's why you and Creed are so intent on keeping the gold."

"We are obligated to keep it. It's the reason we're here in the first
place."

"But where does that leave me? I'm risking my neck for that gold
the same as you and Creed."

"Ma'am, Creed and I feel bad that you're involved in this, but the
gold stays put."

"But I need money or I can't return to Mercy Flats. My sisters may be waiting there as we speak." She refused to allow the thought that Abigail and Amelia had met with an even worse fate than hers.

Quincy's eyes softened. "I'm sorry. I want to help, but my hands are tied."

Her heart sank. *Dear Lord, what am I to do now?* Had her Heavenly Father finally tired of her misbehavior and decided to let her swim in her own deceit?

"Anne-Marie," Quincy coaxed, "if you'll be patient, Creed will see that you're returned to your sisters, unharmed. Once he—"

"Creed doesn't care a whit about my situation."

"You're wrong; Creed's a man who takes his responsibilities seriously, and right now you're one of his responsibilities."

"Yes, and that's all I am—one gigantic pain, a big one he doesn't want." Tears smarted to her eyes. "Quincy?"

"Ma'am?"

"Is it true that Creed is betrothed to Berry Woman?"

"Does it matter?"

She longed to deny that Creed's engagement bothered her. She'd only known the man a short time, but in that short period she had grown fiercely defensive of him. But that was all her feelings were—loyalty and compassion to an injured person. These feelings she was having weren't affection—not even close. They were simply protective ones, like a hen with little chicks.

Quincy took hold of her shoulders and turned her to face him, his long fingers wiping tears from her cheeks. "You're plum worn out, Miss Anne-Marie. Now hear me out because I'm thinking of your welfare. I can't allow you to leave. Whether you like it or not, we're in this together. The snow is deep and travel is dangerous. If you were to do anything foolish, like run away, you'd have a slim chance of survival. Creed will be stronger soon…"

His voice trailed off when Anne-Marie spun on her heel and stalked out of the tent, but she didn't miss his soft, "Ma'am, you sure do try a man's patience. You sure enough do."

Seven

It is good to see you enjoying the fresh air, my brother. But do not linger long. The cold seeps through your injured bones." The young chief tossed a stick in the fire, sat down, and lit a pipe.

Creed nodded, drawing the heavy robe closer. "My duties with the bluecoats have kept me busy. I apologize for not visiting my brother and his family sooner."

Smoke from Bold Eagle's pipe spiraled up in soft wisps. "It is said you work hard for the white man's cause."

"What is said is true."

A twig snapped, sending a shower of sparks through the air. "This is wise?"

"It is what I believe, or I would not risk my life for this cause."

Bold Eagle closed his eyes, clearly savoring the taste of the *kinni-kinnick*. "Bold Eagle does not understand why brother fights against brother."

"It isn't only a matter of brother fighting against brother. The issues are more than a man buying and selling another man. It is economic and social differences, states against federal rights, the

Abolition Movement—even the election of Abraham Lincoln. Much is involved in this war."

"I do not understand this way. The white man fights and dies for the black man, but he takes food, water, and land from the red man without a care."

"This too is cause for a fight." Creed sat up straighter. "The woman? Where is she?"

"She is well."

The numbing effects of the sweet sage smoke and potent medicinal herbs flowed through Creed. "And Quincy?"

"John Quincy Adams?" Bold Eagle smiled. "He too is well, my brother."

Creed shifted his leg and felt a stab of pain in his thigh. Although the wound was healing, it would be several weeks before it became a memory. Passing the pipe to Bold Eagle, he acknowledged, "If your warriors had not come upon Anne-Marie and Quincy when they did, I would not want to think what would have happened. I am in your debt, Bold Eagle."

"There is no debt among brothers." Smoke continued to filter up into the shadows as the wind whistled through the bare tree branches.

Long moments passed before Bold Eagle again broke the silence. "There are men, four of them, outside the camp. They arrived the same sun you did, shortly after you were brought here."

Closing his eyes, Creed eased his injured leg to a more comfortable position. "That would be an outlaw band that's been trailing us."

"You know of these men?"

"I recognize one of them. Unless I miss my guess, he and his thugs are after that gold shipment."

Drawing on the pipe, Bold Eagle stared into the fire. "I know of such enemies and many times I have helped Storm Rider defend his honor; now Bold Eagle will do whatever is needed to help. These men will not enter the camp. Of this I am certain."

"The woman shouldn't leave," Creed murmured as the medicine drew him deeper into unconsciousness.

"Rest, my brother." The man drew the animal hide closer around his friend. "We will let no harm come to the woman or your friend."

Bold Eagle sat beside Storm Rider, the smoke drifting quietly in the cold stillness.

❧

Cortes stamped both boots, trying to force feeling back into his frozen feet.

Cold wind whistled down the collar of his coat as his eyes darted back and forth, trying to ferret out any movement in the camp. He had been standing watch for hours, but the three outlaws were still nowhere in sight. But they could not fool Cortes; he knew they were in there.

His eyes filled with resentment when he studied the circle of tepees. They were in there all right. Huddled near a warm fire, eating wild game. Hot stew.

Such fools. Their buckboard tracks had led straight to the Indian camp. Walker and his party could not leave without Cortes spotting them.

Ollie hunched deeper into his sheep-lined parka when he approached Cortes. The wind tore at the brim of his hat, threatening to snatch it away. "See anything, boss?"

"Only Cortes's breath in cold air."

Squinting, Ollie focused on the camp. "Whaddya think's going on?"

"I tell you what is going on. My eyeballs are frozen to my sockets!"

"Yeah," Ollie admitted. "I know the feeling. We ain't jest gonna sit here all night, are we, boss?" The outlaw's breath formed a frosty vapor in the frigid air when he knelt beside the fire, feeding the dying embers a few scrawny limbs. Flames spurted and flickered in the high wind.

"*Sí*, we sit here," Cortes mimicked. His eyes narrowed sharply. "They can't stay in that camp forever; they have to come out sometime."

"We could always go in after them."

Cortes turned to stare at Ollie. "Them's warriors, Ollie. Cortes does not go sashaying into an Apache warriors' camp like a foolish peacock."

"Yeah." Ollie glanced sheepishly back to the fire. "Don't guess that would be real bright."

"Only if you grow weary of your—how do you say it?—scalp," Cortes grunted.

The outlaw didn't appear to take kindly to the thought. Ollie's eyes switched to the circle of tepees. "You see the buckboard anywhere?"

"*Sí*. Near the large tepee."

Ollie clasped his hat to his head and strained to see around the boss's shoulder. "Is the gold still in it?"

"I do not have eyes like the puma."

The men turned when they heard Rodrigo jump back, hollering as a violent gust of wind shot a shower of sparks up the back of his coat. He hopped around the campsite, slapping at his back.

Butch stepped over to help. "Ah, you've done gone and burned a hole in your coat," he chided. He smacked the smoldering embers with his gloved hand.

Rodrigo glared at him. "Mind your own business."

Butch threw up his hands. "All right, all right, I was just a-tryin' to help."

"Stop your bickerin'," Cortes called over his shoulder. "We have a long night in front of us."

Ollie threw more wood on the fire and the four outlaws hunkered down, prepared to wait out the Indian, no matter how long it took.

"Sure hope they come out soon," Ollie admitted. He blew on his hands.

"You are a sissy pants," Cortes said. "Only Cortes knows *real* danger. Once, many years ago, his ship sank. Not one survived but Cortes. The waters, they were filled with sharks, they come and try to eat Cortes, but he fights them off bare-fisted and swim great distance. On shore, Cortes lost his boots in the water and had to walk five miles to find nearest shelter. There, he had to chase down a wild jackal and kill it with only a tiny blade. Then Cortes must start a fire and there were no stones to strike together…"

Ollie rolled his eyes and bent close to the others. "How many times do we tell Cortes we don't believe his stories? When he gets confused he just gets mad and mean."

"Jest let him talk," Rodrigo advised. "We will close our ears."

⌒

Berry Woman entered the medicine lodge on a gust of heavy wind. "Is he stronger?" she asked.

The old woman nodded. "You still favor this man."

Berry Woman's eyes focused on the injured man. "Storm Rider stole my heart when I had lived but twelve summers." Smiling, she softly traced his sleeping features. "He rode into camp beside my brother, Bold Eagle, and remained among my people, teaching them the ways of the white man. He is wise and strong and an ample provider, having killed more buffalo than all the seasoned warriors combined. Every young maiden in camp envied me because Storm Rider spent his leisure hours with me. When the white men went to war, Storm Rider rode off to fight on the side of the bluecoats. I accepted his absence without question, for I knew, just as *Heammawihio* had promised, that one day Storm Rider would come for me and I would be the envy of every woman."

A smile bowed the corners of her mouth. "Soon the war will be over and Storm Rider will be mine. He will ride into camp, long locks flying in the breeze, a single eagle feather braided in his flowing hair, his bronze chest bare except for the necklace of eagle claws and his splendid form encased in the finest deerskin breeches. His dark eyes will boldly search mine and claim me for his own."

"Storm Rider and Bold Eagle will soon come to a proper agreement, and a wedding feast will be scheduled. It will be a great honor to have such a man for my husband." Her smile faded when the young maiden saw that Storm Rider was trying to open his eyes.

❦

As his vision cleared Creed saw Berry Woman bending over him, her smile as soft and welcome as a summer shower. He tentatively moved his leg, relieved to find the pain was no longer sharp and penetrating. When he struggled to sit up gentle hands lowered him back to the pallet.

"No, you must rest. It is too soon," she scolded.

"Quincy—the gold…need to leave…"

Berry Woman frowned. "Why can you not stay awhile with your people? Why must you always leave?"

"The woman has sisters awaiting her return. I must see her safely back home."

"Why cannot the black man assume the woman's care?"

Pride made him obstinate. "I assumed her care, and she expects me to reunite her with her family."

Berry Woman's jaw firmed. "I do not understand this."

"There's nothing to understand. The woman is not your concern."

"But—"

"Enough." Storm Rider spoke with authority. "You will see to the woman's well-being."

The young woman's eyes lowered submissively. "Forgive me, Storm Rider. I will speak of this matter no more."

Creed's eyes closed and he started to drift off. "You will see that that no harm comes to her…"

Her answer came as soft as a cloud. "Why would you think otherwise? Are our people not kind and courteous? Do we not care for our guests?"

"When I awake, bring her to me."

Berry Woman nodded. "Rest."

❦

Later, the tepee flap opened to reveal a relieved Quincy. Creed looked up from his pallet and answered Quincy's questioning gaze.

"I'm still alive. Much better thanks to Spirit Cloud's healing herbs."

"There was a time I thought you were a goner for sure." Quincy sat down and crossed his legs. "Cortes and his hoodlums are camped half a mile away. No doubt they're after the gold."

"What about the posses?"

"Haven't seen one since we left town. They must have turned back—but those outlaws won't. What are we going to do about them?"

"I'm not sure," Creed admitted. "I do know that we will need Bold Eagle's help in order to get out of camp."

"The chief will help?"

"Yes. Our bond is strong. He will help."

"Want me to take Anne-Marie to her sisters while you recover? The gold should be safe here."

Creed was silent for a moment. Anne-Marie had been nothing but a millstone around his neck. Why should he care if Quincy fulfilled his obligation? She was resourceful—more than capable of caring for herself. She could outthink a man and whip a bull with her free hand. It would serve her right to let her go it alone.

And yet she had practically saved his life. If she hadn't gotten him to Eulalie he doubted that he would be here now. "The woman is my concern, and I will see that she is returned to Mercy Flats." He would never see Anne-Marie again once he delivered her to Mercy Flats, but he would know that he had not fulfilled a man's promise if he sent Quincy in his place. He'd seen what a legacy of broken promises had done to his mother, and he refused to be like his father.

"We'll talk again later," Creed said. His leg was beginning to throb, and he wanted to sleep now. "Send Anne-Marie to me."

"You're sure? She's not in the best of moods today."

"Send her to me." Creed had dealt with every mood that woman could muster up. He welcomed the chance to best her.

"It's your funeral, brother."

Anne-Marie was busy rearranging her bedding when Quincy asked for permission to enter the tepee.

"It's real chilly out there," he began awkwardly when he stepped inside. He wasn't looking forward to the conversation.

"What is it now, Mr. Adams?" She turned her back on him, a clear sign she resented his attempts to keep her in camp. She added more sticks to the fire.

"I just spoke with Creed." Looking at her, he wondered how anyone could ever mistake her for a nun. There wasn't a nun-ish thing about her, all nice curves and womanly softness.

She whirled and a mass of auburn hair tumbled around her face. Green eyes wide with concern faced him. The transformation was nothing short of jaw-dropping. "Is he better?"

"Somewhat." Quincy willed his eyes away from the inviting sight and cleared his throat. "He's feeling stronger. He wants you to come for a visit." He paused. "He was hoping that you would stick around until he can take you to Mercy Flats."

She frowned. "He would do that for me?"

"Yes, ma'am. If you'll just hold on a few days until he's able to ride."

She turned back to the skins. "I'm not making any promises. He doesn't deserve my loyalty—why, he hasn't even asked to see me."

"He just did. I told you, he wants to see you."

"Too little too late."

"Ma'am, he's real sick. Now you need to use some common sense here. You can't take off by yourself. This is rough country. A woman like you wouldn't last any time at all in these wilds." He eyed her appearance. He knew that what he was about to say was highly improper, but he couldn't hold back. "Anne-Marie, would you be offended if I made a simple observation—one any red-blooded man could see?"

Shrugging, she fluffed a robe.

"A man would have to blind to not understand what's got Creed howling up a tree."

"Howling up a tree?" She straightened. "I don't understand."

"Excuse me. I shouldn't have said that. But I want your promise that you won't do anything foolish until Creed is stronger."

"I'll make no such promise. I'm leaving. I have been on my own since I was a mere child, and I know how to take care of myself."

"You've always had your sisters with you. You provided protection for each other."

"Abigail and Amelia know how to take care of themselves. If you want to help, get me a pony."

"I can't do that, woman!" Quincy ran a hand through his hair. "Creed says I'm to keep you here."

"Since when is Creed my keeper? You have no control over my comings and goings. A few days ago we were total strangers. Now get me a few provisions and I'll get out of your hair."

"What hair? I'll not have one left when Creed gets through with me."

"You look like a robust man; surely you can best a sick opponent."

"Creed's not like other opponents." He felt the muscle in his jaw tighten when he shook his head. "No. You are to remain here until Creed is better. Only then will we have this conversation."

With his words, she fell silent.

Turning muley on him. It didn't surprise him. And with what little he knew about her he reckoned she would find a way to leave, one way or the other. He'd have to keep a closer eye on her comings and goings.

"I want your word that you will do as I say."

She turned and refolded a skin.

"Cold shoulders don't bother me." He stepped to the tent flap. "I'm warning you, don't do anything foolish." He lifted the fold and stepped out, confident that he was talking to thin air.

If that lady wanted something, she made a way to get it, but it wasn't going to be through him.

Eight

A half moon slid lower when Anne-Marie slipped from her tent late that night and made her way to where the ponies were tethered. As promised, a brown and white spotted animal stood in the shadows waiting for her. Berry Woman had kept her promise, and why not? She desperately wanted to see her leave camp. *Lord, though I don't deserve Your mercy, look after me*, she prayed silently.

Creed's woman had been more than happy to oblige her requests, and Anne-Marie was more than happy to leave. She couldn't wait for Creed and Quincy and their secret plans. She planned to take every precaution, using isolated back roads to avoid any hint of trouble. She wasn't a simpleton; she was willing to take the risk.

Hitching her skirts above her knees, she grasped the reins firmly and mounted the pony. Snow drifted deep in ditches as she walked the horse to the outer edge of camp, but other riders had cleared a decent path.

The wind savagely whipped her hair as the horse picked its way along the snowy path. Shivering, she huddled deeper into the thin trader's blanket. Berry Woman had not gone to extreme lengths to provide warmth.

Turning to look over her shoulder, she felt her earlier resolve fading. Quincy was right; she shouldn't be so impulsive. She was acting more like Amelia now, flighty and high-strung instead of guided by plain old common sense.

Maybe being under Creed Walker's protection wasn't so bad. She pulled her scarf tighter around her neck. In truth, she was being downright foolish.

❧

Berry Woman and River Woman slowed their horses beneath the barren branches of a cottonwood tree. Snow clouds churned beneath a watery moon.

"Storm Rider will be angry," River Woman warned. The women watched Anne-Marie's horse disappear into the blowing snow.

"Storm Rider will not know," Berry Woman said.

"He will know. When he awakens and finds the woman gone, he will ask what has become of her."

"And no one will have seen her," Berry Woman countered.

"But she goes into the dark—into the coming storm. She will not survive—"

"Whatever happens to her is her own foolish doing," Berry Woman snapped.

River Woman shook her head. "Your coldness saddens me. The white woman does not have the skills to protect herself. She will die."

A smile touched the corners of Berry Woman's mouth. "I do only what the woman asks. Is that not common hospitality? I do only what Storm Rider has instructed me to do."

River Woman's eyes reflected deep concern. "It is not right, Berry Woman. You do not speak the truth about Storm Rider. He would never send a woman into the night alone."

"You worry too much. Come, the wind is rising." Reining her horse, Berry Woman turned and rode in the direction of camp.

She was confused. Anne-Marie had ridden a good distance before she realized that her body was getting numb. Only her feet tingled, and she hadn't been able to feel her hands for a while.

Dawn streaked the sky and she realized she was lost. At one time she thought she was riding west, but now she knew she wasn't. Slowing the pony, she studied the muted rays streaking the cold morning sky. She was no longer riding west; she was riding south. In fact, that stand of trees looked familiar. She had made a huge circle and wasn't nearly as far from the camp as she'd thought. Desperation filled her, and she giggled, realizing that it didn't make any difference what direction she rode in, since she didn't know where she was anyway.

She had to go back now while she could. Quincy was right; she shouldn't be out here alone. She needed to turn back...

The pony sidestepped, catching Anne-Marie off guard. Reacting, she jerked the bridle around and the pinto bucked, crow-hopping blindly in the snow. She struggled to hang on, but the animal's strength was greater than hers.

Pitching wildly, the horse threw her and she struck the ground hard, tumbling wildly down a steep, snow-covered incline.

By the time she reached the bottom, she welcomed the blackness that consumed her.

Smoke from the cook fires hung over the village this morning when Creed stepped outside the tent. Heavy snow covered the ground. Testing his leg, he found his strength returning. He knew if he stayed up too long, he would open the wound again, and he couldn't spare another delay.

Memories flooded him as he drew deeply of the camp aromas.

Though he had spent a good part of his life with Father Jacob, the Indian ways were still a large part of him.

He stood for a moment watching children play as their mothers went about their daily chores and their fathers unloaded slain deer from packhorses. A hunting party had departed before dawn; they were back with a good kill. There would be fresh venison hanging over the fires tonight.

Turning away, he spotted River Woman carrying a bundle of sticks in the direction of her family's tepee.

"River Woman," he called. "Come, sit by my fire."

River Woman's pace didn't slacken as she hurried toward her tent with an armload of wood. "I cannot. Our fire burns low, Storm Rider."

Surprised by her reaction, Creed smiled and called out again. "River Woman, you work too hard. Come, sit with me and we'll talk."

Slowly putting down the wood, the young maiden turned and approached him, her eyes focused on her moccasins. "What is it you wish, Storm Rider?"

"Have you seen the white woman? I don't see her around this morning."

River Woman's gaze stayed riveted to the ground and she murmured, "Not this morning."

Creed frowned. Although yesterday he had asked Berry Woman and Quincy to send Anne-Marie to his tent, she had failed to respond. "You haven't seen her today?"

"Not today."

Berry Woman turned from her fire, her eyes sending River Woman a silent warning.

"I must go," River Woman murmured. "Our fire burns very low."

"If you see the white woman—"

"I will not see her. I must go."

When River Woman walked away, Creed reached out and caught her arm. Studying her flushed face, he frowned. "Is something wrong?"

Glancing at Berry Woman, River Woman shook her head quickly. "Nothing is wrong. Please, I must go."

It was a moment before Creed finally released her. She was acting oddly today. "Give my greetings to your mother."

Nodding, River Woman walked away and moments later ducked quickly into her tent.

Glancing at Berry Woman, Creed wondered about the significance of the look that had passed between the two women.

Meeting his gaze, Berry Woman smiled. "Storm Rider appears much stronger this day."

"Yes, I gain more strength every day. Have you seen the white woman today?"

Berry Woman averted his gaze. "I have not seen her today. Perhaps she gathers wood with Elk Woman."

Creed found that possibility even more remote. Anne-Marie had never volunteered to wander off alone. "Where is Quincy?"

"In his tepee." She turned back to tend the haunch of venison hanging over her fire. Succulent juices dripped into the flames and the scent of cooking meat filled the camp.

He reached out to stop a small boy who was running through camp. "Have you seen the white woman?"

The child shook his head.

"Would you go through camp and look for her? She may be gathering wood with the other women."

The boy spoke in the native tongue and turned to skip off.

"Bring her here when you find her," Creed called after him, and then turned and lifted the thick buffalo fold. Anne-Marie would be angry because he hadn't sent for her earlier, but he had needed time to think without her butting in. She was getting under his skin, yet he was reluctant to have Quincy take her to Mercy Flats. She was his responsibility, and his alone.

She would not leave this camp without him.

By late morning, the child had searched high and low and Anne-Marie had failed to appear. Creed made his way slowly to question River Woman.

When the tepee flap parted, River Woman glanced up. Storm Rider filled the doorway and apprehension mirrored in her dark eyes.

"I asked earlier if you had seen the white woman. I want the truth now," he said.

Glancing away, she said softly, "I have spoken the truth. I have not seen the white woman this day."

"When did you last see her?"

River Woman's silence stretched.

"When did you last see her?"

"I cannot—"

Entering the tent, he knelt beside her, his hands gripping her shoulders tightly. He forced her to look at him. "When did you last see her?"

The young girl still hesitated and he lowered his voice persuasively. "Tell me what you know."

"I know nothing."

"Has something happened to her?"

A sob caught in River Woman's throat. "I cannot—Berry Woman will be angry."

His grip tightened. "Tell me what you know."

"She…the white woman rode away…"

Creed frowned. "Rode away? When?"

"Last night."

"And you didn't tell anyone?"

River Woman shook her head, sobbing. "She rode…into the darkness. Berry Woman and I returned to camp, but I was worried, so I went back out and followed the woman a ways, but then I turned back because the weather was so cold." Her eyes lifted defensively. "Berry Woman said she was only following your instructions."

Creed's eyes narrowed. "Where is the woman now?"

Tears rolled down the maiden's cheeks. "I do not know, the snow blinded me—I can only take you to where I last saw her…"

"You didn't try to help her!"

She buried her face in her hands. "Forgive me, Storm Rider. I should have sent for help, but I feared that Berry Woman would no longer be my friend."

Creed could not believe what he was hearing. Berry Woman would not willingly disobey him when he had given instruction to see to the woman's needs.

River Woman was still explaining. "I did not wish to anger Berry Woman, so I turned back."

The muscle in Creed's jaw flexed when he pulled the girl to her feet. "Show me where this happened."

River Woman drew back in fear. "I must ask Berry Woman…"

Ignoring her defiance, Creed pulled her out of the tent and went in search of two horses.

Silence blanketed the frozen hillsides when the animals pushed through layers of crusted snow. A bitter wind battered the man and woman as they rode in silence, their eyes searching the icy hillsides. The fire in Creed's leg became a roaring inferno.

He and River Woman split up, scouting different areas but keeping each other in sight. River Woman's pony came to a halt in a heavy strand of trees. "Here."

Creed's gaze followed the tracks leading away from the clearing, the buffalo robe lying to the side. Nudging his horse, he traced the tracks a mile or so before he saw signs of a struggle. It looked like a pony had spooked and thrown its rider.

His gaze shot to the deep ravine.

Sliding off his animal, he limped to the edge of the steep divide. Halfway down, he could see a crumpled form lying at the bottom. A blanket of snow covered the familiar skirt and blouse.

Turning, he shouted to River Woman. "Go! Tell the camp I have found the white woman, and she needs care."

❧

Anne-Marie drifted in and out of consciousness, faintly aware that she was dying.

Dying wasn't so bad. Nothing at all like she had thought it would be. There was no pain, just a nice numbness that filled her whole body.

She hadn't heard any trumpets yet, but she expected them to blow anytime. She could picture St. Peter calling his trumpeters together, and right this moment they were getting ready to blow her up through the Pearly Gates.

She had to start taking her faith more seriously. She had always meant to let God know that she accepted Him—she really did, though she often acted nothing like His child. The angels were getting ready to herald her arrival—or were they? She hadn't been the most obedient subject, but she hadn't been the worst. She'd never killed anyone or been unkind—except to Creed. Every misdeed she'd done, she'd done with the purest of intentions.

What you've done, the stealing and misleading, is wrong, Anne-Marie. Selfish, childish, and wrong. You are not representing Christ or any form of His love. He looks upon the heart, not good intentions.

But I meant to tell Him that I do accept Him and I know what I've done is wrong—and now my time for decisions has run out.

She'd thought she had all the time in the world. She couldn't be dying now—not so young. Remorse and panic filled her. Was it too late? "Dear God, forgive me. I want to be Your child..." She forced the long-delayed acceptance through frozen lips. She had been lying in the snow for how long now? An hour? Two hours? Ten hours? It must be closer to ten hours, but then, if it was ten hours and not one hour or two hours, she would surely be wherever she was going by now, wouldn't she?

An ache, deep inside her, made her think that she was still on earth, a place that had nourished and sheltered her and brought her good and bad times. She bit back the urge to cry. Her death would bring such pain to Amelia and Abigail. And the mission sisters—they didn't deserve sad tears.

She didn't want to be the cause of such pain.

The McDougal sisters were all they had and now there would only be the two left to carry on the mission work. In one way she wanted to stay and help, but in another she longed to be where it was warm and dry and...happy.

Creed Walker's face floated above her, and she squinted, trying to see if he had a trumpet to his lips. Wasn't that just like him—always showing up where he wasn't wanted?

Deciding he was trumpetless, she reached out to lay her numb hands against his face. No matter where she went lately, he was there. It was almost like the Good Lord had planted Creed Walker in her life and wouldn't let her lose him.

"Ohhh, you've come to save me again, but you're too late this time," she whispered.

His rugged features swam into focus. Even if he was only a dying hallucination, she was beginning to like him. Really like him, although she couldn't imagine why. He hadn't been particularly nice to her, although she had to admit that he hadn't had much of a chance. What with going to jail and then ending up with a buckboard full of gold and being shot—well, she supposed, under the circumstances, few men would have been overly gracious.

Why, who knows, if she wasn't in the process of passing on this very minute, she might conceivably have fallen in love with Creed Walker. She, Anne-Marie McDougal, who never liked men, in love?

If her lips weren't frozen stiff, she'd laugh.

She closed her eyes when realization flooded her again.

I'm alone. I'm hurt. I can't move. And I'm so very scared. Not one soul cares where I am, or what happens to me—except Abigail and Amelia. And You, God. I have You now. She smothered a sob that tore at her ribs and made breathing unbearable.

Where were those trumpets?

"Breathe deep, Anne-Marie."

A heavy robe settled around her, and she absorbed the heavenly warmth. "Thank You—I was afraid You hadn't heard me."

The time had come: She was gone from this earth.

"Where's your trumpet?" she murmured, wishing He would hurry because she was so very cold. Wait—maybe it was Gabriel. He blew the trumpet, didn't he? "I didn't hear it."

"I didn't blow it."

The voice sounded close, and not at all like an angel. It was deep and masculine and...Oh dear.

Had the devil himself come to claim her? Her heart hammered against her ribs and she tried to open her eyes, but the lids were frozen shut. "I'm sorry...don't take me...There's been a mistake; I accepted the Lord as my savior..."

Gentle hands fastened the heavy robe around her. "Anne-Marie, can you hear me?"

That was Creed's voice. What was he doing here, passing himself off as one of St. Peter's trumpeters?

When she tried to ask him, her lips refused to form the words. She swallowed and tried again, but the sound wouldn't come.

"I'm going to move you. We're going back to camp now. Put your arms around my neck."

"Do I have to?"

"Yes, you must."

Wouldn't you know it? He was trying to boss her around—even now when death was so close.

"You're angry with me. I left and I wasn't supposed to."

"Right now, I don't know whether to kiss you or curse you."

"A kiss would be better." A nice, sweet kiss—she bet he was good at that sort of thing.

A pair of incredibly strong arms lifted her, and she sighed, laying her head on the trumpeter's shoulder, and lapsed into unconsciousness.

Nine

Prickly stinging slowly dragged Anne-Marie back to awareness. Her toes stung like fire, and she couldn't feel her face. Panicked, she struggled to sit up.

"Drink."

She didn't recognize the male voice, but a gentle hand supported her head and pushed a cup against her lips. Drinking greedily of the warm, thin broth, she dropped back into unconsciousness.

Twice more she awoke to find the same compassionate hands urging the cup back to her lips. Once she thought she heard Creed's voice, but it seemed different somehow, restrained, concerned, and she couldn't think why.

The third time she roused, her eyes opened slowly, trying to gain her bearings.

Unfamiliar surroundings met her gaze. Then understanding slowly dawned on her; she was lying in the medicine lodge where Creed had been. The heat, the incredible heat…the place was practically an oven.

Afraid to move, she looked out of the corner of her eye and saw the aged medicine man sitting beside the fire, smoking a pipe.

A burst of cold air swept her when the flap parted and Creed entered to kneel beside her, taking her hand.

Swallowing thickly, she tried to speak, but only a croak escaped her parched throat.

"You have slept a long time."

Frowning, Anne-Marie lifted her hand to her throbbing temple. "What happened?"

His fingers brushed her cheek, and the motion brought about the nicest feeling inside her. "Are you in pain?" he asked.

"Yes," she murmured. Her head throbbed and hot knives sliced her everywhere feeling was left in her body, but she didn't expect his sympathy. What she had done was beyond foolish. Color heated her cheeks. He must think she was an utter imbecile, and her reckless actions only confirmed it.

His gaze swept her gently. "God has again smiled upon you. You have some frostbite, but Spirit Cloud says you will live."

Anne-Marie wasn't sure if she heard relief or regret in his tone.

"How...how did you find me?" Events of the past few hours were slowly coming back: the flight from camp, the worsening snowstorm, losing her direction, the fall from her horse into the ravine.

"River Woman led me to you."

Anne-Marie frowned. "How did she know where I was?"

Creed hesitated, choosing his words. "River Woman saw you ride out of camp. She and Berry Woman followed to make sure your escape was successful."

Sighing, Anne-Marie closed her eyes. "Berry Woman would be happy to see me turn into a stewing hen forever."

He chuckled, a nice, rich-sounding timbre. "Berry Woman feels you are a threat."

Anne-Marie wanted to look him directly in the eyes, but she didn't. Why should the suggestion that he found her desirable be anything but laughable? They had only known each other a short while and they battled each other constantly.

Admittedly she lacked experience where men were concerned, but simple logic told her that few men would be attracted to a woman who had landed him in jail and shot him to boot. "I acted foolishly. Will I lose my toes—or fingers?"

His calm tone soothed her. "You were foolish in many ways, but the frostbite was not severe; there should be no lasting effect." Turning aside, Creed dipped a cloth in a bowl of warm water. "Bold Eagle extends his apology for your injuries. It is not their way to dishonor a guest."

As he talked he smoothed the cloth back and forth across her brow, his touch surprisingly gentle. Anne-Marie wasn't certain if the odd tingling he awakened inside her was the result of his compassion or merely a lingering effect of the recent fall. Either way, she found the gesture agreeable. She found him enjoyable.

"Berry Woman is aware that her actions have shamed her family and her heritage." He tossed the cloth aside.

Drawing a ragged breath, Anne-Marie opened her eyes to meet his direct gaze. "She's deeply devoted to you, you know." The observation was too personal, she knew that, but she needed to know if he returned her feelings.

He was silent for a moment, then: "I am aware of Berry Woman's devotion."

His admission was unsettling. Then Berry Woman was telling the truth. He planned to marry the young woman once the war was over. The thought stung more than the feeling starting to creep back into her hands. "She says you and she will marry someday."

He stood up slowly, towering over the pallet. A mighty sight for any foe.

"Are you in love with her?"

"It is good to know that your tongue is not harmed. But you ask many questions." Moving to the edge of the pallet, he settled his leg more comfortably and changed the subject. "Why did you decide to leave? Were you not treated well?"

In view of what had happened, Anne-Marie realized her reasons for leaving were inadequate if not downright scatterbrained. She hadn't the slightest idea where she would have gone had her ill-fated attempt to escape proved successful. She had no money, few provisions, and her pleas for assistance had fallen on deaf ears in High Bluff.

"I admit running away wasn't the smartest thing I've ever done, but you don't understand how worried I am about my sisters. For all I know they're dead—and for all *they* know, I didn't make it either." She turned curious eyes on him. "I would think you would be relieved to see me gone. I am capable of returning to Mercy Flats on my own." *Though I don't want to*, she added silently. She wanted him beside her, but she had no right to ask his protection—especially if another woman waited for his return.

A dangerous light entered his eyes. "Alone? Are you not convinced of the perils that await a woman traveling alone?"

Her chin lifted. "I know the risks. My sisters and I have traveled alone and no harm has befallen us…until now."

His dark gaze traveled over her slowly, with an assessing interest that Sister Agnes would have thought highly improper.

"You could be hurt by vile men. It would be wise for you and your sisters to reconsider your ways before harm snatches you away."

Every word he spoke was truth, yet she couldn't let him think that she was completely helpless without his protection. She had already decided to change the folly of her ways. "I am a resourceful woman, Mr. Walker. You would be surprised how much I know."

Their eyes held for a long moment.

"No, I don't believe I would be, Miss McDougal."

Anne-Marie looked away first. "If you are engaged to another woman, you should not be looking at me this way," she chided, although his look threatened to rob her very breath away.

He conceded the point with a nod. "You will forgive my temporary insanity." He leaned back, his dark eyes dancing with amusement. He was more male than she cared to notice.

The teasing light disappeared and his features sobered. "I have come to strike a bargain with you."

She glanced up. "What sort of bargain?"

"I have come to ask your help."

Her eyes narrowed with skepticism. "What kind of help?"

"I want you to help Quincy and me get the gold out of camp."

"Why should I do that?" She was already more involved with John Quincy Adams and Creed Walker than she should be. If it weren't for that gold, she would already be on her way back to Mercy Flats.

"If you will agree to help, I will see that a third of the money is yours. You can donate the windfall to your mission, maybe make up for some of your...downfalls."

"A third," she breathed, trying to envision the fortune. Even without prolonged calculation, she knew it would be a lot. A whole lot. "What would I have to do?"

"Come up with a way to remove the gold from camp, undetected." He leaned back, watching her. "You're good at moving without detection."

She wasn't sure if he had given her a compliment or insult, but the idea intrigued her. A third of the shipment. The sisters would be overjoyed with such a gift, and the McDougal girls would never have to swindle another man. Her forehead creased in concern. "Just the gold, or you, me, Quincy, and the gold?"

"All four."

Dear me—he must be desperate! "This must be pretty important to you and Quincy."

The muscle in his jaw tightened. "Very important."

Her eyes narrowed. "Now why do you want to leave your friends' camp—and Berry Woman—undetected? You're a spy, aren't you?"

He gazed stoically back at her. "No."

She recalled Quincy's earlier explanation. "Paid agents?"

He sat up, his eyes pinpointing her. "Quincy has told you this?"

"You *are* a spy. A government spy. I thought something was funny about that gold. But you surprise me. I wouldn't have thought an Indian would take sides."

"I don't." His features remained somber. "The Crow is for his side."

"But you ride with the Union."

"I ride for the side that is right."

"But now you and Quincy need my help."

He shrugged. "If you're willing—a third of the gold and my word to return you to Mercy Flats unharmed."

"You can't promise that—only the Lord can do that."

He bent his head. "I stand corrected. Will you help?"

Well, well, well. So now the two spies were so desperate they were willing to come to her for help.

"Why me? Why not ask Bold Eagle for his wisdom?"

"I've thought about it." His eyes avoided contact with hers now. "You have the greater skills in trickery."

She was getting a little tired of these backhanded reassurances, though the thought of her deceits made her edgy. They sat for a moment in silence.

"Will you do it?"

"I'm still thinking." Closing her eyes, she mulled the situation over in her mind. If she thought hard enough, she could come up with a way to get them and the gold out of camp without arousing suspicion. It wouldn't be easy. Every eye would be watching her to report another break for freedom.

She sighed, wishing for the hundredth time that she had never gotten involved with her dealings. Look where her talents had landed her: half-frozen in a medicine lodge. And because Creed knew about her criminal past, he viewed her as a convenient tool. He'd never look at her with the respect and admiration he reserved for Berry Woman.

Finally he spoke. "Quincy has told you of our mission?"

"Yes—you're an Indian Northerner."

"It wasn't long ago you said I didn't look like an Indian, Anne-Marie.

The me you see is not necessarily Creed Walker. Perhaps when this is over we'll both have a better understanding of each other, but for now you will have to trust me and do what I ask."

"I never meant you didn't look like an Indian—I only meant you don't act like an Indian." Her eyes focused on the skins lining the walls of the lodge. "At least, not all the time."

Their eyes met, and she could see he was assessing her again.

"So, you and Quincy are involved in the war," she murmured. "Where does that leave me?"

Shrugging, he smiled. "It leaves you just as desperate as Quincy and me. The way I see it, we're both in a bad situation."

"I agree. Why should I trust you when my life is in danger?"

"You'll just have to take my word that I'll get you home, I suppose." He fell quiet as he studied her. She squirmed under the close scrutiny. He was trying to decide if he could trust her, and he could. If he saw the determination in her eye or the mulish set to her chin when she made a promise, he'd know that he could.

"All right. I'm going to trust you. Quincy and I were on our way to pick up the shipment of gold when I rescued you from the jail wagon."

"I never saw Quincy during that time," she countered.

"He rode ahead of me. We were to meet within the hour when I encountered you being chased by Comanches. That is why I had such meager provisions the night I rescued you."

"Quincy had your supplies?" That would explain why he had been traveling so light. No food, only one blanket.

Creed nodded. "He carried the supplies that particular day. We don't usually ride separately, but we were in a hurry to break camp that morning."

"You were on your way to pick up the gold?" The irony of it made her laugh. "That explains why it was loaded and waiting on the buckboard."

"No, I don't know why it was loaded and waiting on the buckboard. The city councilman knew we were on our way to get it, but he didn't know when we would arrive."

"Whose gold is it?"

"The funds were donated by a group of wealthy California investors for the Northern cause. The money will enable the North to continue fighting. Quincy and I were sent to pick up the gold and bring it to our commander."

Anne-Marie understood men's belief in a single cause, but a trunk full of gold was a whole lot of belief for any cause.

"Why would California investors donate such a large sum specifically to the Union Army?"

He smiled. "Your naïveté is refreshing. Let's just say the 'investors' like their present affluent lives, and they don't care to lose them."

"Then the gold wasn't donated because the investors have a true sense of right and wrong; they gave it because they're looking after their own selfish interests. It's a matter of greedy men wanting to dominate other men and having enough money to do so."

"It's surprising how astute you are when you want to be, and yes, that unfortunately is the case."

Her jaw firmed with resentment. "It's not fair. The North should refuse to accept the money."

He shrugged. "In war, the end justifies the means."

"Then you think someone else knew about the gold and was in the process of stealing it when we broke out of jail?"

"It's a reasonable assumption, but I have no proof one way or the other."

"Who could it possibly be? Agents working for the South?"

"Maybe."

"A crooked banker?"

"Maybe. Or councilman."

"A crooked sheriff?" She snapped her fingers. "A crooked sheriff and banker? That's it! High Bluff's sheriff and banker are nothing but low-down, cutthroat snakes."

"You are jumping to big conclusions—but you could be right. At this point it doesn't matter. We have the gold."

"And that's exactly how it's going to stay. Whoever tried to steal the gold won't get a second chance." She crossed her arms and winced. Her shoulder muscles still felt like mush. "I refuse to let that gold fall into unsavory hands."

"Then you agree to help?"

Her eyes lifted expectantly. "Certainly, for a third of the gold and your promise that once the gold is safely in your commander's hands, we will ride *immediately* to Mercy Flats."

He stiffened. "I cannot give you my word that I will immediately take you there. I have my duty."

"That's my condition. Take it or leave it."

His brows lifted. "Condition, Miss McDougal?"

She smiled. "Circumstances, Mr. Walker."

A disgusted sound passed his lips. "You are a hard case, lady. The whole Northern cause needs your help and you start bargaining with me."

She smiled. "Good. I'm glad you accept. When do we start?"

He sighed, but she thought she saw a hint of a grin on his lips. "Bold Eagle says those outlaws are waiting on the outskirts of camp; undoubtedly they have their eye on the gold. They're minor nuisances, but they'll be in our hair until we shake them. They must have followed the posse out of town. They know we're in here."

"So I have to figure out a way around them too." The job was getting harder. Maybe she should up her price.

"For you, that shouldn't be difficult. Quincy tells me the so-called gang is led by a bandit named Cortes."

"You know him?"

"We've had dealings in the past."

Anne-Marie frowned. She'd learned from planning her confidence games that the first step was gathering information. "Is he smart? Will he be hard for me to outwit?"

"A man doesn't have to be brilliant to cause trouble."

"Why don't I just go out there and demand to know who they are and what they want? If they're after the gold, I'll just tell them they can't have it."

Creed's jaw dropped. "I don't think so. You have a pretty neck, much too pretty to have it wrung off like a Sunday dinner chicken."

He got slowly to his feet when he saw her energy was draining. "We will speak of this again later. Now you must rest."

"Yes—but come back tonight. Meanwhile I'll give the situation some thought."

When the flap closed behind him Anne-Marie was curious about what had prompted his grudging smile and the gentle way he'd tucked a corner of the blanket closer around her neck. By all rights he should have been angry enough to personally wring her neck for that Sunday dinner.

Ten

Ben!" the sheriff bellowed. "Get in here!"

Deputy Ben Parnell tossed the pail of water out the back of the jailhouse and stepped back into the office.

"What do you want?" he shouted.

"Run this down to the telegraph office." Ferris Goodman handed the deputy a piece of paper with a scribbled note on it. "Have Ladeen send it off to every lawman in a hundred-mile area."

The deputy glanced at the brief message.

> IF A NUN ACCOMPANIED BY A BLACK AND
> A CROW INDIAN IS SPOTTED IN YOUR AREA,
> APPREHEND IMMEDIATELY. WOMAN HAS
> GREEN EYES, SMALL STATURE. WANTED
> IN HOWARD COUNTY FOR CATTLE THEFT
> AND JAILBREAK.

"You think this is really gonna help, Ferris? Cortes and his men have been chasing the three of them for days, and the gold is still in their hands."

"No, I'm sending it 'cause I don't have another blessed thing to do, Ben!" Ferris mocked.

"All right, all right, you don't have to be so cranky. Seems to me a black man, a nun, and an Indian traveling together shouldn't be that hard to spot. If you ask me, which nobody ever does, that'd be a sight hard to overlook."

"Well, now, if you'd stop working your jaws and think about it, Ben, don't you just suppose those three might have enough brains to split up so's they wouldn't be so noticeable?"

Ben frowned. "Well, I allow that's possible—I guess."

Snorting, Ferris stalked back to his desk. "That's mighty big of you, Ben. Mighty big."

Ben's chin jutted. "So, I ain't perfect."

"You gonna go send those telegrams, or do you plan to take root where you're standin'?"

"I'm goin', I'm goin'," Ben mumbled, starting out the door. "But for the life of me I cain't see what good it'll do. Ain't no one seen hide nor hair of those three and I don't likely think they're gonna."

⟶

Creed stepped from the medicine lodge the next morning and walked straight to Quincy's tent.

Thoughts of Anne-Marie continued to haunt him. He found himself looking forward to their daily matches of wit. The woman was not only beautiful, she was intelligent. It was not the keenness of a con artist that attracted him, although he found that aspect of her intriguing, but rather it was her appeal as an independent and rational woman that fascinated him. He knew many women, but none could match this one.

Quincy glanced up from cleaning his rifle when Creed entered his tepee and grinned. "Brother Walker. How's the good sister this morning?"

Seating himself opposite his friend, Creed lifted his hands to the fire. "She is anxious to move on."

"Is she now?" Quincy mused. "And what about you?"

Creed's frown deepened as his gaze centered on the bandage wrapped tightly around his thigh. To all who asked he vowed he was recovering, but his force was slow to return. "The wound doesn't want to heal."

"I wouldn't be too concerned." Quincy spat on the rifle stock and rubbed harder. "Spirit Cloud says these things take time."

"I do not have time." Creed's tone was short now. "We have been delayed too long as it is."

"I could ride ahead, deliver the woman for you," Quincy offered. "By the time I return you will have your strength back."

"No, it's too dangerous to travel alone with such a large amount of gold."

Spitting again on the rifle butt, Quincy polished it to a deep shine with his sleeve.

"And there is the matter of the men waiting outside the camp," Creed noted.

"Hmmm." Quincy glanced up. "Haven't figured out a way to escape the illustrious outlaws yet? Don't figure that noodle-brain Cortes will give us much trouble, but the warriors say the gang is dug in outside the camp."

"Cortes is a headache, not a threat," Creed admitted.

"What does Bold Eagle suggest we do?"

"I don't want to involve Bold Eagle any deeper in this matter. The tribe is small, and the people have already endangered their welfare by taking us in."

"You don't think Bold Eagle would insist on helping? You two are blood brothers, aren't you?"

"Yes, but I'm reluctant to accept my brother's help." There would be no question of Bold Eagle's loyalty if Creed chose to ask.

"One moonless night, and Cortes and his men could disappear, never to be heard from again," Quincy mused. "Two strong braves with freshly honed blades could take care of that problem."

"Killing is never the answer. I will find other ways to evade my enemies."

"Hmmm, Anne-Marie's safety wouldn't have anything to do with this, would it? I thought you would be more concerned about our mission than about her." Lifting the barrel of the gun, Quincy peered through it.

Creed pitched a twig on the fire. "I am concerned for all who are involved."

"We could always leave the woman in Bold Eagle's care and then come back for her later. That way all we'll have to worry about is the gold."

"No," Creed objected shortly. "The woman would not accept it, and I have given my word that once the gold is delivered, I will personally see her to Mercy Flats. It will be far wiser to enlist her help in this matter. She can be, at this point, a help. She is working on a plan and thinking of a way for us to elude the enemy as we speak. I figured if anyone can get us past that gate without detection, she can."

Glancing up, Quincy frowned. "Are you serious?"

"She is wise in the ways of deception," Creed maintained. "She has given her promise to help."

"But we've never had to ask a woman's help before—"

Creed's eyes fixed on the fire and he interrupted. "We have not been in so grave a situation before." Silence fell between the two men.

Then Quincy noted, "I have never known Creed Walker to rely on anyone, much less a woman. Are you convinced there isn't another reason you're willing to jeopardize the mission by bringing her along—asking for her help?"

Creed fixed his eyes on the fire. "If you are implying that anything personal exists between the woman and me, you are wrong. I'm thinking of what is best for all, nothing more."

Quincy released a low whistle. "Brother Walker, just how far will you go to help this woman?"

❧

There is nothing between the woman and me, Creed mentally repeated later when he limped across the open communal area to Bold Eagle's lodge.

Bold Eagle opened his eyes when Creed sat across the fire from him.

"Your wound is better, my brother."

Creed nodded. "Soon I will be able to leave to complete my mission."

"This is good. And the woman?"

"She is eager to leave also, my brother."

"This is also good."

They sat for a while in companionable silence. Their shared friendship was peaceful. As a courtesy, Creed waited for Bold Eagle to break the quiet.

"What does my brother wish my warriors to do concerning Storm Rider's enemies waiting in the trees outside our camp?"

"I haven't decided the men's fate," Creed admitted. "If Cortes's gang is killed, more will come to take their place, and I fear for the safety of your tribe."

"Do not worry," Bold Eagle scoffed. "The Apache are strong. Tell me what must be done and it will be, for I owe you my life as well as the lives of my people."

How could he explain the power of the white man? Creed had listened to Bold Eagle recount the many raids his band had made against the white settlers. How did he tell this noble man that his days were numbered? That when this war ended there would be more and more whites encroaching on the vast Texas plains? That if the outlaws were eliminated, more would take their place? Someday Bold Eagle's band would vanish like the large herds of buffalo that once dominated the plains.

"I don't want anyone uselessly killed," Creed repeated.

"Then we must trick them," Bold Eagle decided.

"That's what I'm thinking."

Bold Eagle nodded. "I will help think of a plan, my brother."

"That's good—you are wise in your ways. And the woman will help."

"The woman?" Bold Eagle bit down on the stem of his pipe, hard. "Has my hearing left me?"

"No, your hearing is fine. The woman is cunning—like the fox. She can be a big help."

"She is bother, like the wolf," Bold Eagle said when Creed rose to leave. "Better my hearing left."

ᥫ

Late that evening Creed returned to Anne-Marie's tepee. She had been moved from the medicine tent and into her tepee where a vat of hot water awaited her. She had finished bathing when Creed's tap sounded at the flap.

She was sitting close to the fire braiding her auburn tresses. The flames from the fire caused her hair to come alive with a fire of its own. Her borrowed doeskin dress clung damply to her soft curves in a way the black nun's robe never had, and Creed felt a disturbing tightening in his stomach. He had seen her in various conditions, but tonight she looked like a wife waiting for her husband.

For a moment their eyes met in mutual awareness until a fire log broke in two, shattering the stillness.

Seating himself beside her, he crossed his legs, focusing on the flames. "You look very pretty tonight. That worn blouse from Eulalie—it does not reflect your eyes, the color of sweet-smelling grass that blooms in the spring."

Glancing away, she remained silent and then said softly, "Creed…"

He placed a finger on her lips to silence her. "Soon this will be over." His fingers lightly traced the outline of her face. "You're feeling better tonight? Our God shined on you—you could have been…"

"I know. And I know how irrationally I acted. I'm sorry."

"Irrational you're not, but leaving was a mistake. Promise me you won't try anything like that again."

"You have my word." Lowering her eyes to the flames, she admitted, "You've saved my life three times now. I will forever be in your debt."

"It was my duty." His tongue twisted in the lie, because he knew that he had gone after her the third time for a reason beyond that of simple obligation.

"Well, thank you again," she said quietly.

"Have you come up with a plan yet?"

"I'm working on it. We could always have Bold Eagle's warriors simply tie those outlaws up until we can get away."

Creed silently laughed at the idea of Bold Eagle's warriors tying men up, but his features remained somber as he answered her, again surprised at her gentleness even toward those who would harm her. "Too risky. They would only break loose and follow." His hand was drawn to a lock of her hair and her eyes closed when he gently wound the silk around his finger. "Cortes would send others to retaliate for their humiliation. We need a more clever way to leave without bringing harm to either ourselves or my brothers."

"Have you spoken to Bold Eagle?"

"Bold Eagle will do as I ask."

She nodded. "I have no real plan," she confessed. "Not without upsetting everyone. What I'm thinking would mean that your friends would have to break camp and move." Their eyes met, and unbidden, the thought came to his mind that he would love nothing more than to take her into his arms and kiss her. Firelight played over her flushed features, drawing him like a flame. "It would be easier for the three of us to escape if we didn't have the gold to worry about."

His expression sobered. "The gold goes with us, or we do not leave."

"But if we—"

He released the curl, scooting to the side. "We don't leave without the gold."

"All right. But you're not going to like what I'll come up with."

He didn't doubt her word, but at the moment he was desperate.

Asking a woman to do a man's work stung, but he admitted she was far more experienced in the art of escape. And common sense told him to let her take the lead. "Just don't get us killed—or lose the gold."

"All right—but you're not going to like it."

"So you have said. I'll cope, all right?"

"All right. I'll try to keep the risk to our necks to a minimum."

Rising slowly to his feet, he extended his hand to her in a gesture of friendship.

Placing her hand into his, she smiled. "I'll have something in a couple of hours."

He nodded. "Send for me when you do." He dropped her hand, more aware than at any time before of the young woman's powerful effect on him. A dangerous effect he could not afford.

&

Thin shafts of light streaked the morning sky. Creed and Quincy sat atop a rise, watching God's morning portrait unfold. Creed drank in deep drafts of cold air. Anne-Marie was a constant thought with him now, an arrow in his heart. She was a mystery far beyond his comprehension. It was not fair that he put her in this situation, and yet—she was willing. Was it possible that in her youth and innocence she risked her neck in order to actually feed and clothe the mission sisters? A man would be hard-pressed to find fault with her motives, though stealing was never right.

Creed rode a paint pony, his eyes assessing the outlaws' camp. A heavy wind kicked up wisps of smoke from a struggling campfire. "They must be freezing their socks off down there."

Quincy shifted on the stallion he was riding. "I still say we leave Anne-Marie here and come back for her later. There's no sense in involving her in something that might get her killed. Once we deliver the gold, we come back for her. Bold Eagle will protect her with honor. It's the only smart way to handle this. We can outsmart that gang."

"And if we can't?"

"If we can't, then we're goners."

Creed's answer was the same. They were in trouble and he'd use any means to escape with the gold intact. "No, and I'm tired of discussing it. She goes with us or we don't leave."

"Well, we'd better come up with something, and pronto." Resignation was evident in his friend's voice. "Bold Eagle can't be happy about those outlaws camped on his doorstep."

The men spotted Anne-Marie approaching the rise. She rode up, wind whipping her cheeks to a rosy fuchsia. "I've got it!" she declared in a breathless voice.

Creed frowned. "It's about time. I sat up half the night waiting for you. You said you'd have it in a couple of hours."

"Sorry, it took longer than expected. Details, you know. But I've got the plan." She addressed Quincy, but her eyes found Creed's.

Quincy frowned.

"Relax. She's the best in her field," Creed said. "What have you come up with?"

"Well, it's lengthy." The three dismounted and walked their horses along the ridge. As they walked, she talked. "What I'm about to say may sound farfetched, but from my vast experiences, I'm convinced it's the only way out of our situation. We'll need Bold Eagle's help—maybe he should be here for this conversation?"

"Let's not involve Bold Eagle until we hear the plan."

"All right." She glanced at Quincy. "I know you're leery, but hear me out. Once we're out, there's that abandoned mission not far from here." Her eyes searched Quincy's. "You know where it is. We were discussing it moments before Bold Eagle's warriors found us."

Quincy agreed that he knew of the mission. "I've seen it many times."

"We'll be safe there until Creed heals. When he does, we'll move on and deliver the gold and Creed can take me to join my sisters."

Creed nodded for her to go on. "The mission is a good place to hide. But how do we get out of this camp without Cortes and his men following?"

Anne-Marie quickly began to outline her strategy. As she talked on in a rush she could see disbelief creep into Creed's expression and outright horror in Quincy's.

"You must be kidding," Quincy said when the plan was laid out.

Creed stared at Anne-Marie as if she had lost her mind. "I thought you were taking this seriously."

"I told you that you wouldn't like it, but it will work."

His eyes darkened. "Impossible. Do you know what it takes to move a whole camp with snow still on the ground? Bold Eagle would never go for it."

"The plan will work. It's positively brilliant; some of my best work," she argued.

"You're both crazy," Quincy declared, "and I refuse to have anything to do with this."

"Do you want to get out of here or stay until summer?" Creed inquired.

"But her plan is nuts!"

"We'll do as she says."

Quincy's mahogany features paled to almond. "Good Lord, please have mercy on our ignorant souls."

"You know of a better way?" she asked.

"No, but this one is insane. With our luck the last thing we need is to stir up a bunch of evil spirits. I don't like it, Creed. I think we'd be setting ourselves up for more trouble than we ever thought about."

"No one said you had to like it," Anne-Marie consoled, patting Quincy's arm. "It is a little uncommon…"

"A little?"

"…but it'll be over before you know it."

"I can't believe this woman." Quincy shook his head like a bear with porcupine quills in his muzzle. "Creed, she's gonna get us all killed."

"Nonsense. Now come along, gentlemen." Anne-Marie swept her hand toward the camp. "We have business to attend to."

Eleven

Bold Eagle glanced up when three sets of eyes appeared in the tepee opening. "Bold Eagle welcomes his friends to his lodge." He motioned for the visitors to sit on the buffalo robes encircling the fire.

Creed lowered himself to the ground. "We have decided on a plan."

"And the three of you agree to this plan?" Bold Eagle questioned. His eyes focused on the woman.

Smiling, Anne-Marie nodded.

Bold Eagle directed his gaze to Quincy.

Quincy nodded his head.

"Tell me of this plan."

"It is one that will take a great deal of courage, my brother, for it goes against our teachings, and it would take much courage to move the camp before the grass is new."

Bold Eagle's features turned stoic. "If Bold Eagle goes against the Wise One Above, he would be doomed forever to walk the Hanging Road."

Anne-Marie crept closer, bending low to speak. "It's nothing like that."

"Continue. Bold Eagle is listening."

Creed took over, unfolding Anne-Marie's strategy. Bold Eagle's brows shot up, finally disappearing into his hairline.

"I am to understand you want my people to prepare your bodies for burial, transport them out of camp on a travois, and place them on sacred platforms?"

Creed's gaze met his brother's unflinchingly. "This is what I ask."

"Before you are dead?"

Creed nodded soberly.

"It is said that the ghosts of the people waiting to be escorted to the Hanging Road walk between the scaffolds. You ask too much, Storm Rider."

"I am aware of the Apache beliefs," Creed continued, "but there is no other way to escape without causing much pain to my brothers. Those outlaws will try to take that gold, and they won't care who gets hurt."

Bold Eagle shook his head. "This I cannot do."

"Please." Anne-Marie reached out to take his hand. "You're our only hope and though the plan goes against everything you hold sacred, can you not help your brother?"

"I cannot."

Creed shifted closer. "I know I ask much—"

"My brother asks too much. Far too much." He crossed his arms over his chest.

"My brother, we need the help of your tribe if we are to be successful," Creed said.

Silence, heavy and foreboding, settled upon the visitors and their host. Only the fire emitted warmth. When the silence grew, Anne-Marie turned her feminine wiles upon the noble leader of his tribe. "Chief Bold Eagle, may I have permission to speak?"

Although women were allowed to give counsel, Bold Eagle eyed the woman in disbelief.

The chief glanced at Storm Rider and he nodded. "Permit her to speak."

At Bold Eagle's nod Anne-Marie began. "Noble Chief, I am a follower of the One Who Is Above." She glanced at Creed. At his nod she continued. "I am here because God guided my steps to you." She waited for confirmation.

The chief nodded.

"I believe that He will protect us—that I am here because He has so willed it."

Bold Eagle turned his attention to Creed. "Do you agree with her words, my brother?"

"Yes," Creed said simply.

Bold Eagle gave him a piercing look and then returned his gaze to Anne-Marie. Bold Eagle had a problem and he must rid himself of this problem; Anne-Marie had given him a way to do so without loss of face, and at little danger to his small band.

As the sun rose higher, Creed, Anne-Marie, and Quincy used their persuasive powers to convince the chief that the plan, though unorthodox, was sound, and there was no other viable solution at hand. "I am committed to respecting the ways of God," Anne-Marie said, "even if my plan involves something forbidden. I am reminded of the story in my Bible when Jesus and His disciples ate grain while walking through a field on the Sabbath."

Creed nodded. "This is true. I have read the story many times."

Bold Eagle grunted with a heavy sigh. "Let it so be."

༄

In the early afternoon Bold Eagle gathered the council and explained, with Creed's help, the steps needed in order to make the escape successful.

Horrified eyes shifted to Anne-Marie. Mutterings in the foreign tongue surrounded her.

The chief stood firm. "Bold Eagle does not like the plan but he will help his brother. It is the only way."

"When?" one brash warrior asked. "When do we do stir up the spirits and bring evil and destruction upon our village?"

Bold Eagle's chin lifted. "Sunrise."

Groans filtered throughout camp and the disgruntled group dispersed, returning to their tepees with dragging moccasins.

When the sun next appeared, the plan was set into motion. Anne-Marie volunteered to be first. She lay down on the tepee floor and crossed her hands.

"I'm telling you, I don't like this!" Quincy's voice shook when squaws wrapped buffalo hides and strapped him onto a wooden rack. "Just the thought of being buried alive makes my skin crawl!"

"You're not being buried. And the time will pass swiftly," Creed assured from across the tent where Berry Woman and other women were swathing his body.

Quincy struggled to break free when the women cinched the straps around him tighter. "I can't move my arms, Creed!"

Creed smiled. "You're dead, Quince. Your arms aren't supposed to move."

Quincy took a deep breath and clamped his eyes shut. "How did I ever get myself in this mess?"

"You have the knife, don't you?" Creed asked, a hint of humor coloring his voice.

"What good's a knife gonna do me? I'm bound up like a Christmas goose, my body wrapped in buffalo hides, and ropes lashed so tight I can't move."

"You don't hear Anne-Marie complaining."

"Of course not," Quincy snapped. "It's her idiotic idea."

"And a splendid one it is. You'll see," Anne-Marie noted.

"Well, I just want you to know," Quincy's muffled voice complained beneath the hides, "this is last time that I'm agreeing to anything that you suggest. Understand? The very last time—if we get out of this one alive."

"Got it, Quincy."

Quincy let out a yelp when his pallet was lifted onto the shoulders of two strong warriors.

Anne-Marie heard rather than saw Creed's pallet being lifted and carried away. She prayed that he could sense the reassuring thoughts she sent his way. She closed her eyes and gave herself over to God. She knew He would protect them.

∾

"Hey, looka there." Ollie elbowed Butch near sunrise when activity in the camp picked up.

"What do you make of that?"

Cortes struggled to see through the cloud of activity that had suddenly enveloped the Indian camp. "The Injuns are leaving," he grunted. They'd wasted days waiting for something to happen and now the redskins were pulling up and high-tailing it out of here? Squinting, he bent for a closer inspection. Cortes's eyes were getting old. Tiny blurs scurried around in the distance.

Something was not right. Indians never moved their camp until the grass was greener and the wind warm.

"See the black and the nun anywhere?" Rodrigo peered around the other men's shoulders.

"Yeah, and the Indian?" Butch cut in.

"Cortes sees many Indians," he snapped, "but he does not see the black or the woman." Cortes saw nothing but blurs.

"What should we do, boss?" Ollie peered over his shoulder. "Looks like they're breaking camp or something. Why would they do that? It's ain't full spring yet."

"How should Cortes know? We watch…and wait to see which way they go." He spat a stream of tobacco on the melting snow. "Our grit has finally scared them out into the open. We will follow the buckboard."

"But, boss, I don't see a buckboard." Butch cupped his hands to his eyes and strained.

"No buckboard?" Cortes flared. "Do you not see the wagon?"

The three shook their heads negatively. Butch ventured. "Do you see it?"

Cortes straightened. "It is in plain sight. They would not leave the gold. They will take it with them, and when they do, we will follow and take it."

Four pairs of eyes watched as the tribe went about striking camp.

"Boss's right. They wouldn't leave the gold," Ollie said. "We'll get it when they come out."

The outlaws kept vigil, their eyes focused on the burial procession that slowly wound its way out of camp.

"Well, will you look at that?" Ollie whispered. "A bunch of 'em must've died off."

"Could be that's why they're strikin' camp, boss," Butch said. "Could be there's a sickness down there like the fever or something. The whole tribe is dyin' off."

"Perhaps," Cortes mused, "or could be just some old people whose time has come."

"I don't think so," Ollie said. "Warriors are carrying the dead. See?" He pointed to the medicine man who walked in front, carrying weapons. "Them's not just old people."

"So?" Cortes wasn't interested in the burial details; what he was interested in was the buckboard, and right now all he could see were figures tearing down the lodges.

Ollie straightened. "You don't suppose those Injuns could have took a notion to finish them three off."

"Enough!" Cortes roared. "You are *muy estúpido*! And if it is the nun, the *indio*, and the black, good riddance. Cortes cares only for the gold."

Frowning, Ollie's gaze followed the slow-moving procession. "I don't know—we might oughta check it out."

Rodrigo's eyes widened. "Are you *loco*? The thought of going into an Indian burial ground—I ain't going. Period."

"*No es necesario*," Cortes stated emphatically. "The *indio* and the black are still down there. I have seen them just this morning. They are no fools. They would not leave the gold. Cortes wait. If they do not come out, Cortes storms the camp."

❧

Anne-Marie was beginning to have second thoughts. She lay nearly suffocating, listening to the wind keening through the trees. How long had she been here? One—two hours? Minutes dragged by. If she only had some water—and she then remembered that a buffalo stomach full of water was hanging just a few feet below her. Food was also left on her scaffolding to provide nourishment for walking the Hanging Road. The Indians had also secured ceremonial weapons to the scaffolding so that courageous warriors would be able to hunt for nourishment.

Right now all Anne-Marie wanted was to leave this smothering cocoon, but she remembered Bold Eagle's warning. They must not leave until well after dark, when the moonless night would effectively cover their escape.

She could barely hear the tepees being dismantled, but she could feel the wind that had sprung up. It swayed her scaffold and caused the buffalo stomach and parfleche to thump against the sides of the poles.

If a person were afraid of ghosts, this could be his undoing.

❧

Creed lay quietly on his platform, awaiting the moment of escape. He counted each hour as time passed slowly. At least another five counts before he could safely escape his bonds. The pain in his thigh throbbed. He'd known, even before he'd accepted the plan, that it would take a toll on his wound. The leg was swollen, pressing tightly into the buffalo hides.

The sound of his rifle thumping against the pole was as comforting as the knife he held in his right hand. Laid to rest among the bones of his brothers. The sooner this was over the better.

Closing his eyes, he saved his strength for the ordeal that still lay ahead.

If Anne-Marie's plan proved sound, they only had a few more hours before nightfall and he could cut his way free of the bindings. A squaw had placed a sharp knife in his right hand and left plenty of room for him to cut the straps. Then he would rescue Anne-Marie and Quincy, and the three would be long gone by daylight, the awaiting gang left in their dust. The plan left ample room for failure, but he prayed that Anne-Marie's assurance that God was with them proved true.

For God was now their only hope.

Twelve

Four riders sat atop a rise, their eyes riveted on the deserted land. Horses shifted, snorting.

"Well, that's the last of 'em," Ollie mused.

"Yeah, that's the last of 'em all right," Butch said.

"We cannot be so sure," Cortes snapped. "We have not seen the wagon carrying the gold. Where is the wagon?"

"It ain't come out, boss," Ollie said. "If you ain't seen the blasted wagon, how are we supposed to have seen it? We've been watching for hours, and that buckboard ain't left that camp."

"He's right," Rodrigo put in. "We watch *mucho* close."

"Well, it's got to be down there somewhere." Cortes spat on the ground and then wiped his mouth on his coat sleeve. "Buckboards do not disappear into thin air." Spurring his horse forward, the boss headed toward what had been a camp only a little while ago. The other three men halfheartedly reined in to follow.

When the outlaws rode into the deserted campsite it was hard to imagine that over a hundred people had lived there not three hours before. Not one scrap of debris was seen. Several horse tracks, as well as two-pole tracks, led off to the southwest, but there was no evidence of a buckboard.

If Cortes had not seen it with his own eyes, he would not have believed that there had once been a buckboard, but he grudgingly trusted the eyesight of the idiots that rode with him.

"Spread out and check every inch of this ground," he ordered as the men sat astride their horses, looking at a loss as to what they should do.

"Maybe they burned the wagon," Butch offered.

"Estúpido!" Cortes exploded. "This is what we must find out! The wagon, it had iron to hold it together, no? Iron does not burn. If we find iron that is not burned, then we know our eyes do not play the tricks upon us." He pointed to several mounds of smoldering ashes and his eyes leveled on Ollie. "You and him"—he motioned to Rodrigo—"go sift through the ashes." Turning to Butch, he ordered, "You, I want you to ride to where they buried their people and look for any sign of buckboard tracks. The Apaches are trying to fool Cortes." His eyes formed wrinkled slits. "This they cannot do."

Butch stared at him vacantly. "Buckboard tracks?"

Cortes spat on the ground, hard. "No, brilliant one, *monkey* tracks."

"But, boss," Butch argued, "we didn't see anyone go near that place once those dead people were put on those platforms—"

Taking a deep breath, Cortes lowered his tone to a threat. "The *carro* couldn't have vanished into thin air. Go!"

Reining his horse, Butch rode toward the burial ground, but his stiff posture told Cortes that he did not like the order.

❧

The sound of approaching hoofbeats startled Anne-Marie. *Stay calm. You're perfectly safe*, she thought. No one, not even those outlaws, would dare desecrate a grave. She couldn't be certain who the riders were; perhaps Bold Eagle had left a couple of warriors to check on their needs until Creed freed their bonds. The chief had been most agreeable once the escape plan was underway. Bold Eagle would surely look after them until they were well away from danger.

⌒

Slowing his horse, Butch shaded his eyes with his hand and studied the tall platforms. There were too many to count, some very old and weather-worn. His gaze focused on the three new structures. Wind kicked up dust, swirling around the high stands.

"Rodrigo? Is the wind making the platforms shake like that?"

"I don't know." His *compadre* glanced toward the narrow path leading away from the burial ground. "I don't like this one bit, Butch. We got no right to be messin' with the dead."

"We got no choice. Do you want your share of the gold?"

"Sure I do, but this is insane—Cortes is *loco*."

"Keep your voice down. He'll hear you."

Butch started when something dropped to the ground. The noise ricocheted like a shotgun blast in the eerie silence.

Every tooth in Butch's head startled to rattle. "I'll never see my sweet Prudy again. My babies won't ever have their papa bounce 'em on his knee or tell 'em bedtime stories." The prediction came out in a parched whisper. He focused on the platform directly above him, and then froze in place. "Rodrigo?"

The platform began to rock as though the spirits were peeling their way through the thick bindings.

"*Sí?*" Rodrigo's answer was a mere squeak now.

"Gold or no gold, I ain't gonna tangle with one of those heathen spirits for anyone—Cortes included. I'm headed home!" Wheeling his horse, Butch whipped the animal's flank and beat it out of the burial ground.

Glancing at the wavering platforms, Rodrigo did the same.

✑

"See anything?" Cortes asked when Rodrigo's horse thundered to a stop in front of him.

"Nothing, didn't see a thing—just some weapons dangling off them spooky-lookin' platforms. Butch cut out on us. Said he was heading home."

"Coward!" Cortes snatched off his hat and flung it on the ground. "No sign of the *carro?*"

Rodrigo looked him straight in the eye. "I looked everywhere. No buckboard, just dead Injuns."

Cortes centered on the deserted campsite. "Well, now, you just ride back up there and help yourself to those weapons. No sense in letting good arms go to waste."

"You talkin' about them spears and stuff tied on those platforms?"

"*Sí.* Cortes can sell them, or put them to use."

"You go yourself. I ain't cuttin' out on you, but I ain't going back in there."

Cortes glanced up. "What do you mean, 'You go yourself'?" He thumped his chest authoritatively. "Cortes gives the orders."

"I ain't going back up there."

Cortes stomped his foot. "Cortes gives the orders!"

Reining his horse, Rodrigo gave the boss an unsympathetic look. "If you want those weapons, you go get 'em."

✑

When the three riders rode past the burial platforms, Rodrigo crossed himself.

"*Uno momento.*" Cortes swerved his horse and urged it up the incline to the entrance of the burial ground.

Ollie groaned under his breath. "He's gonna make us go after those weapons."

"I ain't going near those platforms," Rodrigo vowed. He spat on the ground. "A team of wild boars couldn't drag me back in there. If the boss wants those spears, he can get 'em himself."

"You! Men! Get up here!"

⌒♦

Anne-Marie slowly became aware of riders approaching. Or was it only one rider? She couldn't be certain. She willed her heart to remain in her chest. *It's only the braves or warriors coming to check on us. Lie still.* Her dry mouth cried for water. The canteens were tied on the outside. There was no way to drink until her binds were freed. She made her mind oblivious to the suffocating blackness. Only a thin shaft of air penetrated the casing. It had to be dark now. It had to be—she'd been in this shell for days, weeks? She swallowed back the urge to scream. What if the plan failed? What if Bold Eagle's warriors rode away and Creed was unable to free his binds? Abigail and Amelia would never know what happened to her—not ever. Nor the mission sisters...

She silently began to recite the Lord's Prayer. *Our Father, who art in heaven, hallowed be Thy name...*

"See, such fine weapons, men. They make Cortes very happy." Something was being cut loose from her platform.

"I wouldn't touch those if I were you!" A second man's voice drifted to Anne-Marie. "Those Injuns will come back and relieve you of your scalp."

The outlaws were back, stealing from the dead. Was there no limit to their audacity? Closing her eyes, she set her jaw and began to squirm. It was a risky move, but suddenly the thought of freedom appealed more than the thought of dying in this horrible place. She would be in the outlaws' hands, but that was a thought for another hour. What had she been thinking? The plan was too risky. She would free Creed and Quincy, and they would give the desperados what they wanted: the gold. No amount of it was worth their lives. Better to admit defeat than to die a suffocating death on these poles.

✑

Scoffing at his friends' taunts, Cortes continued sawing. "See, rifles, and knives with long shiny blades, and—"

He glanced up to see one of the bundles shaking. His eyes grew wider as the body started to jerk back and forth, looking for all the world like it was trying to free itself from the platform.

"See," his voice trailed off lamely, "such nice knives..." He fell silent when a wailing moan came from the bundle.

Spurring his horse, Cortes kicked the animal into a fast gallop. The trophies broke loose from his hands when he tried to avoid hitting Ollie's horse.

"Out of my way!" Both animal and rider plunged down a steep incline.

"What's wrong with him?" Ollie shouted when he rejoined Rodrigo, who was waiting below.

"Who knows," the outlaw grumbled. "I told you to stay down here with me."

✑

The sound of men's shouts, horses veering, and beating hoofs pounding the ground in the opposite direction met Anne-Marie in the midst of her escape attempt. Fighting and clawing, she tried to break the binds. "Drat—these straps are so tight..." She wiggled, feeling the platform sway with her efforts.

Still trying to free herself, Anne-Marie heard a familiar voice below her.

"Anne-Marie, it's Creed. Are you all right?"

"Get me out of here!"

"Hold on, I'm going to cut you loose now. Who were the riders?"

"Those crazy outlaws. Hurry, Creed. I can barely breathe."

She felt the ropes give way, and moments later her pallet was slowly lowered to the ground. The bindings were cut away, and she shivered at the sudden chill she felt when her sweat-drenched body was exposed to the cool night air.

"Are you sure you're all right?" Creed whispered.

"I'm fine. What about you? And Quincy?" She tried to wring feeling back into her hands when she noticed blood seeping through his britches. The wound had broken open again. "Your leg—it looks awful."

He busied himself cutting away the last of the ties. "It feels awful too."

"The moment we can, we're going to see a doctor and have that taken care of properly. I'm sorry," she added. She hadn't thought about the effect her crazy plan would have on his injury, but the plan seemed to have worked. With a quick look around, she saw no sign of the outlaws. "Do you think they've gone?"

"We're not sticking around to find out. Let's free Quincy and get out of here."

When Creed cut the binds and Quincy rolled free of his prison, he bent over his knees, sucking in air. "Anne-Marie, if you *ever* suggest such a plan again, remind me to ride as hard and as fast as I can in the opposite direction." He took long, deep breaths.

"Bold Eagle had better be where he said he'd be," Creed whispered. "Let's go." The three struck off in a northwesterly direction under a cloak of darkness.

Thirteen

Three indistinguishable figures rounded a bend in the road and two waiting riders slipped from the shadows. Kneeing his horse forward, Creed rode to greet his brother.

"You have survived your ordeal," Bold Eagle greeted when he drew closer.

"By the Father's grace, we have survived." Creed studied the blood-soaked bandage wrapped tightly around his thigh. The wound was pounding from the arduous walk.

Black Earth and Two Belly brought along a fresh horse. A moment later Berry Woman appeared astride a pony. Slipping from her mount, she ran quickly to Creed's side. "Storm Rider—you cannot continue this madness," she pleaded. "It is not wise."

Anne-Marie glanced away when she saw the possessiveness in the young maiden's eyes. Creed responded to her, taking her hand tight in his. A razor-sharp pain split her heart. She wanted him to hold *her*, to comfort *her*.

The thought shocked sense into her. She was falling in love with this man, a man she couldn't have. Not only did he have feelings for this lovely young maiden, but his emotions ran deep—like still waters.

Quincy was busy examining the buckboard. "I have to hand it to you, Anne-Marie. I had strong reservations about the plan, but I've never seen a slicker operation in all my born days. Breaking down that buckboard and then hauling the parts—plus the gold—out of camp on several travois right beneath the outlaw's noses was brilliant all right, even if a woman did mastermind it."

Berry Woman helped Creed to the back of the reassembled wagon and Quincy and Anne-Marie climbed aboard. Securing the spare horse to the gate, Black Earth and Two Belly dropped back.

"You will rest?" Berry Woman fretted over Creed as she carefully stretched his leg out in the bed of the wagon.

"My sister clucks like a mother hen," Bold Eagle scolded. "Come, we must move on before we are noticed. It is a day's ride to our new encampment."

"Will you go to your summer grounds?" Creed asked.

"It is too soon; the grass is not new, but water is plentiful here and so is buffalo and game."

"I'm sorry for this upheaval."

Bold Eagle rested a hand on Creed's shoulder. "My brother would do the same for me." The men's eyes met and sealed the words with a silent understanding. Bold Eagle drew back and straightened. "I have sent riders ahead with provisions to see you through a short time. You will remain at the mission?"

Creed nodded. "We'll remain there until this thing heals again." Gritting his teeth, he shifted his boot.

"Herbs, fresh kill, and water await you."

"Thank you, my brother."

Leaning forward, Berry Woman whispered into Creed's ear. He nodded, and she returned to her horse.

Turning their animals, the party rode off.

Quincy picked up the buckboard reins. "Well, Miss McDougal. The plan went off smooth as my grandma's Christmas pudding." He chuckled. "I'd sure like to have been there and seen the looks on those bandits faces when Bold Eagle broke camp and rode off. I'll bet they're still shaking their heads and wondering what happened."

✑

At one time the Santa Maria Mission had been a lovely sight. Low adobe structures sheltered with red-tiled roofs dotted the hillside. Now the buildings were neglected and falling into ruin. However, years of disrepair could not detract from the beauty of the twelve arches, some tall, some short, some semicircular, and others majestic and narrow. Their grandeur was still breathtaking.

The outer buildings were crumbling to the ground, but the mission's beauty and serenity still showed through the rubble. Though it would be weeks yet before spring came, Anne-Marie could imagine what a magical place the gardens would be when the heady scent of Castilian roses and myrtle filled the air with a scent sweeter than honey.

High above in the old tower, a bell stood sentry. It reminded Anne-Marie of all the mornings a bell much like this one had awakened her and her sisters for morning prayers. Scampering into their clothes, they had raced giggling to the chapel, to be detained by a stern-faced nun who reminded the impetuous McDougal sisters that young ladies never ran, they walked.

A pain so deep she could hardly bear it flooded her when she thought about those happy, carefree days with her sisters. Would she ever see them again? Yes, they'd outwitted authorities, but Creed had to heal and then the gold had to be delivered before she could even begin the journey to Mercy Flats. Perhaps she could find a way to send a message to her mission and have the sisters inform Amelia and Abigail that she was well and would join them as soon as possible. Time was passing; perhaps they had grown tired of waiting and gone home to seek solace among the nuns. Or they could still be with their rescuers, either captive or unable to return. She would never know until she got home.

Quincy's dark eyes studied the crumbling building. "Doesn't look like much, but I guess it'll keep the rain off our heads."

Anne-Marie agreed without much spirit. She was suddenly very tired.

She drove the wagon under a vine-covered portico. Creed was asleep, so rather than disturb him and start his wound bleeding again, she pulled an extra buffalo hide over him for warmth. They needed to choose a good place to build a fire, assess their supplies, and be sure the deserted mission held no dangers.

Leaving Creed in the buckboard, she and Quincy set out to explore the main building. They entered the dim interior and Anne-Marie wrinkled her nose when the scent of the musty-smelling alcoves reached her. What few pieces of furniture had been left behind were either damaged or broken. All were covered with dust.

They entered the kitchen with its vaulted roof, and a sigh escaped her when she saw the chimney was intact and the kitchen stove still there. It was a huge, monstrous contraption, but at least they would have hot water and a more convenient way to cook their food. Her eyes scanned the room and found the pile of provisions left by Bold Eagle's braves. Meat would be hanging in the smoke house.

"Have mercy," Quincy murmured when they moved upstairs and roamed the empty corridors. Thick walls with innumerable rounded stones rose from the clay floors. They passed through the baptistery and into the large sanctuary.

Light streamed down through a long, narrow, horizontal window, illuminating the reredos with nine statues in various niches. The resplendent altar was elegantly carved with winged cherubim. Pieces of the dais candles still remained, waiting to be lit for prayers.

A bat darted from the high ceiling toward the intruders. They ducked for cover. Quincy shook his head and stepped closer to Anne-Marie.

"This place gives me the jitters."

"A little jitters never hurt anyone," she whispered.

"Why do we always end up in spooky places?"

"It's not so bad." Anne-Marie moved on, with Quincy following close behind. Returning to the kitchen, she parted a layer of thick cobwebs and peered down a black column of steps leading to the cellar.

"Now if you're thinking of sending me down there, you can just get that idea out of your head," Quincy said. "There is a limit to my cooperation—and you reached it with that last plan you hatched up."

"You're such a scaredy-cat," she chided. Searching for a light source, she spotted a candle stub lying near the base of the first step. "You have matches with you, don't you?"

"No, ma'am." His answer was too quick for Anne-Marie to believe him. "Miss Anne-Marie, I have a phobia of dark places. I'd just as soon we didn't go down there."

"All right, I understand phobias. I'm not over-fond of water, iguanas, and spiders, but we do what we must. Give me a match. I know you have some; now give me one."

"Ma'am, you don't want to go down there. It's dark and dirty, and who knows what's at the bottom? I don't want to even speculate on what might be crawling around down there—or even worse, slithering around down there on its belly."

"You don't have to go. Wait here and I'll be right back." The old mission seemed spooky only because it was so quiet and in disrepair. Dark cellars didn't bother her. When she was small, she had fetched potatoes and rutabagas for Sister Delia from the storeroom nearly every day. "There might be something to eat down there," she reasoned. "Something the former occupants might have left behind." Sisters always had large gardens and most likely there were jars of tomatoes, corn, and green beans left behind. Canned goods lasted a very long time.

"By the looks of the place there's been no one here for months—maybe years," he countered. Taking a deep breath, he muttered. "I'll go—just make it quick."

"Your choice. Where's the match?"

He fished the match from his vest pocket and handed it to her.

She struck the sulfur tip on the sole of her shoe and then lit the candle stub, brightening the narrow stairway with enough light to see the way down.

"Oh." Quincy's eyes grew rounder. "I wish you hadn't done that." She felt him cringe when the sound of scampering feet ruptured the silence.

"It's just some old mice. They won't hurt you." Hitching up the hem of her skirt, she stepped down a couple of stairs and then turned to peer over her shoulder. "Are you coming?"

When he didn't answer, she continued in a peeved tone, "You don't have to, but if I should find something, I'll need your help bringing it up."

"What we need is two or three torches instead of one little candle. Why don't you just forget looking for something to eat? Anything you'd find would be spoiled by now, anyway. The last thing we need is a good case of the grippe. And besides, Creed's tribe gave us supplies."

"I just want to take stock of all our provisions," said Anne-Marie.

Quincy jumped back when a mouse darted up the stairway and shot between his legs.

Drawing a shaky breath, he started down the stairs behind her.

Candlelight danced across dirt walls when Anne-Marie stepped deeper into the dank cellar. The sound of dripping water momentarily distracted her. Cool drafts of musty-smelling air threatened to extinguish the candle, plunging the stairway into total darkness.

"Do not let that candle go out," Quincy hissed.

"I'll try not to."

"You do more than try, sister."

Pausing on the bottom rung, she lifted the candle higher, trying to see. It was black as night down here. "See anything?" she whispered.

"Nothing. I couldn't spot a speeding locomotive if it was coming straight at me." Squinting, he slapped blindly at something that zoomed by his ear.

Drifting deeper into the vault, Anne-Marie noted the cellar wasn't as large as the one in Mercy Flats, but it was adequate.

She moved the light slowly along the walls, searching for shelves lined with canned goods. It appeared as if nothing had been left behind.

It was spooky down here.

A man's voice shattered the silence. "What are you two doing?"

Quincy started at the sound of Creed's voice. "What are you doing down here?" Creed repeated when he stepped off the bottom step to join them.

"What are *you* doing down here?" Anne-Marie snapped, shaken at the unexpected intrusion. "I thought you were sleeping."

"I was, but when I woke up and found you both gone, I thought I'd better look for you." His eyes roamed the dark interior. "What are you searching for?"

"I thought the former occupants might have left something we could eat," Anne-Marie murmured. "You never know where a sister might have stored provisions." Canned green beans, corn, tomatoes. Lifting the candle higher, she moved the light slowly through the inky interior. Her hand paused, swinging the light back to the left a little more when she thought she detected a small chamber in the very back of the room.

"Do you see anything?"

"It looks like a room—maybe more storage."

"We're not going in there," Quincy warned.

Brushing past him, Anne-Marie held the candle out in front of her and moved toward the rustic door, her skirt fabric rustling in the shadowy darkness.

Quincy glanced at Creed. "That woman is going to give me the green apple quickstep before this is over."

Brushing aside a layer of cobwebs, she lifted the heavy bar blocking the chamber entrance. When she slid the bar aside it rattled on its rusty hinges, making a menacing sound throughout the small chamber.

Using her slight weight, she shoved against the door. The hinges groaned at the disturbance but refused to budge. Quincy stepped up, laid his shoulder against the wood, and heaved.

The door slowly swung open, yielding an even blacker void.

Three sets of round eyes peered into the gaping edifice.

"See anything?" Anne-Marie whispered.

Creed edged closer. "Nothing. Hold the light higher."

The three pressed close to each other and entered the stale-smelling chamber. The inside was pitch black.

Anne-Marie moved the light along the walls and her gaze anxiously roamed the tight quarters. The room appeared to have no apparent purpose that Anne-Marie could identify.

"Just more empty shelves," she announced.

Sinking back against a ledge, Quincy fumbled in his back pocket for a rag to wipe his brow. "This place is worse than Eulalie's house and that Indian camp put together."

Creed closed the door and slid the rusty bar back into place.

The next morning Anne-Marie was up before dawn. Meals were meager, consisting mostly of a thin gruel, nuts, winterberries, and the venison Bold Eagle had left for them.

After breakfast, Anne-Marie dressed Creed's wound and bandaged it using strips of petticoat that she had washed and hung out to bleach dry in the sun. To her delight, Creed's health gradually showed signs of improvement.

Each hour brought a new and wondrous discovery for Anne-Marie. She found contentment with Creed. A satisfaction she hadn't known was possible. At times she thought she was falling in love and at others she knew it. The idea was so unlikely and complicated that it made her laugh, but at other times she would try to analyze her frightening new feelings. She decided she felt the way she did about

Creed Walker because he was the first man who made her aware that she was a woman. Not by anything he'd done or said, but the way he watched her over the supper table, the way his hand brushed hers when she poured his coffee, or the way he put his fingers on the small of her back to usher her out of a room. His gaze would fix on her at times, following her as she went about her work. Their eyes would lock, and there was something indefinable in his expression. Creed Walker was not the type of man to settle down on a homestead and raise potatoes; he was an adventurous man, one who would eventually return to Bold Eagle's camp and marry the waiting young maiden who had a claim on him.

Sighing, Anne-Marie dunked another dish in the hot sudsy water. There had been little time for daydreaming of late, so she didn't feel bad about taking her time with this morning's dishes, watching robins outside the mission window forage for seed. Lifting the window, she took a long breath of fresh morning air, her mind still on Creed.

For all the times interest dominated his gaze, she had to admit there were often as many times he'd stared at her as if she suffered from a rare brain disorder. Like the night she was invited to share her poetry. She had warned the men that she was only a novice poet, and her attempts were amateurish at best, but they had insisted she recite something she'd written, so she had complied.

"Are you sure?" she asked, afraid she would bore them to tears. Nights were long at the mission and entertainment was as scarce as hen's teeth, but that particular night the men were in a charitable mood.

"Go ahead," Quincy invited. "Recite something for us."

Glancing at Creed, Anne-Marie sensed that he wasn't necessarily the poetic type, but he seemed agreeable. "Well," she began, drawing a fortifying breath, "I'm not as good as my sister Amelia."

"You have to be better than either one of us," Creed said, the corner of his mouth lifting.

They sat on the floor in the kitchen, around the huge cook stove. The fickle spring weather had turned balmy, but there was still a brisk chill at night. May wasn't far off, and Anne-Marie found herself long-ing for the time when honeysuckle, bougainvillea, and jasmine would perfume the mission air.

"I wrote a poem about robins once. Would you like to hear that one?" she asked.

"Sure." Quincy lay back, resting his head on crossed arms.

"Shoot," Creed said.

"All right." She curtsied and, clearing her throat, she began:

> The robin hopped, the robin sang,
> The robin fell, and hurt his wing.
> He got right up and chirped some more
> And found some crumbs upon the floor.

She drew a deep breath. "The robin—"

Creed's brow lifted. "*Sang* and *wing* don't rhyme."

Her face clouded. "I told you—I'm not very good." That was one occasion when he looked at her as if he doubted her sanity.

Later that night the conversation had turned to the gold.

"The buckboard's well hidden?" Creed asked.

Quincy nodded, pouring coffee from the pot that sat on the kitchen stove. It wasn't real coffee—just the chickory brew Creed carried in his saddlebags. "Well hidden. No one could spot it, even if they got this close."

"Where?"

"In the mission courtyard, beneath a thick growth of tangled vines."

Creed toyed with his cup. "I don't know, Quincy. I think the hiding place would be pretty obvious if one had a mind to do some looking. Maybe we should move the shipment to a safer place. That wagon is our only means of transportation if we're forced to leave on short notice."

"It's seems safe to me, but if you want it moved I'll move it. Are you thinking what I am? That squirrely outlaw Cortes is still hanging around, looking for us?"

"His type doesn't give up easy."

Anne-Marie supplied the logical solution. "Why not store the gold downstairs?" She glanced at Quincy, aware he wasn't comfortable with the idea of going into the basement again.

Quincy had two words. "No. Way."

"Think about it, Quincy. What better way to assure that the gold will be safe? No one but us knows the room's there, and even if those outlaws find us, they know nothing about that room."

"That outlaws aren't going to find us," Quincy stated.

"They might."

Quincy shook his head. "Cortes isn't smart enough to blow his nose on a hanky. I'll wager he's given up and gone home."

"I wouldn't be so certain about that." Creed got up to stretch, still favoring his wound.

"Are you siding with her?"

"Yes, because she's right, Quince. That gold isn't safe where it is."

"Now look, you two. Do you understand the meaning of *fear*? I'm not just afraid; I get paralyzed in dark, cramped spaces. Can't get my limbs to move. Creed can't carry the gold to the cellar; he's still babying that leg. So who does that leave to move the gold down there? John Quincy Adams, that's who. I'm not going near that room, so don't ask. Someday I would like to settle down, marry me a fine woman and have sons and daughters. If I stay with you, the prospect is looking less likely every hour."

"If a light were on it wouldn't be dark." Anne-Marie tried to make the task more tolerable. "I'll find a larger candle..."

Quincy wasn't buying it. He set his jaw, crossed his arms and stared at her.

Sighing, Anne-Marie got up to stir the fire.

When the silence lengthened, Quincy grew more vocal. "I know what you're doing; you two don't fool me. You're trying to make me feel guilty about not doing my share to get us out of this, but you are wasting your time. Period. That gold is fine right where it sits. There hasn't been a sign of those outlaws for days, so you might as well get it through your thick skulls I am not going back to that cellar."

Creed calmly turned to Anne-Marie. "Do you have any more robin poems?"

She frowned. "Really? You didn't think the other one was awful?"

"Pretty awful, but I'll listen to another one."

"No. I think I'd rather just sit and think."

Silence stretched. Creed lay back, closing his eyes. Night birds called back and forth in the courtyard.

"You're not going to shame me into that cellar," Quincy said. "I'm not going in that dark hole again. It isn't like the gold is in any danger."

Moving back to the pallet, Anne-Marie sat down, gathering the hem of her skirt between her legs. Loosing the pins from her hair, she absently ran her fingers through the thick mass.

A slow awareness crept over Creed as he studied her movements beneath hooded lids. Candlelight caught the fiery silk highlights and he wanted to run his fingers through the thick layers, draw in her sweet feminine scent. His gaze moved to her mouth and lingered.

When she absently glanced up and caught him staring, color filled her cheeks and she quickly looked away. He was waiting when she lifted her eyes again and their gazes touched. What would she feel like held tight against his chest, listening to his heart's erratic thump? Berry Woman was nothing more in his mind than a young girl; Anne-Marie was a woman.

"Oh, all right!" Quincy shoved back. "You're not going to let up until I move that blasted gold."

Startled, Creed broke eye contact with Anne-Marie. Quincy stalked to the door, jerked it open, and left.

Glancing back to Anne-Marie, he frowned. "What got into him?"

Shrugging, she got slowly to her feet. "He must have changed his mind about moving the gold. He'll need my help."

Before Creed could argue, she followed. Quincy was still grousing. "I have lost my mind. I swore I would never go back into that cellar, but here I go, like the numbskull that I am. They got a place for men like me, insane asylum…wouldn't be surprised if they already had my name on the door 'cause that's sure where I'll be heading when this little farce is over…"

Fourteen

Sheriff Ferris Goodman sat across the table from Loyal Streeter in the Gilded Dove saloon. The men had kept company for over an hour, and Loyal was getting restless. He kept toying with his glass, sending nervous looks toward the door.

"Relax, Loyal. Cortes is gonna show up any minute now."

"Where is that buffoon?"

"We're gonna get the gold back," Ferris assured the councilman. "The job's just takin' a little longer than expected."

Loyal tossed down another drink. "It's like the earth opened and swallowed that Indian, black, and woman alive."

"There's an Apache camp the other side of Brittlebranch. Fifty or so tepees."

"You think they went there?" Streeter blanched, and then shook his head. "Cortes ain't got the guts to confront a band of Apaches. The man is crazy, but not that crazy. Those outlaws would be nuts to mess with an Apache—unless the Crow's in cahoots with the chief."

"Well, you never know. If the Indian's desperate enough, and I'd say right about now he is, he might try anything to hold on to that gold shipment."

"Maybe—but I'm still puzzled about what part the black has in this. And what about the nun? Why is she with them? Seems real strange she'd be in such company. You think she's a captive?"

Loyal signaled to the bartender for another refill. "I don't know, but you can bet your life the Indian's not worried about the black or the woman right now. He's looking after his own self."

Ferris frowned. "Them redskins are smart—and wily. Suppose the Crow knows something about that gold? It was plain bad timing that we moved the shipment when we did. I should have been more careful."

Shrugging, Loyal tossed down another drink. Shoving the glass aside, his gaze focused on the empty glass. "Nah, those three couldn't have known about the gold. No one knew about it other than me and the officials."

"Dirty agent?"

"You know I don't reveal my contacts." Loyal glanced back to the doorway. "Where is that two-bit outlaw? I should have insisted that you put someone other than Cortes in charge."

Goodman's face clouded. "Relax. He'll show up. He's on to something, or he would have been here by now."

Shoving out of his chair, Streeter tossed a coin on the table and reached for his hat. "Time's running out, Goodman."

Ferris nodded. "The South can't hang on much longer without funds." He paused, eyeing his companion. "You're not thinking of doing anything crazy, are you, Loyal?"

Loyal paused. "Crazy? What kind of fool question is that?"

"Just wondering. You wouldn't be thinking of pulling a switch, would you? I've seen the look in your eyes lately, that greedy look you get when you're busy hatching a plan. I don't know what you got in mind, but it's a pretty safe assumption that the Confederacy isn't going to see a single coin of that gold."

Loyal's voice tightened. "If you haven't heard from Cortes by sundown, send someone out to find him."

"I will—if he don't show up before long."

Striding across the saloon, Streeter shoved the double swinging bar doors open and left.

"Yeah," Ferris muttered. "Whatever you're up to Mr. Streeter, it's a safe bet it stinks to high heaven."

ᥱ

"You have family, Quincy?" Anne-Marie stacked another bag of gold. She was hoping that idle chatter would keep Quincy's mind off his work.

"Got three younger brothers at home."

"You said you were from Alabama."

He nodded and then paused to wipe the sweat rolling from his temples. The cellar was cool, but the gold was heavy and he'd worked up a sweat.

She hefted another bag onto a shelf. "You said you hoped to marry one day, have children, settle down." He had not looked up once, fixing his eyes on his work.

"That's what I plan, if I live to see the day." He strained to lift the bags of coins, taut muscles working in his corded arms.

"Got any particular woman in mind?" There must be a long line of willing candidates awaiting him back home. His tall, muscular frame, deep brown eyes, and molasses-colored skin were sure to attract women, but it was his good nature, his ability to make her laugh and want to choke him at the same time that had found its way into her heart. Her life would feel hollow when the three parted.

"If she's out there, she hasn't made herself known yet."

"Guess you'll be real happy when the war is over and you can go home."

His tone turned wistful. "Yes, I sure will be."

"How many children do you want?"

"However many the good Lord sends—I'd like to have a couple of sons, maybe a daughter."

"I'm sure your family misses you." Anne-Marie barely remembered her papa. She couldn't have been much more than a toddler when she and her sisters were left at the mission by kindhearted neighbors when both of her parents were waylaid on the way to town to purchase supplies. When the sheriff came to inform the family he found her and her sisters alone and frightened. Their closest neighbor would have taken the girls, but they could barely feed their flock, so she and her sisters were taken to the mission. But she remembered Papa's booming voice. Loud and spirited, Irish McDougal's voice made everyone grin. Irish must have inspired many a winsome thought among women in his younger years, but it was Mary Catherine McCurdy who had won his heart.

Memories didn't sadden her. The good Lord had provided shelter and food at the mission; the sisters were like mothers. Strict but fair.

"Creed thinks the war can't last much longer," she said quietly.

"Don't see how it can last, but man's got a stubborn streak. They'll get their fill of death and bloodshed one of these days and the fight will be over."

Anne-Marie paused to catch her breath. "You're still worried about the gold, aren't you?"

Quincy's solemn gaze met hers. "I'd just as soon it was in the commander's hands," he admitted.

"It will be—the moment Creed's able to travel."

"Well," Quincy tucked the last bag among the others. He didn't have to say that he was mighty relieved to have the job finished; his strained features told Anne-Marie as much. "I hope you're right."

"Why wouldn't I be? We outsmarted the outlaws, didn't we? They haven't a clue as to where we are right now."

"Yes, ma'am—maybe it's safe."

She hated it when he "yes ma'amed" everything she said. His superficial answers meant that he didn't share her optimistic view.

"What're your plans once you and your sisters are reunited?" Quincy slid down the wall and stretched his long legs in front of him.

"Well…" Anne-Marie thought before answering. Before their arrest, she and her sisters had planned another scam near Dallas County…but she was through with thievery. Never again would she take anything that wasn't hers. "I guess we'll return to the mission and help the sisters. They're all very old now."

"You ever thought about marrying, settling down?"

"No. No I haven't."

"Your sisters. Have they…"

"No."

Quincy leaned back, smiling.

"What are you grinning about?"

"You're downright funny."

"I don't mean to be." And she resented the observation. Having a genial personality was one thing, but being the butt of someone else's joke was another.

"How old are you?" he asked.

"Old enough to know a lady never tells her age."

Sighing, Quincy said, "I remember when I was your age. Nary a brain in my head."

Anne-Marie focused on his earlier remark. "Is that why you think I'm funny? That I don't have a brain in my head?"

He continued as though he was talking to someone else. "Pretending not to have an interest in men, pretending to be a nun. When are you going to tell him?"

Her heart leaped. "Tell who…what?"

"Creed. Tell him you're in love with him."

Denial sprang to her lips and she clamped her teeth on her lower lip. She'd promised God to never lie again. Did that mean she could skirt the issue? Lacing her fingers through her hair, she closed her eyes. "What a fine mess I've made of everything. Creed will never forgive me."

"Forgive you for what? He's a reasonable man and you've been more than cooperative."

"Reasonable enough to forgive a foolish young woman for dragging him around the countryside, shooting him, demanding that he take me to Mercy Flats above his duties to his country?" She slumped against the wall, fighting tears. "What man in his right man would forgive a woman for driving him to complete madness?"

Silence filled the small room. She needed to get Quincy out of here and into the sunlight, but she didn't have the energy.

Quincy finally broke the stillness. "He's pledged to Berry Woman."

"I am well aware of Creed's...situation." If she knew nothing else, she knew about Berry Woman. In camp, someone went out of their way to remind her everywhere she went. Her voice took on a small, soft quality. "Do you think he loves her? I mean, the way a man really loves the woman he's going to marry?"

"Well, that's hard to say. Creed never mentions her, but then, that doesn't mean much. Creed doesn't talk about his personal life."

"Yes, I suppose men don't talk about things like that—not the way women do," she admitted. She and her sisters would sit up half the night talking, but men were different. But then..."Don't you think if a man truly loved a woman that he couldn't do anything but talk about her?" she persisted.

If she loved someone that much, it wouldn't bother her one bit if the whole world knew it. She'd shout it from the highest hilltop; stop strangers on the road and tell them.

"You don't know men," Quincy said.

"I don't. I haven't been around men for any length of time. Tell me, why doesn't Creed talk about Berry Woman?" Berry Woman's life and his were so different now. They were both Indian, but Creed had learned the white man's way. Was it possible he wanted to return to Berry Woman's way of life? He and Bold Eagle were closer than brothers.

"You don't know much about the Crow, either."

"No," she admitted. "Nothing." She'd seen Indians all her life, and she had heard tales about how they not only fought each other, but also had to fight to protect their territory from a variety of enemies, including miners, settlers, and soldiers.

Quincy's expression sobered. "A Crow's marriage is also a treaty between clans. It's not only about love. It's about honor and duty. The Crow's idea of an ideal marriage is one between a man with honor to his name and a girl who is no clan or kin relation. So it doesn't matter if he loves her or not, he'll marry her."

Meeting his gaze, Anne-Marie couldn't hide her emotions. "But why—if Creed doesn't love her?"

"No one but Creed can say if he loves her, but he has given his word to his blood brother, Bold Eagle. Nothing"—Quincy's eyes searched hers—"and no one can alter his pledge."

"Then you admit that Creed may not be in love with this woman?"

Anne-Marie didn't know why the speculation should make her so happy. Whether he loved Berry Woman or not, Quincy had just said Creed would marry her regardless.

Getting slowly to his feet, Quincy dusted off the seat of his breeches. "Won't do any good to dwell on it, little sister. As soon as the war's over Creed's going to have to sort through this and find his answer."

Anne-Marie stood up and stuck the lid back on the Wells Fargo box, refusing to face him. She couldn't take her hurt out on him. He was only trying to soften the blow, but she didn't want him to see tears. He didn't need a stricken woman on his hands.

Resting a large hand on her shoulder, he made a final observation. "Nor will it do any good to brood about it, child."

It was impossible for Anne-Marie to hide her feelings. After all, a woman's eyes never lied. Tears spilled from her lids. "I wouldn't waste time brooding about some man." She turned away, snuffing back emotion. "Let's get out of here."

ꙮ

Creed shifted, finding the wound much less painful.

"See, it's better today." Anne-Marie studied the bandages the following morning, obviously proud of her handiwork. After only a few days at the mission the wounded leg looked much better, although he'd had to endure her reminders several times a day to keep his weight off the limb.

"We'll need to leave soon," she observed when her eyes centered on the dwindling pile of makeshift bandages. "I don't have much petticoat left."

Creed's sober eyes focused on her when she wrapped the clean bandage neatly around his leg. Her hands were small and her touch was as light as a hummingbird. The past few days had revealed a different side of Anne-Marie McDougal. A softer, more vulnerable side he found very appealing. In the beginning he had thought her more man than woman with her rowdy ways and rapier tongue. Now he realized he had been wrong. She would bring honor to the man she chose to marry.

He had begun to think about the time he would take Berry Woman as his wife. The war could scarcely last any longer, and once those dark days were past Bold Eagle would be anxious for the ceremony to take place.

Creed had learned the white man's ways, and many of those ways he found practical. Like the white man, when he married, he desired a woman of faith, gentle ways, and quiet strength. He would be her one weakness. This woman would come to him in her need when no other could comfort. To her husband she would give her deep and abiding love. Together, they would become one heartbeat, one soul.

"There now." Anne-Marie drew Creed back to the present when she patted the bandage into place. "All finished."

He smiled, resting his hand upon hers. "Your touch is gentle."

Turning aside, she asked, "Would you like to see some pictures I found this morning?"

"Pictures?"

"Yes, I found them in one of the chambers earlier." She left the kitchen, returning shortly carrying two large canvas paintings.

Propping the canvas against the wall, she considered them for a moment. "Admittedly the pictures are unusual in content, but the artist's efforts were not in vain. What do you think?"

Creed assessed the two canvases with a critical eye. "I'm not an art connoisseur, but the color's richness and clean, broad strokes are evident." One painting portrayed a dilapidated house, the other an eroded field. "Odd."

"Aren't they, though? I suppose a sister—or a monk—must have painted them in their spare time." She broke into a grin. "Let's play a game."

She could practically hear his mental groan, but there was little else to do. The dishes were washed, Quincy was off hunting, and it was a long time yet until the noon meal needed to be prepared. She and her sisters had often played the game she had in mind to while away the hours.

"What kind of a game?" he asked, skepticism lacing his voice.

"We'll each make up a story about the pictures. Whoever makes up the best story wins."

A smile played at the corners of his mouth. "And the prize?"

She thought for a moment and then smiled. "Whoever loses cooks the evening meal."

Leaning forward, he whispered, "I don't want to play games. I'd rather just look at you." Resting his hand across hers, he met her gaze.

She dropped hers, blushing under his eyes.

His fingers curled under hers. "I find you most charming—a little stubborn and rebellious, but nevertheless feminine and…" He paused. "Men are not so frightening. Honorable men." His fingers moved to gently tilt her face, forcing her to look at him. "I frighten you?"

"It's just that…you are promised to another and I know—and I agree that you should honor your word." Sighing, she gazed back at him and then, as if sanity returned, she sprang to her feet.

"Don't run from me, Anne-Marie," he whispered softly when she bolted for the door. How could he explain that his feelings were every bit as tormented as hers?

❧

The thick double sanctuary doors were open. He found her kneeling before the lighted candles. With head bowed and hands clasped tightly together, she appeared to him as a saintly picture of contrition.

A shaft of sunlight slanted through the narrow window above Anne-Marie. It caught the lustrous glint of her hair, bathing her in radiance. The scene before him took on an ethereal quality. She looked so small, so vulnerable, so much in need of being protected, cared for, and loved. He wanted to be the one to do all those things for her.

The knowledge shocked him almost as much as the desire that she caused in him. Desire he'd felt for no other woman.

Her soft voice came to him in the quietness. "Why do your feelings for me frighten you so?"

A voice drifted to her from the back of the room. "Why do your feelings for me frighten *you?*"

Tensing, Anne-Marie clamped her eyes shut tighter. "Because I don't want to love you," she whispered brokenly. "Love hurts."

Her admission echoed hollowly in the chapel. Creed took a few quiet steps toward her. "Love should not frighten you. I feel this power between us," he confessed.

"Doesn't it bother you?"

"Love does not frighten me. Commitment is my enemy. When a man gives his word there is little that he can do but keep it."

Moving up to the altar beside her, he knelt, grimacing when his leg touched cold stone. "Don't look at me or dare touch me," she begged. "A mere touch would undo my most sincere effort to preserve your integrity."

"Speak to me of your fears, Anne-Marie."

"I'm not afraid to love. I just don't want to love *you*—" She broke off, her words catching in her throat as the tears welled up in her eyes.

The planes of his face remained impassive. "I understand, but often love doesn't ask why."

"Until you came along, I was happy."

He sighed. "And I have made you unhappy."

"No, you haven't made me unhappy. Considering the agony I've put you through, I fear it is I who has made you miserable, but you've taken away my contentment and my freedom, whether you meant to or not. I want the carefree life I had, when all I wanted or needed was Abigail and Amelia."

"I have caused you this despair? This was not my intent."

She turned to face him, tears rolling from the corners of her eyes. "You love another woman."

Pain crossed his features.

"Isn't that so?"

"Love? I belong to another, but I am not in love with her."

"And yet you would marry her? How can you sit here and ask me why I can't let myself love you when you can't return the sentiment?" Her words tumbled out in a rush.

"Anne-Marie." He took her hand. He knew that his eyes spoke of his great love for her, but she refused to acknowledge it. "It is my honor and principle that binds me."

She stood up. "I assumed if a man loved a woman he would go to the ends of the earth to claim her." She stood up. "I'm glad we've had this conversation. It has not only cleared the air between us, but it has cleared my foolish head where you are concerned. I would share a cup of cornmeal with another woman, but never the man I loved."

And most certainly, she would never share Creed Walker. What difference did it make if he revered her? He planned to marry another. "It's time to choose, Creed Walker. You either love me or another."

She fled the chapel, slamming the doors on her way out.

Fifteen

Mission supplies dwindled to a critical low. Creed and Quincy knew it, but neither seemed inclined to do anything about it. As promised, Bold Eagle had kept fresh meat on the doorstep, but Anne-Marie needed flour and cornmeal—something that would stick to a man's ribs. She had to deal with the problem daily, while the men seemed content to eat the thin gruel she prepared each morning, noon, and night without complaint. Rhubarb wasn't in yet, so that left only chokecherries and wild turnips as staples.

"Don't wander away," Creed warned on various occasions, and at first Anne-Marie obeyed. Now she was seriously considering going against his wishes. Creed and Quincy wouldn't do anything about seeing that they were fed, and she was tired of being hungry. Besides, Creed's wound would heal faster if he ate properly. But she'd need money for supplies, and she knew of none except the gold hidden in the mission cellar. One single coin wouldn't be missed. And besides, she and Creed were going out of their way to keep from talking. So what he didn't know wouldn't hurt him.

Any gold she took would be for a worthy cause. They had to

keep up their strength. The gold would never reach the commander's hands unless they delivered it, and they couldn't deliver it if they were emaciated and half-starved.

The decision made, she planned to start off early the next morning—right after she dressed Creed's wound. She was confident he wouldn't miss her.

⁀

Creed silently handed her his empty plate after breakfast. He touched her a lot lately, always spontaneously, but with enough feeling to heighten her awareness of the strong pull between them.

Guilt brought her cheeks to a rosy red. She should tell him something about her brief absence. What if he came looking for her? "I thought I might look for mushrooms today."

"You are to stay close by," he warned.

"How far could I go?" The paths surrounding the mission were overgrown with weeds. It would be all she could do to find her way out.

On the way here they had passed the small community of Brittlebranch. The town wasn't more than an hour's ride away, so if she left now, she'd be back well before dinnertime. Oh, Creed would be angry when he discovered she had disobeyed him, but his anger would fade once he enjoyed a pan of cornbread tonight. There would be plenty of money left and she would give it to him, so he couldn't scold her too much.

The plan was simple, and she could pull it off with her eyes shut. She would be in and out of Brittlebranch before a cat could give itself a bath.

"Well." Quincy got up from the table to hand her his empty plate. "I'm going fishing this morning."

She dunked the plate in a pan of hot water. "Fishing?"

"Yes, I spotted a little stream about a mile up the road. I thought I'd try my luck at getting us a fish for our supper tonight. 'Course," he added wistfully, "a nice fat catfish is going to be mighty tasty, but there won't be any cornbread or fried potatoes to go with it."

Don't be so sure about that, she thought. There just might be a big pan of cornbread, some nice creamy butter, and a huge pan of fried potatoes waiting when he got back with his catch. But she played right along. "And with what do you plan to catch a fish? You don't have a fishing pole, a string, or even a hook."

"Why, ma'am." Quincy held up both hands. "I have two of the finest fishing poles the good Lord ever created." Grinning, he walked out of the kitchen, merrily whistling as he struck off for the stream.

Rinsing the last plate, Anne-Marie laid it on the countertop and then wiped her hands on her skirt. She silently stepped around Creed and reached for her coat.

The moment she was out of sight, she raced out of the kitchen and down the cellar stairway. Sliding the heavy bolt aside, she lit the candle stub, took a deep breath, and entered the dank chamber. Then taking one gold coin from the bag nearest the door, she slipped it into her pocket, turned, closed the heavy door, slid the bolt back into place, and raced back up the stairway.

Blowing out the candle, she laid the stub on the first step and firmly shut the door. Leaning against the wooden frame, she paused for a moment to catch her breath. So far, so good. Giving a hurried glance to the back of the mission, she breathed a sigh of relief when she saw that Creed was already engrossed in chopping wood.

Now all she had to do was get to town and back by suppertime.

❧

Sunshine warmed Anne-Marie's back as she straddled the horse. Hitching the buggy would make too much noise and Creed would hear her, so she took the mare. It was a beautiful morning and Anne-Marie was tempted to dawdle. But she had to complete the errand and return to the mission as quickly as possible.

A gentleman in a passing buggy tipped his hat to her, and she returned his smile as the horse clomped merrily along the road. The last thing she needed to do was draw attention. She must be careful to hurry about her purpose and remain as inconspicuous as possible. A passing stranger would think that she was merely a woman on her way in to town to purchase supplies—which was mostly true.

As she entered Brittlebranch, several more gentlemen tipped their hats, bidding her a pleasant morning. Nodding demurely, she acknowledged their greetings.

Riding straight to the mercantile, Anne-Marie dismounted and entered the store.

The proprietor glanced up when she walked in. Smiling, he walked toward her. "Morning, ma'am."

Anne-Marie nodded. "Good day, sir."

She was delighted to see that the shelves were adequately stocked despite the war. Quickly gathering the needed supplies, she lingered before the sugar, thinking how nice it would be to have some, but decided on a jar of honey instead. Selecting six nice plump apples from a barrel, she placed them on the counter beside her other purchases.

When the clerk saw that she had finished, he turned from where he was busy stacking canned goods and began to total her selections. "That about do it for you?"

"Yes, this should be sufficient. Thank you." Anne-Marie fished inside her pocket and handed him a gold coin.

The clerk examined it closely, but he made no comment.

"You're new around here," he observed when he boxed her purchases.

"Yes." A small, pretty porcelain music box caught her eye. It was lovely and she still had plenty of money left over from her purchases, but she didn't dare. Creed would understand the need for supplies, but he wouldn't condone a foolish whim like a music box.

"Right pretty, isn't it?" the clerk remarked. He must have noticed that she couldn't take her eyes off the trinket.

"Yes, that it is," she agreed.

"Make you a real good price on it," he offered. "Stocked it for Christmas, but with the war and all, I didn't have any takers."

"It is lovely." Anne-Marie picked the box up to admire it more closely. The detail was exquisite. Tiny engraved flowers and vines encircled the lovely porcelain box.

"Quality craftsmanship," he remarked.

It was indeed; the finest Anne-Marie had seen. Amelia was fond of doodads and she would love the music box. Before prudence intervened, she hurriedly laid the box beside her other purchases.

The clerk's brows arched curiously. "You don't want to know the price?"

"I'm sure it will be fair." Anne-Marie glanced anxiously out the window. "Add it to my other purchases, please."

"Be glad to. I'll even wrap it for you," the clerk said obligingly.

"Thank you, that's most kind of you—if it won't take too long." Anne-Marie's eyes returned to the search the empty streets.

"Looking for someone?" The clerk tore off a sheet of heavy brown paper and began to wrap the delicate box.

"No—oh, would you stick in a few pieces of the peppermint candy?" Creed and Quincy would like the special treat.

The front door opened and a woman holding a small child's hand entered.

"Mrs. Bigelow."

"Morning, Mr. Kinslow."

"Be right with you."

The young woman browsed while the grocer completed Anne-Marie's order. Handing her the basket, he smiled. "Be glad to carry this to the wagon for you, ma'am."

"Thank you, sir, but that isn't necessary. I'll manage on my own."

Emerging from the store, Anne-Marie glanced up and down the street before hurrying to the horse rail.

A speck of violet hanging in Harriet's Millinery caught her eye. Her footsteps slowed when she spotted the exquisite display of finery.

Drawn closer to the sight, she admired the beautiful straw hat.

Violet and white plumes adorned the sides. She had never seen anything so lovely. Slipping her hand into her pocket, she closed her fingers around the remaining coins left from her purchases. She had more than enough to buy the hat. After all, she had gotten the music box for Abigail, and Amelia would surely feel slighted if she didn't receive a similar token of her sister's affection.

Impulsively her hand closed around the doorknob and she entered the shop. When she emerged from the store a few minutes later, she was carrying a large box gaily tied with a red ribbon around the middle.

She paused, wondering how to safely carry the box and her basket of supplies, when a steely hand closed around her shoulder. Her heart sank when she met the cold, hard eyes of Cortes.

"Morning, Sister." The outlaw flashed a nasty grin. "I've been hoping to bump into you."

✺

"Are you sure you haven't seen her?" Creed paced the kitchen floor, his frustration mounting. For over two hours he had searched for Anne-Marie, but she was nowhere to be found. When he returned to the mission for dinner and found her and the horse missing, he had immediately begun to search.

"I saw her the last time you did," Quincy told him for the hundredth time. "This morning at breakfast."

Creed's strained features darkened when he strode back to look out the window again. "Where could she be?"

Shaking his head, Quincy admitted that her disappearance had him stumped. "I've spent the last half hour scouring the gardens and the surrounding area and there isn't a sign of her anywhere. The horse is missing too."

Creed frowned.

"She told me she was going to pick mushrooms. I should have

known she was up to something." He started for the door. "I'll have to go after her."

"We'd better get started. It'll be dark soon." Quincy reached for his coat.

"You stay with the gold." Creed's eyes met Quincy's and a look of understanding passed between them. "She's my responsibility."

Nodding, Quincy stepped aside. "Feels like she's gettin' to be a whole lot more than a responsibility."

⌒

"For the last time, I'm not telling you anything." Anne-Marie stared straight ahead, determined to die before she told Cortes where the gold was hidden. The streets remained empty and she wasn't sure if the store clerk had noticed the encounter. Should she scream, or quietly bluff her way out of the situation?

"*Señorita*, you are most unwise." Cortes paced before her, hands clasped behind his back, looking pensive. Sunlight caught the dented badge on his chest. "And most stubborn, but Cortes has yet to meet his match." His voice dropped menacingly. "Move her to the alley, men."

Anne-Marie squirmed when Ollie stepped up and shoved her to the alleyway. Not a soul stirred there.

"Now." Cortes's squat frame pinned her to the building. "You will tell Cortes where that gold is."

Her insides quaked, but she wouldn't let him see her fear. She set her jaw. "I have no idea what you're talking about." *Lord, please don't let him hurt me. I can't tell him where that gold is—I won't betray Creed.*

"Ohhhh, the woman has an obstinate *disposición*! Cortes, he appreciates a sense of humor, but I'm afraid he must resist the urge to laugh." The strange man's eyes turned steely. "You will tell Cortes, *señorita*. Where is the gold?"

"I will not."

"You will tell Cortes!"

She stared straight ahead.

Ollie and Rodrigo exchanged anxious looks.

"The black man and the *indio*—where are they?"

"They don't tell me where they go."

"You lie!"

She fixed her eyes on the alley entryway. Not one man had rushed to her rescue.

Anne-Marie shook her head. "I mind my own buisness. You should too."

Ollie pointed out the obvious. "She ain't gonna tell us."

"Yeah, but leastways we caught up with 'em again," Rodrigo noted. "It was a sure stroke of luck that we were still in town this morning."

Ollie shifted his stance. "If she refuses to talk, boss, there ain't much we can do about it."

"Oh, no, you are wrong, *señor*." Cortes spat, and then wiped his mouth on the sleeve of his shirt. "There are ways to make her tell us what it is we wish to know."

Rodrigo stirred uneasily. "I don't know, boss—"

"Do we not know of ways to loosen her tongue?" Cortes prodded. "The well?"

Rodrigo shifted. "Are you talking about that old shaft we came across a few months back? The one with all those creepy slimy things crawling around? We gonna throw her down there?"

"Can you think of a better way to make her tell us what she knows? We put her there and when she is ready to talk we bring her up. If she still isn't persuaded to say where the gold is, then we leave her there."

Ollie shook his head. "Those iguanas would loosen about anything in a body."

The men turned pensive.

Rodrigo finally broke the silence. "I don't think we oughta. After all, she is a woman. I ain't a religious man, but it does seem downright mean mistreating a woman."

Anne-Marie blinked. At the mention of iguanas her pulse threatened to thump out of her neck. Her heart was throbbing so painfully against her ribs that she could barely breathe. *Stay calm. Stay calm.* No matter what they said or did to her, she would never tell them where Creed and the gold were. Nothing they could do—including throwing her down some old well—would make her further endanger Creed's mission. She refused to cause him another ounce of trouble.

Cortes spat on the ground. "I will know where she has hidden the gold. Put her on the horse and we will take her away—somewhere no one will hear her screams."

Anne-Marie dropped the music box and supplies when Rodrigo grasped her by the arm and dragged her to a waiting horse. Squirming, she bit into his hand and fought until he stuffed a dirty rag in her mouth.

Manhandling her into the saddle, he mounted up behind her.

"What about the Indian?" Ollie called. "Are you figuring he'll come after her?"

"He will come. Then Cortes will have the gold."

The three riders thundered out of town to the deafening sound of hooves.

Sixteen

It was nearing dark when Creed entered Brittlebranch on foot. The storefronts were dark, the shops closed for the day.

Piano music filtered from the saloon when he slipped through the shadows on the sidewalk. When he saw that the clerk in the mercantile was just locking up, his pace quickened.

The clerk glanced up when confronted by a pair of hard black eyes. For a moment he couldn't find his voice as he stared eyeball to eyeball with the Crow.

Nodding solemnly, the Indian spoke. "I am looking for a woman."

"Good heavens, man. I can't help you. You'll have to find your own women."

"No, a particular woman. Small, pretty, red hair, dressed in a worn blouse and skirt. Have you seen her?"

"Yes, she was in earlier in the day. Bought some staples and a music box," the grocer said.

Creed stared at the storekeeper. "A music box?"

He nodded. "Yeah, a right pretty one, porcelain—real dainty like—"

The Crow interrupted. "Did you see where she went after she made her purchases?"

"Yes."

"Where?"

"To the millinery."

A muscle tightened in Creed's jaw. Where was she getting the money for this burst of frivolous shopping?

"She came out later carryin' a big box. Must've bought a real nice hat," the clerk said.

A hat and a music box? "And then?" Creed probed.

"Then I don't know where she went," the clerk said. "Mrs. Bigelow needed some kerosene, and I had to go to the back room to get it for her. When I looked out later, the lady's horse was still there."

Thanking him, Creed slipped back into the shadows. A music box and a hat. He was going to wring her neck. Having that kind of money meant only one thing. She had gone against his orders and had dipped into the stash of gold. She had done exactly what he had told her not to do.

At the edge of town Creed quickly located horse tracks and the footprints of three riders. The trail was easy to read—too easy. It appeared that whoever had taken her wanted to make certain Creed followed. His hand settled around the handle of his knife. He knew who had her.

His temper darkened with fury when he thought about the consequences she would face because of her reckless actions. But his fury was tempered with fear—a fear that he wouldn't reach her in time. Something stirred within him, an emotion deep and disturbing.

Slipping back into town, he untied Anne-Marie's horse from the railing in front of the saloon and walked it quietly out of town.

❧

"Where is the *oro*?"

"He didn't say where he was going." The words barely escaped

Anne-Marie's parched throat now. For hours she had been sitting beside a pit, her hands bound. Pain wracked her body, and she was faint with hunger.

But Cortes refused to concede defeat. "*Señorita*," he cajoled, "you have only to answer my simple question. Once you have spoken the truth, Cortes will give you some nice warm tortillas, beans, and something to quench your most terrible thirst."

The crazy man's swarthy features wavered above Anne-Marie, but she was barely conscious of him.

"See the pit?" he said. "See, it is filled with lizards. Many large lizards. Iguanas, *señorita*. Do you know the word *iguana*?"

Bile rose to Anne-Marie's throat at the mention of lizards. She hated lizards.

"If you do not tell Cortes what he wishes to know, he will have no choice but to throw you into the pit of iguanas. This would not be so nice. This would spoil the *señorita's* whole day, *sí*?"

Anne-Marie felt herself growing dizzy. His threats seemed to be coming at her through a fog. Somehow it no longer mattered what he was saying. She was paralyzed with terror.

Cortes grasped her by the shoulders and shook her until her teeth rattled. "The gold. Where is it? Speak!"

Anne-Marie reeled when his hand cracked across her cheek. Shaking her head she dropped back to the ground, welcoming the blackness about to consume her.

The Mexican's voice lowered. "You are most stubborn, fine lady. Now you have pushed Cortes's patience to the limit." He straightened, his eyes focused on the pit. "Perhaps if Cortes gives you time to reconsider your ill-advised ways, you will have a change of heart."

Barely hearing his voice, Anne-Marie swam in and out of consciousness. Nothing mattered anymore. She was going to die. She was going to be thrown into a pit full of lizards and be eaten alive. *Creed. Where are you, Creed?* He would know she was gone by now, but would he look for her? Her heart ached with the realization that he might not. He had no reason to further jeopardize his mission in order to save her from the consequences of her own willful ways. The gold was safely hidden in the mission cellar, and she would die before she would let this evil man know where it was—but oh, how she prayed Creed would search for her.

Ollie sat on his haunches. "Boss, don't you think she's had enough? She ain't gonna say where that gold is."

Rodrigo focused on the comatose woman lying on the ground. "You really gonna throw her down that well?"

The outlaw's eyes returned to Anne-Marie. *"Sí,"* he announced dispassionately. "I have been kind for too long."

ᥱ

Creed lay on his belly outside the perimeter of Cortes's camp, his gaze alert for any sign of Anne-Marie. Cortes had left a track as evident as a locomotive. A broken horseshoe. Small bushes uprooted and stacked in the middle of the road. Creed wouldn't have been surprised to see a large red arrow pointing the way.

The moon slid low, casting yellow light on the rough patch of ground. A small fire dwindled to glowing red embers.

With catlike stealth, he inched toward the camp, his hearing alert for any unusual sounds. Two mounds lay beside the fire in sleeping blankets. There had been four men last time he looked. Had Anne-Marie managed to break free?

Or had he miscalculated? Maybe she wasn't with the outlaws—and all this time he had been wasting hours on a wild goose chase. Panic gripped his chest. Where was she?

Three unsaddled horses stood in a thick grove of cottonwoods to the right of the camp. Pulling himself slowly along on his elbows, he inched closer, his body silently skimming over the hard ground.

His gaze traced the large hole dominating the clearing, and he frowned. An abandoned well? The opening was large enough to shove a person down. A stake and the dusty footprints beside the site spoke of recent activity.

Rage welled deep inside him when he thought about Anne-Marie's fate. Her foolish nature might well have gotten her killed this time.

Focusing on the nearest sleeping bag, Creed elbowed closer. A mockingbird called as he slithered closer. There—ahead. Sounds were coming from the bush. A man's low tone, laughing.

He strained to hear, searching for a woman's voice. Nothing came to him.

Pulling himself forward on his elbows he approached the bush, the blade of his knife between his teeth.

A woman's high-pitched screams rent the night, and he recognized Anne-Marie's voice. He sprang toward the sound, knife in hand, and in one long leap, the Indian charged.

Shouts rang out and fists flew as Creed lunged at Cortes. Bare knuckles met flesh.

The Crow was strong—very strong for an injured man. Cortes's head rang when fist after fist slammed his head.

"Ollie! Rodrigo!"

Another fist and Cortes tasted blood. Bunching his paws, he swung through the air, hoping to strike his aggressor. Around and around they went, both men swinging and connecting.

"Rodrigo!"

The Indian dove and Cortes's feet flew out from under him. His head hit the ground and his teeth rattled. Stars exploded.

"Ollie!"

The two outlaws appeared, waving pistols in the air. More scuffles. The men's grunts reached a high-pitched frenzy. Ollie and Rodrigo manhandled Creed to the ground and Ollie swung the butt of his pistol. The sharp crack put an end to the fight.

Panting hard, the two outlaws faced Cortes, who had conveniently stepped aside. He now stepped up. "Cortes will show this insolent Indian who is boss."

Ollie held him down while Rodrigo wrapped a thick cord around his hands and ankles. "What do you want to do with him, boss?"

Cortes's eyes narrowed as he deliberated. "Perhaps the woman will no longer be necessary, *Señor* Ollie. Perhaps if the *indio* is willing, he will keep the woman from further harm." He laughed, showing a mouthful of horse-like teeth in the flickering firelight.

Creed was starting to come around. "Let the woman go."

"I shall, my good friend, I shall, but Cortes's plans have changed."

Creed struggled to sit up, but Ollie slammed him back to the ground.

Squatting, Cortes bent over Creed. "You can save yourself and the woman if you tell Cortes where to find this gold."

"Release the woman and I will take you to it," Creed said.

"No. I do not trust you. You must tell Cortes where it is. He will go and get it himself."

"That's not possible." Creed sat up, rubbing the back of his head. "I'll have to show you where the shipment is hidden, but I won't unless you release the woman."

Cortes spat on the ground. "You are a stubborn man, as stubborn as the female." He straightened. "Cortes grows weary of the games."

"Let the woman go, and I will take you to the gold," Creed repeated.

"*Silencio!*" Cortes started to pace. "It would seem that I cannot do this in a reasonable manner. Very well, Cortes wants the gold, and he is willing to play rough. Bring the woman here," he said to Ollie and Rodrigo.

Ollie grimaced. "We've got the Indian now. He knows where the gold is. Why get her all upset again?"

"Upset?" Cortes roared. "Why should Cortes care if the woman is upset? Bring her to me."

"That's not necessary." From a short distance away, Anne-Marie struggled to her feet. "I'm right here."

The men turned at the sound of her voice, and Creed breathed deeply. *Thank You, God, for keeping her alive.* He shook his head at her. "Stay out of this."

"I am here," she repeated. "I will take you to the gold."

The outlaw motioned with his head. "Get her and the Indian on the horses. Now Cortes will find the gold." The bandit paused. "Wait. Cortes thinks this is another trick." His eyes squinted and then he glanced at Ollie. "Throw the *indio* down the well."

"But boss, we don't how deep that hole goes—"

"Throw him down the well. We do not have to worry about him."

"You gonna just leave him there?"

Anne-Marie stepped up to take Creed's arm. "You do that and I'll never tell you where that gold is hidden."

Cortes turned to Ollie. "You stay here. If Cortes has not returned by dawn you will abandon the site. If she takes us to the gold I will permit her to return and save the Indian."

Anne-Marie pounced to stop the outrage, but Cortes restrained her while Ollie and Rodrigo dragged Creed toward the shaft. Her eyes searched Creed's.

"Give them the gold," he said calmly.

"Creed—"

"Give them the gold. When they ride off, you know where I am."

"I don't know if I'll be able to find my way back!"

Oblivious to the woman's desperate pleas, the two outlaws dragged Creed toward the well. Rolling him onto his side, Ollie grinned when he placed his boot in the middle of Creed's back and shoved hard.

Seizing Anne-Marie by the arm, Cortes dragged her to the horses. "Now, my lovely, you will show Cortes where the gold is." Swinging her into the saddle, he grabbed the reins and quickly mounted his own animal.

"Ollie, you make sure that our *indio* friend"—he chuckled—"is comfortable."

"*Sí*, boss."

"If we have not returned in a reasonable time," Cortes ordered, "we meet in High Bluff at sunrise. The *indio* is to be left in the well."

Ollie nodded. "*Comprendo*, boss."

Wheeling their horses, the riders departed with the sound of thundering hooves.

Seventeen

Quincy paced the kitchen floor of the mission, beside himself with worry. Creed had left hours ago, and he wasn't back yet. That could mean only one thing. Trouble with a capital T. If he had found Anne-Marie, he would have been back by now. No one, not even Anne-Marie, picked mushrooms in the dark. Maybe Creed had located her and they had run into problems, possibly in the outlaws' camp. Muttering under his breath, he pulled on his jacket and exited the mission through a side entrance.

If he lived through this, it would be a miracle.

❧

Two riders pushed their animals hard through the fading light. Anne-Marie clung to Cortes's back, her mind reliving the shocking image of Creed being shoved into the well. Biting back a sob, she closed her eyes and tried to stay calm. She would be glad to get rid of the gold; the shipment had brought them nothing but heartache.

When the mission came into sight Anne-Marie's thoughts turned to what she would tell Quincy. She was heartsick that once again her carelessness had not only endangered the men's purpose but their lives. Quincy's concern for Creed would override his instinct to protect the gold, but Anne-Marie now began to fear for Quincy's life. What if Cortes decided to shoot Quincy once the gold was in his hands?

Choking back a sob, she realized that the McDougal luck, which had never failed her, was about to run out. Every breath felt like a desperate prayer. She'd been headstrong and set her own rules for years, and now someone else had the reins. *Not for my sake*, she prayed silently. *But God, don't let Creed and Quincy come to harm because of me.*

The horses were lathered and breathing heavily when the riders approached the mission.

Quincy, please don't shoot, Anne-Marie whispered silently when Cortes galloped the horse straight to the overgrown gardens near the kitchen door.

The outlaws dismounted and she held her breath as they made their way through the tangled thicket. Overhead, a night bird called, further fraying her ragged nerves.

Cortes and Rodrigo dogged her steps, their hands resting on their gun handles.

"The negro," Cortes whispered. "Where is he?"

"He was here," Anne-Marie said. "I don't know where he is now."

Cortes scowled. "If you speak the lie, he is a dead man."

Please Quincy, be gone fishing, she thought. Or maybe he had decided Creed needed help and had gone to look for him. She reached for the handle on the kitchen door.

Undoing the wooden latch, she stepped inside. Except for the dying embers in the mammoth stove there was no sign of life. Behind her, Cortes's heavy breathing filled the room.

"Quincy?" Anne-Marie called. Her voice echoed back to her. When there was no answer, she called again. "Quincy?"

Moving through the kitchen, she hurried toward the cellar door.

"Where is the negro?" Cortes demanded.

"I don't know. We'll find him—and if we don't, I know where the gold is hidden."

"He is hiding," Cortes said. "He is the weakling."

"He wouldn't hide." And Quincy was far from a weakling. The outlaw might soon discover Quincy's wrath.

Cortes, visibly uneasy, motioned for Rodrigo to stand watch at the door.

Kneeling in front of the cellar doorway, Anne-Marie searched for the candle stub. Locating it, she struck a match and light flooded the narrow stairway.

"It would not be wise to try to trick Cortes," the outlaw warned.

"It's no trick. This is where we hid the gold."

Cortes batted a cobweb away. "I am not the coward; Cortes prefers to see his enemy."

Anne-Marie started off, winding her way down the dark staircase. A cool, musty scent rose to their noses. Upon reaching the bottom, she hurried to the partially hidden door and quickly slid the wooden bar aside.

"What is this you do?" Cortes barked.

"I'm getting the gold. This is where we hid it."

The man's tone faltered. "Cortes smells a trick. A most reckless one."

The door creaked when it slowly swung open to reveal an even darker abyss.

Straining to see around Anne-Marie, the Mexican squinted into the blackness. "It is dark in there."

"Yes," she said.

Dampness surrounded them as they entered the chamber. The flickering candlelight cast eerie shadows on the walls. Lifting the candle above her head, Anne-Marie allowed the light to play over the coins. She heard Cortes's sharp intake of breath.

"We thought the gold would be safe here," she said.

"*Sí,*" the Mexican replied, his voice wavering now.

"Well." Anne-Marie stepped back. She would lead him to the gold, but she wasn't going to gift-wrap it for him. She pointed to the empty Wells Fargo box sitting on the floor. "There's the box it came in."

Cortes stared at the crate and his gaze worked its way to the gold. Swallowing, he reached for a coin, grasping it quickly.

Working feverishly now, he stacked the prize in the wooden crate. When the coins had been retrieved, Cortes fastened the lid on the crate, shouting for Rodrigo.

Rodrigo appeared in the doorway, gun trained on Anne-Marie.

"Quick!" Cortes panted. "Help Cortes carry the gold up the stairway."

"Sí," Rodrigo said.

The two men grunted and struggled up the narrow flight of steps, lugging the heavy crate and a candle between them. Moving through the kitchen, they dragged the crate across the floor and outside.

Extinguishing her light, Anne-Marie laid the stub on the step and then hurried behind them. When she emerged from the mission, the men were already sticking the gold into their saddlebags. "There is too much, boss," Rodrigo grunted. "The horses can't carry the load. We'll have to come back."

"Never. We take it all now. The animals, they are strong."

"You have the gold. Can I leave now?" Anne-Marie was anxious to return to Creed. She suppressed a shudder of repulsion, picturing him in that pit of lizards. How would she get him out? How would she ever overcome her intense fear of iguanas long enough to help him—assuming he was still alive?

"Cortes does not care what you do." He laughed, his evil voice piercing the air. "He has the gold!"

"What about Ollie?" Anne-Marie asked. She didn't want him around when she came for Creed.

"Who cares about this fool, Ollie?" The outlaw laughed, tossing a grin at Rodrigo. "Please inform him that he no can have any gold."

Tossing the empty crate aside, Cortes swung onto his horse. He leered down at Anne-Marie, tipping his sombrero to her. "*Gracias, señorita.* You have been most helpful."

Giving another maniacal laugh, he spurred his horse and the animal sprang forward. Rodrigo wheeled his animal and fell in behind him.

Anne-Marie waited until the two riders disappeared through the thicket and then raced to the carriage house. She grabbed the horse and needed supplies. Minutes later she emerged and rode swiftly to rescue Creed.

She had taken time to locate two long, thick ropes, fashion a kerosene torch, and secure the items to the saddle horn. When she located the well, she saw Ollie leaning against a rock, arms crossed, snoring. Her arrival stirred him, and he stared up sleepily. "Does the boss have the gold?"

She debated whether to tell him immediately about his misfortune. He wouldn't take kindly to being shut out from the take or stick around to help her with Creed. The news would enrage the outlaw.

Sliding off the horse, she nodded. "He has it. You need to help me get Creed out of the well."

"Well," he crossed his arms smugly. "Maybe I don't. Did the boss say I had to?"

"You'd better hurry. Cortes is riding into High Point right now to divide the gold."

The outlaw's face fell. "We'll need a rope."

"I have one, and a torch." She untied the hemp and light from the saddle horn.

"Creed?" Anne-Marie raced to the well and fell on her stomach, peering into the gaping pit. *Dear Lord, please don't let those crawly things have eaten him.* "Are you still in there?"

"Yes, I'm so comfortable I hate to leave."

Incredulity and relief spilled over inside her. His voice didn't sound as strong as it should, but it was Creed's voice. He was alive!

"I can't believe it." She peered deeper into the pit, squinting to find him. Nausea threatened when she saw the dim outline of a lizard. "I can't find you."

"I'm on a ledge just to your right."

"The lizards didn't eat you?"

"You don't know anything about iguanas, do you?"

"No—and I don't want to."

"They spit on me."

"What?"

"They spit on me," he repeated.

"Why would they do that?"

"That's their nature."

"Oh. How far down is the ledge?"

"There is one ten feet down from the lip of the well. I'm sitting on a second ledge close to twenty feet below you."

She thought for a moment, wishing it wasn't pitch black, wishing she'd never gone to town for that silly cornmeal.

"Hold on, I'm coming after you." She handed Ollie the lantern. "Hold this steady, and throw the rope when I tell you to." She met the outlaw's eyes sternly. "It is important that you do as I say and help me rescue Creed…or you won't get any of the gold," she added. The backhanded announcement was as close to telling him about his misfortune as she planned to come.

She saw the thought of riding off had crossed his mind, but he shrugged. "If that's what the boss wants, but I'm not going down there."

"You don't have to; I am."

"Good, 'cause I ain't."

"That doesn't surprise me."

"Don't do anything foolish." Creed's voice echoed back to her.

"Hush up. I'm coming down."

"Anne-Marie! No. There are lizards down here."

Aware that what she was about to do was perhaps the most daring act that she'd ever performed, and perhaps the last thing she'd ever do,

Anne-Marie dropped a leg over the side of the pit and searched for a foothold. His injury had left Creed immobile. He would not have the strength to pull himself up. The toes of her boots scraped the sides until she found a niche. Testing its strength, she shifted her weight to one side, blindly groping for a second hold with the other boot.

"Turn around and go back," Creed ordered.

"You're not the boss now." Step by agonizing step she made her way down the side of the crevice. Twice her foot slipped and she caught her breath, terrified by the thought of what lay below.

"Be careful," he urged.

Hand over hand she lowered herself, scraping her knuckles against the sharp rocks that cut into her hands, praying that if she reached his shelf she wouldn't knock them both to the bottom. Her rasping breath echoed harshly against the rock walls of the pit.

"Don't look down," Creed warned. "You won't like what you see."

"I don't plan to look."

"You're afraid of lizards."

"Don't remind me, but I've grown accustomed to your face and I hate the thought of not seeing it every day."

"I can take this as a compliment?"

"Sort of." Grunting, she eased with a snail's pace down the wall of the shaft.

"Go get Quincy—"

"Can't talk right now. I have to concentrate."

She continued her descent, searching for footholds and handholds, knowing that if she thought too much and too long about what she was doing, she would be lost.

"Careful." When her foot touched his ledge his hand shot out to steady her.

"Creed?"

"I'm right here." His hand grasped her ankle and he pulled her down beside him.

"Creed? Oh, Creed!" His chest felt solid and reassuring. Burying her face in the curve of his neck, she held tightly to him for a moment while she caught her breath. "I thought you would be gone by now," she whispered.

He held her close, smoothing her hair. "Tell me, how are we going to get out of here?"

She pressed tighter, seeking his quiet strength, agonizingly aware of the lizards who were trying to claw their way up the sides of the walls. She turned to look down, but his voice stopped her.

"Don't look down."

Shielding her from the sight, he turned, pointing to the ledge several feet above their heads. "See that ledge?"

She nodded.

"If I can make it up there, I can get us out of here."

"I can help you up. That's why I came down here."

"You honestly think Ollie is going to stick around and help?"

"He'd better."

"If I can get to that ledge, I can get us both out," he assured her.

Anne-Marie viewed the ledge some ways above her head and then said quietly. "You can stand on my shoulders."

"I'd crush you."

"I'm stronger than I look," she said. "Ollie!"

Eyes peered through the shaft. "What?"

"Throw down that second rope."

A length of rope suddenly dangled above her. Creed reached and snagged it. "Ready?"

Anne-Marie hesitated, glancing down at the lizards and then quickly up again. "I'm ready."

"Good girl. You'll have to prop me up. We'll need to work together on this."

"Just tell me what you want me to do."

"First, I want your promise that if I start to fall, you'll let go of me. I don't want to take you with me."

She felt dizzy. "Not my wish either."

"I want your word, Anne-Marie." He took hold of her face. "For once in your life, do what someone tells you."

"You have my word," she promised. "I won't do anything to make us fall in a pit of lizards—even for you."

"Be careful, and stay close to the wall."

Creed leaned heavily on her, and she realized he was hurt worse than he was saying.

Balancing on her shoulders, Creed hefted himself up on the ledge. Anne-Marie helped to support him so he would exert as little weight on the injured leg as possible. The moments ticked by with agonizing slowness.

Leaning down, he extended the rope to her. "I'm going to pull you up. Hold on as tight as you can."

Nodding, she grasped the rope and held on tightly as he eased her slender form upward.

When she reached him he quickly tied one end of the rope around his waist and then tied the other end around Anne-Marie's.

"Hold on tight."

"You don't need to remind me. I planned to."

With slow precision, he began to skim the dirt wall, his boots throwing dirt. The opening edged closer, but the remaining ten feet may as well have been a hundred. Anne-Marie had lost all track of time. Her muscles screamed with the pull of the rope, and the tips of her fingers were bleeding from gouging into the sides of the jagged rocks. The only thing that kept her sane was the certainty that Creed was hurting worse than she. If he could keep moving, so could she.

"You all right?" he grunted.

"I'm…I'm okay. Just keep going," she panted.

When he reached the edge of the pit, he held on to it for several long moments and then hoisted himself over the rim. Grasping her forearm, he heaved her over the edge, and they collapsed in an exhausted heap.

Drained, they lay on their backs staring at the sky for several moments, the only sound coming from their labored breathing and the rustling in the bottom of the pit of restless lizards.

Ollie's voice broke the silence. "Can I go now?"

"Leave," Creed ordered.

The outlaw sprang for his horse and rode off.

"He's going to be very upset when he learns that the others have cut him out of his share of the gold." Anne-Marie took deep breaths.

"I wish I could be there to shed a tear for him."

She rolled over, propping herself up on her elbows.

"Do you realize that all we've done in the short time we've known each other is get into trouble?"

"I have noticed."

He smiled and his hand came out to cup her cheek. "My friend the priest once told me that in China when a man saves the life of another, the one must serve the other until the debt is paid."

She grinned, a warmth rushing through her. "Are you saying you have to serve me until a debt is paid?"

His fingers slipped into her hair and he pulled her face down to his. His lips were warm and supple on hers. When she opened her eyes a moment later, she saw a warm smile.

"You're laughing at me again." Twining her arms around his waist, she held him and closed her eyes to savor the rare moment, relishing the feel of his powerful muscles rippling beneath bronzed skin.

"You feel good in my arms," he said softly.

Reluctantly, he pulled away, his eyes searching the area. "I'd better get a fire started and then see if I can scare up something to eat."

℮

Later, Anne-Marie fed dry twigs into a bed of coals while Creed searched for dinner. He returned within the hour with two freshly dressed rabbits.

"What about the gold?" he asked. He fashioned a spit from two thick branches and hung the meat to roast.

She resented the thought that despite their efforts, Cortes had won. "It's gone. That vile man and his partner took it all."

The telltale muscle flexed in Creed's jaw. "What about Quincy?"

"I don't know where he is. He wasn't at the mission when we got there."

Staring into the fire, Creed turned pensive.

"I think he's probably looking for us," she said.

Nodding, he fed more twigs into the fire.

"This man Loyal Streeter. He and the sheriff are working together?" She recognized the cattleman from their earlier encounter. She tensed. He would surely be put out with her and her sisters for selling him a herd of cattle that wasn't theirs to sell.

"That's how Quince and I have it figured. Now that Cortes has the gold we need to move to the second plan. It's more risky, but I think it will work."

"You're going after the gold *again*?" She would never make it back to Mercy Flats.

"Did you think I'd just walk away and let Streeter have it?"

"I think that would be wise in view of all the trouble that shipment has caused us."

"Well, I've never been accused of being wise, only good at my job."

"By now the outlaws are on their way to turn that gold over to Streeter or whomever they're working for."

"Most likely." He glanced up. "Which means we have to move all the faster."

She gently tipped his face to look at her. "Why don't we just give up?"

He stole a brief kiss. "Sorry, I never learned how."

"We've gone to all this trouble, risked our lives for that shipment, and we're going to turn around and put our lives in harm's way again?"

"You can drop out if you want." His gaze softened. "I can find you a room in High Bluff and keep you safe until this is over."

"No." She set her jaw. "I started this whole ugly mess; I'll see it through to the end." She sighed. "What now?"

"Now? I'm more concerned about Quincy. The meat will be done in a few minutes. We'll eat and then ride back to the mission."

She opened her mouth to argue, but he stood up and walked away, bringing an abrupt end to the discussion.

Abigail had been right about one thing: Men could be one big headache.

Eighteen

The gold?" Quincy asked. He carried a cane pole and a small stringer of fish. Creed and Anne-Marie had searched the area late into the night and found no sign of him.

"Gone. The outlaws outsmarted us," Anne-Marie dished up a plate of eggs, avoiding Quincy's eyes. She couldn't stand to see the disappointment there. If it hadn't been for her, the gold would still be in their hands. Creed appeared to be taking the loss better than Quincy. Maybe because he was still bent on regaining that shipment.

"Here." She set the plate in front of Quincy. "Eat. Creed's wound is bleeding."

"Cortes and his thugs could be counties away by now." Quincy picked up his fork.

"Maybe, or maybe like us they might hope to get a decent night's sleep before they move on."

Anne-Marie knew she should be moving on herself. She still had her sisters to consider. Yet she couldn't bring herself to go.

A cold wind rattled the old mission windows and whistled down the chimneys. Thunder rolled overhead, and lightning lit the kitchen as bright as day.

As if they didn't have enough trouble, more arrived when they were about to turn in for the night. The sound of an approaching rider brought Creed and Quincy quickly to their feet.

If Cortes had returned, she hoped Creed would shoot him this time. She was sick of that man and his evil ways. Absolutely sick of him. Because of him, Creed's mission had failed and the North would suffer even more.

Stepping away from the window, Creed went outside to greet the rider. Anne-Marie followed. They were met by a solemn-faced Bold Eagle.

Creed frowned when he approached the lathered horse. "What brings my brother out in such a storm?"

Rain pelted from the sky and thunder rolled as the chief faced them astride his war pony.

"Bold Eagle comes with bad news, my brother."

Creed's smile faded. "What is this news my brother brings?"

Emotions played across the chief's features. Pain, anguish, deep sorrow. "Bold Eagle brings his brother Storm Rider sad news of Berry Woman."

Creed stepped closer, his features a mask of concern. "Is Berry Woman ill?"

Bold Eagle's composure broke now, overcome by the heavy burden he carried. "My sister is gravely wounded."

Anne-Marie felt Creed tense. "When did this happen?" His voice was barely audible above the wind and thunder.

Straightening, the chief fixed his eyes beyond Creed, his features contorted in pain. "Yesterday."

"Yesterday? How?"

Bold Eagle's tired features showed the strain of the past few hours. His shoulders stooped, and he looked much like a defeated man.

"Berry Woman was digging wild roots. When Plain Weasel heard her cries, he raced to help her, but there was little he could do." His voice broke. "My sister happened upon a *nahkoheso*—she was not swift enough—"

Creed recoiled. "A bear attacked her?"

A soft gasp escaped Anne-Marie. Bold Eagle fixed his gaze straight ahead as another thunderous explosion split the sky.

Turning back to Creed, Anne-Marie saw he was standing, head bowed, trying to absorb the severity of Bold Eagle's words. Finally he lifted his eyes and met his brother's solemnly.

"I am deeply saddened, Bold Eagle. Thank you for making the long ride in the storm to bring me this news."

"The Wise One works now to spare my sister's life."

"Berry Woman is strong," Creed told him.

Nodding, Bold Eagle turned his horse slowly and rode into the worsening storm. When Anne-Marie turned after watching him depart, Creed was gone.

Stepping into the chapel later, she found him sitting in front of the railing, knees crossed, studying the large crucifix. Quietly seating herself beside him, she shared his grief in the lonely silence. Berry Woman was young—too young to face death like this. Many times in Anne-Marie's years, the subject had troubled her. She and Sister Agnes had shared long talks about dying and about eternal life. Considering all the rules she broke, even as a young girl, Anne-Marie often worried about where she would spend eternity. How could she ever become good enough—change enough—to be worthy of heaven one day? Yet Sister Agnes had reassured her that Christ had paid the price. Throughout this long journey she had gained a sense of peace about the matter. And tonight, sitting in the chapel listening to the rain and thunder, she felt no fear. Instead she felt a gentle peace for Berry Woman. If a power so strong could create the sun, the moon, the thunder, the lightning, and the wind, then that same power would have the power to welcome a lovely young maiden into the folds of His love.

It was a long time before Creed finally broke his silence. Anne-Marie waited, respecting his burden.

"I learned about God from Father Jacob." He spoke quietly, his voice lacking its usual assurance. "I still do not understand why He permits these things to happen."

Sighing, Anne-Marie studied the image hanging on the cross before the altar.

"I don't think He brings bad things upon us purposely. Sister Agnes thinks our hurts and joys are a part of life. She says if we didn't hurt, then we'd never know the full degree of happiness."

"I do not understand this way," Creed repeated.

"No one understands. God doesn't ask that we understand, only that we accept what is entrusted to us."

"I want to go to Berry Woman, yet I cannot."

"Why not? Quincy and I can look after things here. The gold is gone and we're not likely to regain it."

"I cannot. My heart is not only with her. My going would be unfair. You have accepted many things in your life," he said. "You have spoken of losing both parents when you were very young. You speak of the strong bonds that tie you and your sisters. I too have felt this bond with Father Jacob and Bold Eagle. Yet at this moment, confronted by death, I cannot feel the forgiving spirit that lives in your heart."

Outside, the howling wind and rain lashed the mission, almost as if venting nature's rage at life's unfairness.

"You really do love her, don't you?" Anne-Marie knew her timing wasn't the best, but the words slipped out in a whisper.

He took a long time to answer. "Bold Eagle is my brother, and I would have honored my brother's wishes."

She turned to face him now, her eyes shining in the flickering altar candles. "She is still alive, and there is the matter of miracles."

"These miracles you speak of—do you believe they happen?"

"Sometimes—not always, but if we both pray, the Lord might see fit to answer our prayers. He loves and responds even to the weakest prayers."

"Then we must pray."

Getting to their knees, they bowed their heads and closed their eyes.

"Creed?"

"Yes?"

"You do love her? I mean, you're not just fond of her like a brother would be for a sister, but you honestly, deeply love her?"

"If she is spared, I will marry her. I have given my brother my word."

"But you've never said you were in love with her."

Creed's eyes returned to the cross and remained there. "So many things fill my mind. So much has happened in so short a time. I respect Berry Woman very deeply, but the woman who now sits beside me creates a sense of longing within me, a sense I have never known before."

Anne-Marie reached for his hand and held it as they knelt side by side. Christ prayed for those who were crucifying Him; she could pray for His grace to spare Berry Woman.

Anne-Marie loved Creed. How would she feel if he were the one lying near death instead of Berry Woman? The resulting pain made her petitions to God more urgent.

Then they sat in silence, hand in hand, until the cry of a rain dove ushered in a new day.

๛

Loyal Streeter patted his lapels and watched the last of the gold being stored in the icehouse. "That's it, boys—handle it real easy."

Ferris Goodman stood beside him, overseeing the activity. When Cortes had appeared toting the gold, Ferris had been surprised. He hadn't expected to ever see it again, but then Cortes had been promised a hefty reward for returning the shipment.

"You done a good job, Cortes, good job—and you'll be rewarded for it," Loyal had promised.

"*Sí, señor*." Cortes had flashed a proud grin.

When the last bag of coins was safely tucked away, Loyal turned, leaving the gold under heavy guard. Walking toward the saloon for a celebratory drink, he appeared to forget Ferris for the moment.

Ferris quietly fell into step behind him.

"Mind if I join ya, councilman?"

Grunting something that sounded to Ferris like, "Do whatever you want," Loyal headed for the Gilded Dove. He didn't take his customary table this afternoon, but headed instead to the bar.

Ferris noticed this. If he didn't know better he'd be tempted to think that Loyal was trying to brush him off today. He didn't know why. After all, he'd gotten the gold back for him, hadn't he? He'd done his job.

The two men engaged in stilted conversation as they stood at the bar drinking. Ferris knew something wasn't right, but he couldn't put his finger on it. Loyal should have been doing back flips that the gold was here—and he was, to a degree. But it was a reserved degree.

"Guess you'll be wantin' to move that gold on to proper channels," Ferris remarked. He toyed with his half-empty whiskey glass.

Tossing the last of his drink down, Loyal didn't answer him.

After a few strained moments Ferris tried again. "I'll put a couple of men on it first thing in the morning. The quicker the gold is out of our hands, the quicker we can relax."

When Loyal still remained silent, Ferris continued. "Should be able to have it signed, sealed, and delivered by this time tomorrow night."

Loyal reached into his vest pocket and drew out his watch. Checking the time with the clock hanging across the room, he wound the stem and absently returned the timepiece to his pocket.

Ferris was positive that Loyal was ignoring him now. "Somethin' troublin' you, Loyal?"

Loyal glanced around the nearly empty bar, lowering his voice. "There's been a change of plans."

"Concerning the gold?"

"Yeah."

Ferris lifted his glass. This didn't surprise him. Loyal had been acting real antsy lately. "What's the change?"

"You've read the latest paper, haven't you?"

Ferris nodded. Richmond had fallen. Lee was making a desperate push to regain ground, but the situation looked grim.

"The South can't hold out much longer."

"Looks that way," Ferris agreed.

Motioning to the bartender, Loyal drew his handkerchief out of his pocket and mopped his brow. Last night's storm had blown in some unusually warm spring air, and inside the stuffy bar it was already hotter than a smoking pistol.

"What're you tryin' to say, Loyal? That you're keepin' the gold? That there's no sense wasting good money when the situation looks hopeless?" Ferris had given the idea thought, but he wasn't a crook. He loved his country.

Ferris didn't know until that moment that he'd figured it out. Sure, that was what was eatin' Loyal. He'd been acting real strange all week, so his decision to keep the gold didn't come as a surprise.

"Can you think of any reason why we shouldn't?" Perspiring heavily now, Loyal mopped at the sweat streaking the sides of his face. In his youth he had been a handsome man, but time and too much drink had altered his features.

"I can think of one. The South is dependin' on that gold," Ferris returned quietly.

"With the war over, the South's gonna have to fend for itself," Loyal grunted. "I've worked hard for the Confederacy and haven't heard one word of gratitude out of them."

"The Confederacy's in bad shape, Loyal. They'll need that gold to rebuild." Pushing his glass aside, Ferris turned to confront Streeter. There wasn't a thing that he could do to stop him from keeping the gold, but it wasn't right. "I can't do anything about your plans, but Cortes and I want our share, Loyal."

Loyal looked up. "Of what?"

"Of the gold. I was responsible for gettin' it back for you, just like I said I would. If you're plannin' on keepin' it, then we split it three ways—you, me, and my men."

Sipping from his glass, Loyal appeared to consider the ultimatum. "You know too much, Goodman. And you'd just as soon cross me as spit in my face; you think I don't know that? Loyalty flies right out the window when the chips are down."

"I haven't betrayed you. I've kept my word and I promised I'd pay Cortes and his men handsomely if they got the gold back. We want our cut."

"All right." Loyal tossed the last of his drink down and then set the glass back on the counter. "A fourth. You can split it up anyway you like. In return, I have your word you'll say that the woman, the black, the Indian, and the gold were never found."

"What do you plan to do? Stash your part, live high on the hog until the next shipment comes along?"

"Your job is to do as I say. I am in charge of that gold."

Ferris eyed him. "And I'll bet you will. Squirrel it away until the ruckus cools down and then take your cut and leave town. Or take it all when nobody's looking."

Loyal's gaze fixed on the mirror over the bar. "A fourth. That's the offer. Take it or leave it."

Ferris fell silent. The clock ticked on the wall. Not a breeze stirred. Then, "You got my word."

Loyal smiled. "I thought you might see it that way. The men who stored the gold in the icehouse will be easy enough to pay off. A couple of bottles of rotgut whiskey and fifty dollars and they'd betray their own mothers."

"Then I guess we've got ourselves a deal."

They sealed the agreement with a gentlemen's handshake.

Smiling now, Loyal appeared to relax. "What're you planning to do with all that money, Ferris? You'll never have to work another day of your life."

Ferris settled back, thinking about the cushy life that lay ahead. It was a shame for the South, and his conscience might dictate that he throw in a few coins for the cause. You win some and you lose some, and Ferris just happened to have won the big one. "Guess I'll buy me that hundred acres I've had my eye on just east of town. Settle down, maybe find a woman who'll cook and clean for me—who knows, might even have me a young'un." He chuckled. "I'll have to leave my fortune to someone."

Elbowing him, Loyal winked. "Don't plan to work that land, do you?"

"No, don't plan to work it." Ferris grinned. "I'll just sit back and take it easy. Real easy."

Smiling, the two men slapped each other on the back.

"We'll make the split first thing in the morning," Loyal promised.

Ferris nodded. "I'll wire the sheriff in Firebrand and turn in my badge tonight."

The two men left the bar together.

❧

When Loyal entered his office he motioned for his clerk, Jake, to follow him.

"You want somethin', boss?"

"Tell Skid Baker I need him."

Jake's brows drew together. "The hired gun?"

Loyal nodded. "Have him here within the hour."

The clerk hurried off to do Loyal's bidding and the councilman walked to the window. Striking a match on his thumbnail, he watched Ferris walk jauntily toward his office.

A fourth of the gold. There were times his job came too easy. Like taking candy from a baby.

❧

High Bluff citizens awoke the next morning to tragic news. Overnight, four killings had taken place. Four. That was unheard of in High Bluff, a town whose folks prided themselves on law and order. Three were in the saloon. Nothing but broken glasses and occasional fistfights happened there. The night of March 18 would go down in the history books as one of the bloodiest the town had ever sustained. Three men were shot to death in a ruckus over a card game. Cortes and his two cousins, Rodrigo Moreze and Oliver—known as Ollie—Dunby. Eyewitnesses swore the bar fight broke out so fast no one was able to tell who shot whom. By the time the smoke cleared, a gunman had run out of the bar and disappeared.

To top it off, Ferris Goodman, the town sheriff of over fifteen years, was gunned down by a lone assailant who broke into the jail and shot him in cold blood. Ferris was respected by almost everyone—a close friend of Loyal Streeter, the town's honorable councilman. Not a single person could think of anyone who would want to harm a hair on Ferris's head.

Streeter, the town's honorable councilman, was so outraged by the violence that he ordered the town to shut down for a full day out of respect to the deceased.

Like Loyal said, the citizens were shocked by such brutality and they weren't going to put up with it.

Nineteen

Anne-Marie stored the last of the supplies in the buckboard with a heavy heart. She had urged Creed to go to Berry Woman, and early this morning he had announced his departure.

"You and Quince load up." The three had gone over the new plan during breakfast. The outlaws would still be in the area and couldn't be hard to track. Quincy and Anne-Marie would locate the tracks and trace them to Cortes's location.

Anne-Marie had tossed and turned last night, alternate plans skipping through her head. They could go after the outlaws and regain the gold. They could trick them, telling them they would pay double for the shipment, and when it was loaded Quincy could cause a distraction and she could ride off with the gold…but Cortes wouldn't fall for anything that apparent. Yet with a little tweaking she could pull the wool over that sneaky little outlaw's eyes. She wasn't sure she had the strength to keep up with Quincy on yet another wild goose chase, but she wouldn't be left behind and they would not give Cortes the satisfaction of victory.

She noted approaching footsteps, and her pulse quickened when she saw Creed walking toward her.

Smiling, he slipped his arms around her waist, drawing her to him. "Take care of yourself."

"I wish you didn't have to go—but you must. Berry Woman needs you." The words stung but they were heartfelt. If the situation were reversed and she lay near death, she would want this man's comfort.

Delicious warmth spread through her when he held her tightly for a moment. "I hate to leave this place," she admitted. Here with him she had found a sense of completeness, and she didn't want to abandon the emotion.

Turning her around, he drew her closer to his chest. The scent of his warm skin set up an even deeper longing. Quincy came out of the mission whistling and they stepped apart. Creed strode to the front of the buckboard to check the rigging and Quincy stored his gear in the wagon.

"Why the grim look?" Quincy teased.

Sighing, Anne-Marie started to help. "I don't know. I guess I should be happy that all this gold misery is finally about to end."

"Yes ma'am. You'll be back with your sisters in no time at all."

The happiness she felt at the thought of being reunited with her sisters dimmed when she considered that Creed was about to be taken away from her.

In such a short time he had become a necessary ingredient in her life, an ingredient that she would dearly hunger for.

Sneaking a longing glance at the one she loved, she was reminded that leaving, no matter how painful, was the right choice. She had become far too dependent on a man she could never have. The journey had been long and arduous but she had discovered the power of love and how one man could stir feelings that she never dreamed existed.

After adjusting the bit in the horse's mouth, Creed returned. "Well, that about does it."

His eyes searched hers. "My visit will be brief. Quincy knows where to meet up. Your job is to find Cortes and the gold."

Quincy shook his head. "Personally, I am getting a little weary of that squirt."

Creed and Anne-Marie had not privately spoken of the time when they would part, but the unsettling thought hung over Anne-Marie like the pox.

Casting a fond glance at the mission, she lifted her hem and climbed into the wagon. Adjusting her skirt primly around her knees, she kept her eyes trained straight ahead, fearing Creed would see the tears that threatened to give way. She had a hunch this was one man who didn't like women who cried in the face of adversity.

Quincy climbed aboard and settled himself on the narrow seat. Scooting across the bench, Anne-Marie made room for the lunch basket she had earlier prepared. Creed mounted up. Moments passed as the three sat watching the wind gently swaying the limbs of the old trees.

"It's been real peaceful here," Quincy admitted. Was that a touch of regret she heard in his voice?

Creed and Anne-Marie focused on each other, emotion raw in their eyes.

"I don't want to leave," she whispered, flinching when she saw Creed's jaw clench.

"I will make my journey brief."

"Well." She sat up straighter, her spunk returning. "Quincy and I have work to do." Pausing, she ventured, "Locating Cortes isn't going to be easy. By now he's long gone—or I would be. Can I suggest an alternate plan?"

Creed shifted. "Anne-Marie, we have a plan."

"You don't have this one. I've come up with something I think might work better. Let's forget Cortes for the time being. He's undoubtedly delivered that gold to Streeter. Why not go after the councilman?"

Quincy groaned aloud. "I don't want to hear this."

"No, listen," Anne-Marie faced both men who plainly were going to be mule-headed about this. "It's a solid plan, really."

"I'm sure it is, ma'am. I recall all too well your last brilliant plan. I still have nightmares about being bound up on those platforms."

She scooted forward on the wagon bench. "Wouldn't you rather return to your commander bearing the gold instead of bad news?"

Creed and Quincy shared a glance, mutual acknowledgment of the truth of her words creeping into their eyes.

"See! You know you would."

"All right," Creed said. "What is this new plan?"

"You're not going to like it."

"Creed!" Quincy objected. "We are *this* close to getting out of this mess by the skin of our teeth."

"We owe her the courtesy of listening."

"Why?"

"Because she's part of this, like it or not."

"I don't like it."

"Then don't listen."

Groaning, Quincy wrapped the reins around the brake handle. "I have a hunch the worst is coming in on a fast freight train."

"Here's the plan." Anne-Marie outlined her ideas and Quincy shifted on the seat, muttering under his breath. Rolling his eyes, he groaned and moaned when the new strategy unfolded. Sweat rolled down his face when she told them her scheme. By the time she was finished even Creed was skeptical.

"That would never work."

"Why not?" She gazed back at him. "I've hatched up plots that were crazier than this one and they've worked."

"It won't work," Creed reiterated.

"It will!"

"Where do we get the clothing? The gold is gone. We don't have a coin between us. We're destitute."

She sobered. "I have some money left from the coin I took. I got a lot of change," she admitted. "A whole lot."

Creed rolled his eyes.

She supposed she had that coming. "Well, where would we be if I hadn't taken that one precious coin that will never be missed anyway?" she accused.

Creed and Quincy answered in unison. "We'd still have the gold."

"Oh, you two. I knew you'd throw that up at me."

They sat for a moment discussing the pros and cons of the new plan. To be sure it was unorthodox, but then so was Anne-Marie. Quincy was firmly against it, but after a while Creed was won over.

"Well, it might work," he reluctantly admitted. "The North desperately needs that money. Lives will be saved. Shoes, uniforms, warm coats—the men need everything they can get their hands on."

"No!" Quincy protested.

Creed and Anne-Marie faced him and said in unison, "Yes!"

"If this plan backfires, we're all goners."

"We know," Anne-Marie said, brushing off the possibility. She didn't have time for negativity; her plan was better than theirs. "Okay, here's what we do. Quincy, there's a casket in the cellar. Get it and make sure the following items are in place." She rattled off a list.

"Lord, can't You please have mercy on this poor soul?" Quincy grumbled when he climbed back out of the wagon. "This female's gone clean out of her mind."

"High Bluff is a small town. It shouldn't take us long to discover where they've stashed the gold if Cortes has brought it to Streeter already," Creed said.

"Quince and I can do this. You go and be with Berry Woman."

"I'll delay my journey long enough to help with the plan. I should be with Berry Woman by tomorrow afternoon."

"All right." Anne-Marie took a deep breath, smiling. She wasn't in any hurry for him to leave.

"We make one brief stop in Brittlebranch to purchase appropriate clothing, and then we proceed to High Bluff." Scrambling out of the buckboard, she marched back to the mission, fire in her step now. "Then, Mr. Loyal Streeter, we'll just see who gets that gold."

⁀

Loyal Streeter glanced up to see a young woman standing in the doorway. Though she was dressed in black mourning attire, she was still a stunning sight to behold.

Getting slowly to his feet, his gaze locked on the vision of loveliness. "Yes, ma'am? Something I can do for you?"

"Yes, sir. I'm looking for a Mr. Loyal Streeter," the young woman replied in a thick Georgia accent. Her voice was as sweet and melodious as a nightingale's.

Bowing from the waist, Loyal smiled. "Loyal Streeter at your service, ma'am."

Taffeta rustled as the woman entered the office. The severe cut of the black gown couldn't begin to hide her delectable curves. Loyal fixed on the full, ruby-red lips. He quickly offered her a chair.

Thanking him, she seated herself and continued, "I'm here to ask a great favor of you, Mr. Streeter."

Loyal smiled. "Ma'am, I am most eager to do anything possible to assist you. Anything, Miss…?" He searched for a name.

"Willingham. Lillie Belle Willingham."

Lifting a gloved hand, Loyal placed a kiss on the back of it. "And what might I do for you, Miss Willingham?"

"I would like permission to make use of your icehouse," she replied.

For the briefest of moments Anne-Marie thought she sensed him tense, but he quickly regained his composure.

His smile faded. "The icehouse?"

"Yes," Anne-Marie said demurely. "I know it seems a most inappropriate request, but I'm afraid I'm just in an awful ol' predicament."

His smile quickly returned. "And what quandary is that, Miss Willingham?"

"My sweet, dear ol' daddy passed on yesterday, Mr. Streeter. He had been in ill health for some time, and I'm afraid—" She paused, lifting the hem of her veil to dab the corners of her eyes.

"Permit me to offer you a cool drink of water," Loyal insisted. "Spring has arrived in full force; it's dreadfully warm in here."

"Why, that would be most gracious of you, Mr. Streeter." She batted her long eyelashes up at him.

"Jake!" Loyal barked.

The clerk's head appeared in the doorway. "You called me, boss?"

"Bring Miss Willingham a dipper of cool water."

Jake was back almost immediately with the requested item.

"Thank you ever so kindly." Anne-Marie drank daintily from the dipper before handing it back to Jake with a grateful smile. "I was shocked to hear of the terrible hostilities that took place in your small town last night. I overheard someone say that many men were killed—even your sheriff."

"Yes, ma'am. The whole town's in mourning. Terrible turn of events—but do go on, Miss Willingham. You lost your father…" Loyal prompted.

"Yes, yesterday, and my two servants and I are taking Papa's remains to be buried alongside Mama's in Georgia."

"Please accept my heartfelt condolences," Loyal soothed, reaching for her hand.

"Thank you so kindly, Mr. Streeter. It has been a most dreadful time. Just evah so taxing on my strength. I am accustomed ta having my dear sweet daddy take care of simply everything for me, and now…now…he's…" Overcome by emotion, she reached inside her pocket for a handkerchief.

"There, there, my dear," Loyal consoled. "You have encountered some trouble?"

"Yes, it seems—well, it seems indelicate to speak of, but due to the unseasonably warm weather that has set upon us we need to keep him someplace cool while we stop for the night."

"Traveling by rail, you say?"

"Yes, we are. Fortunately there are only a few others, Mr. Streeter. Two or three more, and myself and my two manservants. Although the others haven't complained, the situation is most unpleasant."

"Well, I wish I could help, Miss Willingham, but the icehouse is full—all those good men gunned down last night—"

Lillie Belle quickly laid her hand across his jacket sleeve. "If you refuse me, sir, I haven't any other place to turn." Her voice broke with emotion, and he frowned when she began to weep.

"But, ma'am—"

"The casket would only take up a small area in the icehouse," she pleaded, "and we'd be gone by early light." Her voice lowered to a whisper. "Please, do not refuse me this little bitty ol' favor. If Papa's remains aren't cooled immediately, we'll not be able to continue on. Why, I'm afraid I will have to ask that you arrange for Papa's immediate burial if you can't oblige me, and I did so want to bury him next to my dear sweet mama. Papa would be crushed if he knew he wasn't lyin' next to Mama. Why, he'd nevah forgive me. Nevah."

Anne-Marie wrinkled her brow in consternation, blinking her eyes to hold back the tears. Sniffing loudly, she fumbled for her handkerchief.

Loyal paled. His jaw worked as he mulled the dilemma. Anne-Marie knew what was going through his mind. Like any gentlemen, he would be thinking how bad it would look if he refused this sweet, innocent woman her touching request. Why, he'd be a cad of the worst sort not to help her out of her awful predicament.

But then there was that little matter of the gold in the icehouse, he'd be thinking. It had taken Anne-Marie, Creed, and Quincy longer than expected to find the stash, but a coin and a bottle of rum loosened a vagrant's tongue and he admitted he'd seen men unload a trunk of what appeared to be gold in the icehouse the night before all the shootings took place.

The councilman bit his lip indecisively.

"My two servants will assume full responsibility for the casket," Miss Willingham assured him. The councilman's intense inner

struggle had become apparent. She was close—very close to persua-
sion. Abigail would be proud of her—

*Lord, You do understand this isn't the same as my old life. This isn't
the councilman's money, and it isn't my money. It's Your children's money.
The soldiers need shoes, clothing, and food... but then I guess You feel the
same about Your children fighting on the other side. But You're the wise
one. You choose how this turns out.*

"Because of the"—she paused—"odor, my servants will carry the
casket in and out so no one will be affected."

By now he had to realize that she had him between a rock and
a hard place. The gold was in the icehouse. No one but his trusted
employees knew that, and she was quite certain that he didn't want
anyone else to know. It was risky, to be sure.

Lifting her hand to her forehead, Anne-Marie feigned
lightheadedness.

"Are you all right, Miss Willingham? Perhaps you would like more
water, or might I fetch you a refreshing sarsaparilla?" Loyal offered.
He lifted a hand to summon Jake again when she stopped him.

"Please, I'm just weak with hunger." Her voice sounded very small
now. "I have eaten very little in the past few hours." She peered up at
him. "You do understand."

"Of course, Miss Willingham. Most understandable."

She believed that she was about to set the hook. She was such a
winsome creature, small and vulnerable. *Perhaps he's thinking he could
make this one harmless concession.*

She started to rise and then wilted back into the chair.

"I must see to my servants' needs," she murmured. "One is blind,
and the other is...dimwitted. They look to me for their welfare." She
sighed.

"Well, perhaps we can arrange something," Loyal offered. She
smiled. Who would be so heartless to deny her? If one servant was
blind and the other witless, then surely there could be no danger in
letting her use the icehouse. After all, like she said, it would only be
until morning.

"Where are your servants now?"

"With Papa."

"On the train?"

She nodded, dabbing at her moist eyes again.

"Come then, Miss Willingham." Loyal offered her his arm and she stood up, placing her small hand on his wrist. "Once we have your papa settled, you will join me for supper."

"Oh, I couldn't," she protested. "I have imposed enough on your kind generosity."

"Nonsense. I'll see that your servants are fed and bedded down for the night. Then you and I will enjoy a leisurely dinner in the finest café in High Bluff."

"Well, if you insist," she said, demurely offering him her most radiant smile. "You are just evah so kind."

⌇

Creed and Quincy were sitting in an empty boxcar when Anne-Marie stepped out of the councilman's office on the arm of Loyal Streeter. The men sat up straighter. "Can you believe this?" Creed said. "Looks like she's done it."

"Yeah, she's done it all right," Quincy murmured. "I figure she's done it up real good this time." He glanced down at the flour sack breeches and gunnysack shirt. "I feel like a fool."

"You look like a fool," Creed agreed.

"I'd laugh if you didn't look worse." Quincy burst out laughing anyway. "You got the same breeches and torn shirt, except that you're barefoot and Anne-Marie wants you to be the 'simple one.' Now me? I'm luckier. She merely struck me blind."

Anne-Marie and Streeter approached the rail car and her laughter floated to the men.

Heat coursed through Creed. When he had seen her dressed in her fine gown and hat, he knew what a magnificent woman she was. She would meet no resistance capturing the heart of any man she wanted.

The recognition had hit him hard. Loyal Streeter would answer to him if he so much as indicated anything other than compassion for her situation.

ℯ

Approaching the train, Anne-Marie nodded solemnly to her two manservants.

"Tobias, Malachi."

Two men climbed out of the boxcar and lowered their heads subserviently.

"We are in luck," she called brightly. "Mr. Streeter here has been evah so kind and graciously offered his assistance."

Quincy nodded. "I cain't see you, Mr. Streeter." He stared ahead sightlessly. "But you'se surely a good man—a good man."

Streeter nodded absently. "You men carry Miss Willingham's papa on up to the icehouse now. Afterward," Loyal offered, "go around to the back of the jail and someone will feed you. You boys can bed down in the railcar tonight."

"Oh, thank you, Mr. Streeter, thank you. We shore nuf do thank you," Quincy intoned.

"Mr. Streeter has graciously invited me to take supper with him," Anne-Marie warbled, bestowing a winning smile on Loyal.

The muscle in Creed's jaw tightened when Anne-Marie slipped her arm back through the councilman's.

"Once Papa's in the icehouse, Tobias, you take Malachi and go over to the jail. Then you be sure that both of you get to bed tonight and get a good night's sleep, for we'll be leaving first thing in the mornin'."

"Yes'm, we will, ma'am. Don't you worry a bit 'bout us."

Creed and Quincy jumped out of the railcar when Anne-Marie and Loyal turned to go. With Quincy loudly giving instructions to Creed, they unloaded the casket from the train and waited for Anne-Marie and Loyal to lead the way.

Loyal held a hanky to his nose and approached the armed guards, who lifted their rifles when the small procession approached. One's eyes widened and he gave Loyal a censoring look.

"Miss Willingham has asked permission to store her papa's remains in the icehouse," Loyal explained when the two guards viewed the casket suspiciously, "and I have granted her wish. Unlock the door, Boyd."

Boyd stepped up and removed the lock, and the two guards stood back to let the men carry the casket into the icehouse.

Creed's features remained expressionless when he set the coffin down beside a bag of what could only be gold coins.

"It shore do seem cool and nice in here," Quincy drawled.

Creed remained silent, maintaining his simpleton facade.

Groping his way, Quincy turned and led Creed back out of the icehouse. The guards stepped forward to relock the door and then resumed their stance, rifles in hand.

"Well, I do declare," Anne-Marie said, breathing a sigh of relief. "I believe my appetite is returning. Shall we go to supper, Mr. Streeter?"

"As you wish, my dear."

Turning her, Loyal Streeter pointed her in the direction of the café, where private dining quarters awaited.

Once he was turned toward the jail, Quincy blindly stumbled his way along, dragging Creed behind him.

Glancing over his shoulder, Creed saw the councilman slip his arm around Anne-Marie's waist as they stepped onto the hotel steps.

"That pompous idiot better keep his hands to himself," Creed muttered.

e

Loyal Streeter proved to be nothing less than charming over supper, regaling "Lillie Belle" with stories about High Bluff. The roast pheasant, boiled potatoes, and string beans tasted marvelous after the venison she'd been living on at the mission.

"More pheasant, Miss Willingham?"

"No thank you, Mr. Streeter. I do declare I'm stuffed up to the brim."

Rising from his chair, Loyal offered his arm. Accepting it, she stood up, bestowing a tremulous smile upon him. "You're evah so kind, Mr. Streeter."

Loyal nodded, patting his rather portly middle. "Fine meal, fine meal."

"Simply divine."

Arm and arm, they strolled along the plank sidewalk, enjoying the cool night air. There were few people on the streets now, most having gone home to their families.

As Anne-Marie kept step with his long stride she wrinkled her forehead.

"Is there something troubling you tonight, Miss Willingham—other than your father?"

"No, I was just thinking. Perhaps I should check on my two men."

"Oh, they're quite all right," Loyal assured her. "I have seen to their care."

"But if I could speak to them briefly, assure them that all is well," she persisted. "They were my father's favorites, you know, and I'm sure at this moment they are very confused. Perhaps if you'd be so kind as to allow me a moment to put their fears to rest?"

"Very well," Loyal conceded. "If you must."

The councilman and his lady veered toward the tracks. Loyal nodded to a passerby, who greeted him by his first name.

Snapping her fan open, Anne-Marie stirred the air, stepping a little faster. She didn't know why, but she had an overwhelming urge to see Creed. The long day had taken a toll on her nerves. Creed had promised to stay until the gold was back in their hands, but the ploy had taken much longer than she'd anticipated. Now it was dark and he still waited with Quincy in the boxcar when he should be on his way to be with Berry Woman.

When the couple approached the box car, Creed and Quincy sat up. Both men had been lying on a mound of straw.

Creed's eyes locked with hers. For a moment they watched each other before his dark gaze shifted to focus on Loyal Streeter's hand on her arm.

"Dat you, Miss Willingham?" Quincy stared sightlessly up.

"It's me, Tobias. Hope we're not disturbin' you," she apologized.

"No ma'am, you'se not disturbin' us. We's just relaxin' for a spell. Hope you don't mind."

Lifting the hem of her skirt, she approached Creed, casting a coy glance in his direction. "Well, you certainly look well fed."

"Oh, yes'm, yes'm, we'se had real good eats," Quincy assured her. "Plenty o' beans and hardtack."

"That's nice." Her eyes fixed on Creed's stoic features. "And you, Malachi? Did you eat well?"

"He did, ma'am. He shore did," Quincy answered for Creed.

Patting Creed on the shoulder, she turned to smile coyly up at Loyal. "They're such fine men. I don't know what I would evah do without them." She paused, smiling when she saw Creed scowling beneath the slouch hat.

"Mr. Streeter and I just had a long, nice supper. Excellent fare. We had browned plump pheasant, delicious potatoes, and string beans." She smiled again. "Did you say you had beans and hardtack?"

"Yes'm."

"Mmm. Sounds good."

"Yes'm," Quincy returned tightly.

She placed her hand over Loyal's, her gaze returning to Creed.

"Well, I'll be getting on back to the hotel," she said. "It has been a very long day." Hooking her arm through Loyal's, she smiled at Creed. "Sleep well, you two."

On the walk back to the hotel Anne-Marie's conscience pricked her. She hated to cause this delay for Creed. He could be with Berry Woman at this very moment, comforting her, holding her hand, yet he'd remained here throughout the long day until the gold was back in their hands. Now it would be another day before he joined the injured girl. Anne-Marie didn't want to make him angry; he'd been patient with her, considering all she'd put him through. In the morning she would be up even earlier than planned and move that gold shipment out from under Loyal Streeter's eyes. The crooked councilman would never know what hit him until it was too late to do anything about the ruse.

Loyal escorted her to her room, extracting her promise that the very next time she came through High Bluff they would have supper together. When he squeezed her hand possessively, she tried not to shudder. This man was nothing like Creed. She wanted Creed's arm to protect her.

⌒

The sun was just topping the hotel roof when Loyal Streeter stepped out the next morning, escorting Miss Lillie Belle Willingham. Lillie Belle's two servants somberly fell into step behind the couple when they crossed the street and walked toward the icehouse.

As the entourage approached, the guards moved to unlock the door. Once the heavy padlock had been removed, they stepped aside, allowing room for the men to enter.

Anne-Marie ignored the trickle of sweat rolling down her back. If Quincy and Creed didn't come out soon, Streeter was going to get suspicious. Anne-Marie could see the man was already pacing back and forth, his eyes trained on the icehouse door.

Moments stretched into long minutes. The whistle blasted again, warning of the train's imminent departure.

Clearly uneasy now, Loyal started for the icehouse door when it suddenly opened and Quincy and Creed emerged, carrying the heavy-laden coffin.

"There you are," he said. "I was just about to come in after you. Now come along, all of you. The train is eager to leave."

Loyal took Anne-Marie's arm and walked her away as Creed and Quincy followed, weaving their way down the small incline to the railroad tracks.

The conductor and another man were waiting to help the two servants hoist the casket aboard the waiting rail car.

"Must have been a hardy soul," Anne-Marie heard the conductor say as he strained to help lift the cumbersome load. Pulling his handkerchief out of his pocket, the conductor mopped at his forehead. "What's in there? A dead bull?"

The engineer tooted the train whistle again, and Anne-Marie turned to Loyal, extending her gloved hand. "I shall remember you always, Loyal. I just don't know how I can evah repay your generosity. You've just been such a sweet South'n gentleman."

Bowing from the waist, Loyal placed a kiss on the back of her hand. "I shall never forget you, Miss Lillie Belle Willingham."

Anne-Marie smiled. "I suspect you won't, Mr. Streeter. Indeed, I suspect you won't."

"Now, don't you forget to come on back here once all the unpleasantness has been attended to," he reminded. "And we'll have supper."

The train began to move as she daintily lifted the hem of her skirt and Loyal helped her aboard. Moving to the back of the car, Anne-Marie waved her hanky at Loyal's disappearing figure.

"Don't forget, Miss Willingham! You promised to stop off here again and have dinner with me," Loyal called.

"I shan't, Mr. Streeter. I shan't."

Be back, she added beneath her breath. A cheerful "Lillie Belle" waved and waved until the train finally rounded the bend and was out of sight.

❧

Patting his lapel, Loyal drew a deep breath when the train disappeared. Now there was a woman.

Turning, he strode back to the icehouse to check on his gold. When he stepped inside, it took a moment for his eyes to adjust to the dim interior. When they did, he blinked, and then blinked again, unable to believe what he was seeing. The empty trunk lay open in front of him, a piece of paper sitting in the bottom. Loyal's face drained of color as he read the terse note:

A fool and his money are soon parted.

Cursing, he ripped the paper in half.

❧

Some miles down the track, the train once again pulled to a grinding halt. Passengers groped for support and a grumble went up at yet another unexpected delay.

The conductor walked through the cars, soothing frayed tempers. "Just be a moment, folks, and we'll be on our way again," he assured them.

Outside, two men loaded the heavy casket onto a waiting buckboard overseen by three Apache warriors.

Nearby, an Indian chief dressed in a war bonnet sat astride his horse, watching the activities. A servant approached the warrior and they exchanged words.

Shortly, the train released its brakes and steam billowed from the smokestack. The conductor blew the whistle and cars began to rattle on down the track.

Anne-Marie ran over to stand beside Creed when the train picked up speed and disappeared around the bend. "Did you ask Bold Eagle about Berry Woman? Is she..."

"She is stronger. Medicine Man believes that she will live, but it will be a long and painful recovery. It seems that Plain Weasel has not left her side."

"Good. I'm...I'm glad for you. For both of you." And then she grinned. Both he and Quincy had to admit the second plan had gone off without a hitch. "Nice job, huh?"

"Very nice job," he agreed.

Twenty

"How long will it take to deliver the gold?"

Anne-Marie, Creed, and Quincy loaded the wagon the following morning. Creed lashed the gold shipment to the buckboard with a thick rope. "Three—maybe four days' ride from here."

The distance was small considering time already spent on the trail. At least there was now an end in sight to this reckless but unforgettable journey. In so many ways Anne-Marie longed for the ordeal to end, but in others she dreaded the moment when the gold was handed over and she was free to return to Mercy Flats.

When Creed brushed past her, he gently squeezed her shoulder in an act of assurance. The gesture brought little warmth to her heart.

Good weather followed the three travelers. Other than an occasional spring shower that started and stopped almost as fast as it arrived, nothing but bright skies, robins, and early spring crocuses accompanied the group.

At the end of the third day the party rode into the encampment as dusk fell. Creed and Quincy accepted Commander Lewis's praise with dignified modesty. Only Anne-Marie knew the real price that had been paid for this victory.

"We have so many stories to tell you," she blurted to the commander. "You will not believe what we've gone through to deliver this gold."

"I cannot wait to hear these stories." Lewis motioned for men to take the horses. "Come, warm yourself by the fire."

"I want to offer my share of the gold for the Union cause," she had offered.

Commander Lewis's appreciative smile had melted her heart. "That is most kind, young lady. Come now. You'll have a warm meal and then a good night's rest before you leave." He slapped Creed on the back. "And you and I will have time to catch up on all these stories the young lady speaks about—including why the young lady is with you." He raised an eyebrow.

"Sounds good, sir."

There was a large celebration in camp that night. The causes of the festivities were twofold. Word had come early that morning, Palm Sunday, that Robert E. Lee had surrendered his starving ragged Army of North Virginia to Ulysses S. Grant.

The war was finally over. Giddy with the news, Anne-Marie had hugged Creed, Quincy, and every man, woman, and child in sight and then watched as grown men wept and others fell to their knees to thank God for their deliverance. Thousands of slain fathers, sons, and brothers were not here to witness the historic event. The North had won, but any sane man would concede there was no victor in this war. A nation had been split apart, its countrymen left with unspeakable loss. Perhaps the only blessing the weary soldiers carried was a sense of personal valor—a realization that when adversity comes, the most ordinary people can show that they value something more than they value their own lives.

The fighting over, the men were released from duty and told to go home. The gold would help many to begin to rebuild their lives. Soldiers would return to burned-down homes, looted farms, and fields littered with the remains of war. For others, God willing, there would be wives and children waiting for husbands and fathers to return.

"If only the gold could have come earlier," Anne-Marie mused.

"I am thankful no matter the timing," the captain said. "I just thank God the fighting is over."

~

The following morning, Anne-Marie watched as Quincy strapped the last of his belongings into his knapsack and hefted it onto his back.

"Are you going to ride or walk?" she teased.

"Both. I have shoes and a strong back; I'm going home." He turned to shake Creed's hand, his eyes filling with unshed tears. "It's been a pleasure knowing and working with you, Creed Walker."

Creed's features turned somber when he clasped Quincy's hand, his eyes confirming his deep respect for his trustworthy friend. "Our lives have been on the line many times, and you were always there for me. Thank you, Quincy."

"If you ever get near Coleman Flats, Alabama, be sure to look me up," Quincy said. "I'd be real honored to have you meet my family."

"I'll make it a point to ride that way," Creed assured him.

Glancing at Anne-Marie, Quincy cleared his throat.

Smiling, she stepped up, hugging him tightly around the neck. "I hope the invitation goes for me as well."

"Yes, ma'am." That twinkle she loved sparkled in his eyes. "Especially for you." He hugged her back, holding her firmly for a moment. "When you're back with your sisters, you bring them to Coleman Flats, Alabama." He shook his head, grinning. "Lord have mercy not only on me, but the town. Two others like you."

Shaking hands one final time, Quincy turned and started through camp, saluting others as they called out to him.

Anne-Marie followed, tears wetting her cheeks when she watched him set off down the road. They had shared a lot in the past few weeks. She finally understood the passion behind those who had fought this war. If she were asked to give her life in order that Quincy's future sons and daughters would live in freedom, she would gladly do so. These courageous fighting men had proven that the color of one's skin didn't matter. It was the man who made the difference.

Then it was time for Anne-Marie and Creed to leave. Anne-Marie prepared for the final journey ahead with a heavy heart. There was a time when she would have anticipated the return home with a child's enthusiasm. Now the realization of what lay at the end of the journey was bittersweet.

Creed checked the horses' bridles. Even though she was impatient to be reunited with Abigail and Amelia, how would she ever be able to say goodbye to the man with whom she had shared her deepest secrets and thoughts—her very soul?

Turning, he caught her staring. For a moment their eyes met, affection mirroring in each of their depths. He finally broke the silence. "Commander Lewis has offered us an escort. I told him we wouldn't need one."

"No," she murmured. She wanted their last hours together to be spent alone. Moving to her horse, she mounted before he could see dampness building in her eyes.

Creed swung into his saddle and, with a final salute to Commander Lewis, turned his horse.

Anne-Marie brought her animal in behind him, and they rode out of camp while the others stood watching.

For two days they rode side by side, speaking of nothing more serious than how pleasant the day was and how enjoyable the Baby Blue Eyes, Bird Cherry, and Coltsfoot were blooming along the ditches and ravines.

Creed pointed to a robin pulling fat worms out of the moist ground, and they laughed, savoring the shared intimate moments. Another time he spotted a cottonwood tree, and they left their horses to peel back the bark of the tree and scrape the spring sap that flowed upward. The jellylike froth was sweet and creamy. They devoured the delicacy like two small children.

Lying under the stars that evening, Anne-Marie rested in her bedroll, trying to hold back the sunrise.

"I'll miss you," she confessed. The fire had dwindled low. Overhead a canopy of stars saturated the sky.

"I'll miss you too."

"A lot?"

"More than you'll ever know."

Rolling to her side, she tried to memorize his features, every curve of his jaw, the bronze skin, and the eyes. Those beautiful coffee-colored eyes.

"Do you think things might have been different—if the circumstances were changed?" She longed to know that although he couldn't speak of his feelings for her, they were as deep and troubling as hers.

He sat up, threading his hand through her hair. "Yes, things would be different."

"You would choose me?"

His eyes softened. "I have chosen you. It would be impossible for any man to love you more than I do at this moment." He didn't touch her, didn't reach out for her, but even so she was surrounded by the warmth of his arms. She studied the stars, determined to savor the moment and push aside the grief of goodbye that lay ahead.

Even as they drew nearer to Mercy Flats, nothing was mentioned about their future because there was none.

So many thoughts troubled Anne-Marie. Abigail, Amelia. The pact they had made as young girls, vowing to stay together forever. How could she break this promise, even though she loved Creed Walker more than she loved her life? She found herself consumed by guilt. She had betrayed those she loved by falling in love with a man, and yet she would never speak of her love for Creed. She would stay there in Mercy Flats and grow old and crabby with Abigail and Amelia. She would never admit that she so foolishly had fallen deeply in love with a man who belonged to another woman.

When the horses topped a rise the final day, Anne-Marie's pulse quickened when she saw the small community of Mercy Flats spread out below her. For a moment she was swept over with homesickness. The old mission looked achingly familiar and reassuring. Her life had been simple here, so uncomplicated.

They rested their horses side by side as Anne-Marie gazed down at the tranquil setting below them. Creed had said very little the last few miles.

"There have been times when I didn't think I'd ever see it or my sisters again," she admitted, fighting the rising lump in her throat.

"You must consider the possibility. It is conceivable that Abigail and Amelia's rescuers were not able to elude the Comanches." Reaching for her hand, he squeezed it supportively.

Smiling back at him, she bit her lower lip to still its trembling. "Will you ride down with me?"

She knew she shouldn't ask. He wasn't hers to invite, but oh, how she needed him to ride the last mile with her.

His eyes filled with love when he gazed back at her. "It is very hard for me to let you go. If I ride the last mile with you, I may find it impossible to turn back."

She summoned up every last ounce of courage she had. "Ride with me anyway, Creed Walker."

Nodding, he released her hand and Anne-Marie allowed her horse to begin to pick its way down the small ravine.

Approaching riders caught her attention and she reined up. Creed pulled up beside her. "Maybe your sisters have spotted you?"

"Maybe." Her heart skipped with the thought of uniting with Abigail and Amelia. There had been times when she believed that she would never see her sisters again. When the party drew near, she identified the intruders. Bold Eagle and two warriors.

Creed frowned. "Berry Woman must be worse."

The small party drew up, their war ponies winded. The colorful assembly fascinated Anne-Marie. The ponies bore the same pattern and colors his warrior used for his face and body and his weapons. The newcomers made a splendid sight in the balmy spring air. Bold Eagle's large stallion crow-hopped and he brought it under control.

Creed walked his horse toward the chief. "You bring further news of
Berry Woman?"

Bold Eagle focused on Creed. "May I speak in front of the
woman?"

"Speak."

"Perhaps we should talk in private."

"No." Creed glanced her way. "She can hear whatever you have
to say."

The chief hung his head. "I bear bad news."

"Berry Woman has passed."

"Better that she had." The man shook his head. "Berry Woman has
brought shame and disgrace on Bold Eagle."

Creed eased his horse closer. "What are you saying?"

"My sister—I don't know how to say this, my brother—she has
married Plain Weasel."

It took a moment for the words to register. Anne-Marie blinked.

Bold Eagle lifted his head to meet Creed's eye. "Forgive me. My
sister shames me and her people. Plain Weasel has been a thorn in
my side since the day he was born. He runs wild in the camp with the
other young boys, always kills too many buffalo, and will fight until
the death. When Berry Woman looked at him I saw her interest, but I
reminded my sister she was taken. I thought she heeded my warning."

Creed laughed. The sound was one of pure relief or disbelief.
Anne-Marie wasn't sure. "Berry Woman is well enough to marry?"

The chief nodded. "Against my wishes, but she cried and wailed
and threatened to leave the camp if I did not perform the ceremony.
She said that I, her brother, would ruin her life if I made her marry
a man who loved another. She assures me that her love for you was
faithful until…" He glanced at Anne-Marie. "It seems my sister
chooses Plain Weasel over you. Finally her…" He searched for a word.

"Nagging?" Creed supplied.

The chief nodded. "Nagging has worn me down." His shoulders
slumped. "Day and night, night and day she sobbed. She does not

eat or drink. Bold Eagle finally had enough and I married the couple this past week. Berry Woman is now Sits-Beside-Her-Husband wife."

Anne-Marie rode closer. "But I thought she was so very sick."

"In the head," Bold Eagle muttered and then recovered. "She is very weak, but she will now be the weasel's nuisance."

The news finally registered and Anne-Marie broke into a wide grin. "Be sure and give Berry Woman and Plain Weasel my best wishes. I hope that she and her new husband will have a long, happy life together."

It felt so good to say that about the woman who had put fire ants in Anne-Marie's pallet. She had to be making some progress.

Bold Eagle focused on Creed. "I will make amends. Ten horses, three chickens, fifteen of our best hides."

Creed shook his head. "I don't need horses or chickens, my brother. Your apology is enough." He stepped up and the two men shook hands. "Tell Berry Woman I wish her much happiness."

Bold Eagle solemnly nodded and then turned his stallion. "I go now. My stomach is soured."

When the party was about to ride away, Creed whistled. Glancing at Anne-Marie, he said, "Stay here. I want to talk to him alone."

Nodding, Anne-Marie stepped her horse back to allow privacy.

❧

Swinging off his horse, Creed walked to Bold Eagle's animal. The chief peered down. Creed glanced at the two warriors and then told Bold Eagle, "Lean closer."

Bold Eagle bent and Creed whispered, "Don't beat yourself up over this. It was only a matter of hours before I would have come to you with the same news."

Surprise registered in his eyes. "What does this mean?"

"It means I was about to come to you and break my word. I am sorry, brother, but my love for Anne-Marie is stronger than my blood bond to you." Creed met his friend's eyes. "Can we just call this a draw?"

The chief thought for a moment, and then slowly nodded. "This is wise."

"All is good between us?" Creed extended his hand. "We are still blood brothers and we shall never speak of this matter again."

Bold Eagle agreed. "This is good. I would have spent sleepless nights knowing my sister nagged you like she does me."

"Give Plain Weasel my best." The men shook hands.

The chief nodded, a spark of mischief now dancing in his eyes. Straightening his shoulders, he said, "He will need it."

The small party rode off and Anne-Marie turned to Creed, her grin still in place. "So."

A wicked smile curved at the corners of his mouth when he remounted. "So what?"

"So. In case you hadn't noticed, Berry Woman just jilted you. That spoils your commitment excuse. What's your argument now?"

Reining his animal around, he walked the horse to stand by hers. Bending forward, he pulled her roughly to him and kissed her long and hard. The embrace left her reeling. Every emotion he had he articulated in that kiss. Every crazy corkscrew sentiment she was feeling erupted in a ball of fire during the heated embrace.

When their lips parted, he whispered. "Who said I want an excuse? I prefer White Man's wisdom when choosing a wife. I want to spend my life with the woman I love." He inclined his head toward Mercy Flats. "Lead the way, Miss McDougal. I think it's time that Creed Walker met the family."

About the Author

Lori Copeland is the author of more than 100 titles, including *A Kiss for Cade* and *Under the Summer Sky*. Her beloved novel *Stranded in Paradise* is now a Hallmark Channel Original Movie. Her stories have developed a loyal following among her rapidly growing fans in the inspirational market. She lives in the beautiful Ozarks with her husband, Lance.

Sisters of Mercy Flats

LORI COPELAND
BESTSELLING AUTHOR

Sisters of Mercy Flats
By Lori Copeland

The three wily and beautiful McDougal sisters can swindle a man faster than it takes to lasso a calf. But their luck is running out, and they're about to be hauled off to jail. When the wagon carrying them falls under attack, each sister is rescued by a different man.

Unfortunately for Abigail, she's grabbed by a twit of a shoe salesman, Mr. Hershall Digman. She steals his horse and rides off to the nearest town, not giving him another thought...until she discovers those secret papers in his saddlebags. Could such a dandy really be a Confederate spy?

As if to prove it, the man who comes storming after her is no shoe salesman, but a handsome Rebel captain who wants his papers back...at any cost. And Abigail wants a ride back home. Will the two of them ever resolve their differences? And will they ever learn to trust in the God who won't seem to let them go?